State College

at

Framingham

7500-1-64-932122

The Road to Beersheba

This is the story of the exodus from the small Palestinian town of Lydda, which was occupied by the Israeli troops in the Arab-Israeli war of 1948, when, with the refugees from Ramleh and the surrounding villages, some hundred thousand people, mainly women, children and old men—the young men having been rounded up—trekked through the burning wilderness to Ramallah, which was in Arab hands. Thousands died of sunstroke, exhaustion and thirst.

In this story, Butros Mansour, a distinguished Christian Palestinian landowner of Lydda, does the trek with his English wife and their twelve-year-old son, Anton, and other members of the family. The terrible experience makes a profound impression on the boy. His father never recovers from the ordeal and dies the following year at the family house in Jericho, and Anton and his mother go to her parents in England.

For Anton England is exile, underlining his part in the Palestinian diaspora. He is obsessed by the idea of infiltration along the road to Beersheba, which also fell to the Israelis in 1948. With a Moslem friend, a refugee from Beersheba, he has looked along this road, now in No Man's Land, and it has come to symbolize the impassioned Palestinian dream of returning home. He sees it as the road he must eventually tread.

This story of the *other* exodus, the Palestinian exodus, has never been written before, and the author's passion for justice and deep humanitarianism present it in its full pity and terror, in what we believe will be regarded as a memorable novel.

BY THE SAME AUTHOR

Novels

MARTHA
HUNGER OF THE SEA
SOUNDING BRASS
PILGRIMS
GREEN WILLOW
CRESCENDO
CHILDREN OF THE EARTH
RAGGED BANNERS
LINDA SHAWN
VENETIAN BLINDS
MEN ARE UNWISE
CACTUS
THE PURE FLAME (Sequel to *Cactus*)
WOMEN ALSO DREAM
ROSE AND SYLVIE
DARKNESS MY BRIDE
JULIE
ROLLING IN THE DEW

RED ROSE (A novel based on the life
    of Emma Goldman)
CAPTAIN MOONLIGHT
THE BLOSSOMING BOUGH
PROUD HEAVEN
LUCIFER AND THE CHILD
THE DARK FOREST
COMRADE, O COMRADE
LATE HAVE I LOVED THEE
EVERY MAN A STRANGER
BAVARIAN STORY
AT SUNDOWN, THE TIGER
THE FIELDS AT EVENING
LOVER UNDER ANOTHER NAME
THE LIVING LOTUS
PITY THE INNOCENT
FRAGRANCE OF HYACINTHS
THE BLUE-EYED BOY
SABISHISA

CURFEW AT DAWN

Politics and Ethics

WOMEN AND THE REVOLUTION
    (Secker & Warburg)

COMMONSENSE AND MORALITY
CHRISTIANITY—OR CHAOS?

BREAD AND ROSES (Macdonald)

Short Stories

GREEN FIGS
DRYAD
THE FALCONER'S VOICE

NO MORE MIMOSA
THE WILD SWANS (Three Tales based
    on the Ancient Irish)

SO TIBERIUS . . . (A Novella)

Travels and Memoirs

CONFESSIONS AND IMPRESSIONS
ALL EXPERIENCE
FOREVER WANDERING
SOUTH TO SAMARKAND
PRIVILEGED SPECTATOR (Sequel to
    Confessions and Impressions)
MOROCCAN MOSAIC
TWO STUDIES IN INTEGRITY
    (Gerald Griffin and the Rev.
    Francis Mahony—'Father Prout')
LAND OF THE CRESTED LION (A
    Journey through Modern Burma)

CONNEMARA JOURNAL
GERMAN JOURNEY
JUNGLE JOURNEY (India)
THIS WAS A MAN (Some Memories
    of Robert Mannin)
THE COUNTRY OF THE SEA (Some
    Wanderings in Brittany)
BRIEF VOICES (A Writer's Story)
THE FLOWERY SWORD (Travels in
    Japan)
A LANCE FOR THE ARABS (A Middle
    East Journey)

Child Education

COMMONSENSE AND THE CHILD
COMMONSENSE AND THE
    ADOLESCENT
ANN AND PETER IN SWEDEN (Muller)

ANN AND PETER IN AUSTRIA (Muller)
ANN AND PETER IN JAPAN (Muller)
WITH WILL ADAMS THROUGH JAPAN
    (Muller)

ETHEL MANNIN

The Road to Beersheba

'And I have given you a land for which
ye did not labour, and cities which ye
built not, and ye dwell in them; of
the vineyards and oliveyards which ye
planted not ye do eat.'

JOSHUA xxiv. 13

HENRY REGNERY COMPANY
Chicago, Illinois

Second Printing, 1964

Manufactured in the United States of America
Library of Congress Catalog Card No. 64-15767

2|65

To and for

THE PALESTINIAN REFUGEES

who, in all the Arab host-countries,
said to me, 'Why don't you write *our*
story—the story of the *other* exodus—
our exodus?...'

Author's Note
and Acknowledgments

This is a story of a small part of the exodus of a million Palestinians during the Arab-Israeli war of 1948—the exodus from the town of Lydda, and the surrounding villages, on July 12, in which some hundred thousand people were involved, mostly old men, women and children, trekking through the wilderness to the town of Ramallah on the Arab side. The incidents described are as told to me by people who took part in this terrible trek. The characters are fictitious.

I am indebted to a number of people, both Palestinian and English, who assisted the work on this book by their patient answering of my many questions, and to His Excellency, Mr. Adel Zawati, the Governor of Hebron, for permission to travel along the old Beersheba road as far as the Demarcation Line, and for facilitating this.

And to my old friend Gilbert Turner, for assistance with proofs, as always.

E. M.

Contents

Foreword by the Author

Some explanation is necessary.

Until November 29, 1947, there was a country called Palestine, the ancient Philistia of the Philistines, a predominantly Arab country. At the time of the Balfour Declaration, in November, 1917, when the British government declared itself in favour of the 'establishment in Palestine of a national home for the Jewish people', the vast majority of the population, over 90%, was Arab. There were about 50,000 Jews in Palestine at that time, and some 670,000 Moslems and Christians. But already in 1915, in a memorandum entitled *The Future of Palestine*, Sir Herbert Samuel, himself a Jew and an eminent Zionist, had advocated the immigration into Palestine of three or four million Jews, under British protection. It was an unequivocal statement of Zionist aspiration: what had to be established was not a national home, a refuge for Jewish victims of persecution in various countries, but a fully fledged Jewish State. The Balfour Declaration, nearly three years later, envisaged something very much less than that; the obvious solution was so to intensify Jewish immigration into Palestine that the Jews became a majority. In 1919 Dr. Weizmann, then the Zionist leader, made his famous declaration of policy that Palestine should become 'as Jewish as England is English'.

In 1920 the Balfour Declaration was incorporated in the terms of the British Mandate for Palestine—the Arabs, fighting with the Allies in World War I against the Turks, had believed they were fighting for their independence; instead they got British and French Mandates. An attempt was made to control Jewish immigration, but there was an increasing illegal immigration, with a forged passport bureau in Berlin. The hostility of the Arabs was intensified, and there was rioting, strike action, and martial law, as part of the nationalist struggle for independence. The Jewish national home was not yet a reality in terms of a self-governing state, but already by the outbreak of World War II the Jewish population had increased from 50,000 to 600,000, and the operation of the Mandate gave the Jews an increasing economic hold on the country. Zionist industries were government-protected, Arab villages were demolished to make place for Zionist settlements, and the Jews had their own hospitals, schools, political institutions, and preferential treatment from their British sponsors.

Just as World War I had held up Zionist aspirations, so World War II held up Arab nationalist aspirations, and the Nazi persecution of the Jews in Germany proved a powerful ally of Zionism. An Anglo-American committee—three of the six members of which were ardent Zionists—visited Palestine in 1946 and in their report recommended the immediate admission of 100,000 Jews into Palestine, the figure President Truman had urged, with the door left open for further immigration. When the Palestine Conference in London in 1946-7 reached no agreement, because the Arabs represented at it demanded an independent democratic Arab state in Palestine, the 'Palestine question' was taken to the United Nations and a special session convened to deal with it. Under Zionist pressure and with United States backing the United Nations Special Committee on Palestine recommended Partition.

On November 29, 1947, Palestine was partitioned by the U.N.O. General Assembly in Washington, by thirty-three votes to thirteen, with ten abstentions—of which Britain was one. Of the Zionist pressures and tactics brought to bear to secure this overwhelming majority, Truman has something to say in his Memoirs. 'Not only were there pressure movements around the United States unlike anything that had been seen there before,' he wrote, 'but . . . the White House, too, was subjected to a constant barrage. I do not think I ever had as much pressure and propaganda aimed at the White House as I had in this instance. The persistence of a few of the extreme Zionist leaders—actuated by political motives and engaging in political threats—disturbed and annoyed me. Some were even suggesting that we pressure sovereign nations into favourable votes in the General Assembly.' The Under-Secretary of State,

Robert Lovett, declared that he had never in his life been subjected to as much pressure as he had been during the final stages of the voting.

The U.N.O. plan for Partition gave 60% of Palestine—and that the most fertile areas—to a third of the inhabitants, the Jews, and a million Palestinians, almost the entire population, became displaced and dispossessed in the Arab-Jewish war which followed. All that was left of the ancient predominantly Arab land of Palestine, on the west bank of the river Jordan, was added to Trans-Jordan, the east bank, and the Hashemite Kingdom of Jordan established. A narrow strip along the Mediterranean coast, five miles wide by twenty-five miles long, all that remained of the province of Gaza—of free Palestine—was administered by Egypt. It was given a Constitution by President Nasser in 1962. It is little more than a vast refugee camp.

Of the million or so Palestinians who fled as the result of Israeli terrorism, such as the massacre at Deir Yassin in April 1948, or were ejected from their homes (which the Zionists strenuously deny, in the face of all the evidence), more than half have been rotting in camps in subhuman conditions, supported by the United Nations Relief and Works Agency, since the end of 1949. The rest have been absorbed into the host-countries, but all demand not rehabilitation but repatriation. Not one of them, in the camps or outside, has received a penny compensation for their houses, lands, capital, in the hands of the Israelis. Every year the U.N.O. General Assembly, reaffirms the right of the Palestinian Arab refugees to return to their homes, or, if any do not wish to return—to be second-class citizens in the Jewish state—to full compensation; but the resolutions are never implemented. On the contrary the Israeli Foreign Minister, Mrs. Golda Meier, has categorically declared, 'Our policy remains unchanged—not one single refugee!'

Other countries have been partitioned, but have continued to exist as countries, named as such on the map, and occupied by their own people; Palestine ceased to exist, as a name and as a country, and Palestinians as a nation. It is the era of the Palestinian diaspora.

PART I

Exodus

I

THE temperature in the coastal plain was over a hundred in the shade—the thin shade of the olive trees, the red shade of the rocks. Only the compulsion of terror made it possible to walk in that heat, over that terrain. Israeli troops drove the people off the roads and deeper into the wilderness, deeper into the endless bare hills.

The earth was made of sand, too hot to be touched by the naked foot; it was made of sand and stones and grey boulders and clumps of bleached thorn. It was undulating land, flowing away to the hills, which, fold upon fold, melted into a sky heat-drained of all colour. The landscape was vast, flowing away to infinity in all directions; the vast Jordanian wilderness, teeming now with people, mostly women and children, like a scattered army, stumbling over the stones, picking a way through the boulders, toiling up the sandy hillocks, drenched with sweat, stumbling, falling, rising and stumbling on again, women clutching babies, dragging old people, and the old collapsing and unable to rise again. But always the onward surge of people, driven by fear, stumbling on urgently through the blinding sunlight, placing one foot before the other among the stones, because not to do so was to die, of sunstroke, or thirst, or exhaustion.

And always the fear of the small black civilian planes, coming in low, so low you could see the men in them, hovering and swooping like birds of prey, as they had come in the night—that last terrifying night in Lydda.

Long afterwards Anton Mansour remembered the peculiar sound of those planes, different from the sound of any other plane, and the peculiar fear they evoked, different from any other fear he had known in his twelve years of life. Something in his head seemed to burst with that sound, and the blood poured continuously from his nose. At first his mother had stopped as they trekked and tried to stanch the bleeding, but after a time she had no more energy left—barely enough to turn her head and glance at him, none for any words. No one looked at anyone any more, spoke to anyone, did anything for anyone. There was nothing left in anyone but a stubborn will to live, to survive the heat and the exhaustion and the devouring thirst. There was no thought any more, only fear; no emotion, only misery.

From time to time Anton turned and looked back at his mother, to make sure she was still there—it was easy to lose anyone in that vast crowd. There were children blundering about among the boulders crying, having lost their parents; no one took any notice of them; those they clung to, sobbing, shook them off. Women regarded them, dully, without pity. Dazedly Anton watched a woman suddenly fling the baby she had been carrying into a gully; it lay there screaming. The woman staggered on; they all staggered on, the sun beating down on them trying to kill them, the black planes hovering like waiting vultures in the molten sky, the unrelenting earth throwing back the heat, savagely.

They were all making for the little hill town of Ramallah, a few miles from Jerusalem, but driven far out into the wilderness, the road no longer in sight, only a few of the younger ones had any real sense of direction. The rest walked blindly eastward; all that mattered was that Lydda should be behind them—Lydda in whose streets that morning the loudspeakers of the victorious Israelis had commanded them, 'Get out! Go to King Abdullah!'

With Anton walked a blind boy, a little older than himself, the son of a servant on his father's estate. They walked with Anton's right hand clasped with Amin's left and their two hands raised and held close to Anton's shoulder, so that the blind boy was pressed close to him. They spoke very little, neither complaining.

Anton's father, Butros Mansour, trudged along with his brother, Farid, two heavily built men who normally never walked more than the few steps to their cars, men of substance, for whom life had always been, physically at least, easy. Their women followed them, Marian, the English wife of Butros, Majdeh, Farid's wife, and

Nadia their eldest daughter. Nadia's two young children stumbled along beside them, whimpering and endlessly complaining that they were tired, that they were thirsty. Their parched lips were rimmed white, as with salt. Marian and her sister-in-law took turns in carrying them for short spells at a time, staggering and stumbling over the rough ground. Nadia walked with her head down, indifferent to their sufferings, sealed off in her private hell. She wished she were a Moslem, so that she might hide her face behind a veil.

A few days before, when men of all ages had been rounded up by the Jewish troops and concentrated at the mosques, the grand mosque and the small Dahmash mosque, her husband Nasri had been among them, with her father, uncles, cousins, brothers; but yesterday when the men had been released Nasri was not amongst them, for all men of military age had been sent to a concentration camp . . . all, that is to say, from the big mosque; no one of any age, from the three hundred men concentrated there, was freed from the other mosque; there had been a little trouble, which was dealt with by machine-gun fire, after which there was no one to release; no one at all.

At first all the men sheltering in the Mansour house had been in favour of going to the Dahmash mosque; it was nearer, and it would save walking through the town, to be taunted by Israeli soldiers of both sexes—for there had been the astonishing sight of female soldiers, carrying sten-guns and wearing short shorts revealing plump bare thighs. It was Butros who had argued against going to the Dahmash mosque, urging that it would be better to go to the grand mosque and stay near the gates, for it had been rumoured that three armoured cars of the Arab Legion had turned up outside the town, and they would surely be followed by soldiers of the Legion in force. Liberation would come first to the big mosque. Butros was listened to with respect, as the head of the house, and to a man they had gone with him to the big mosque.

It was before the men had returned that the two Israeli soldiers had come to Darat el Kheir, the Mansour house, asking for water. Nadia, and a servant girl called Randa who looked after the children, and other women had peered out at them from behind the iron bars of a first-floor window. They were very frightened, but Nadia had found the courage to call out, 'What do you want?'

The two young soldiers looked up, laughing.

One answered in bad Arabic, 'Don't be frightened—we're Hagana, not Stern. We only want water. We're hot and thirsty. Be so kind!'

He said something to the other soldier, who laughed, and they both unslung their sten-guns and leaned them against the trunk of a dusty casuarina tree facing the entrance porch of the house. Then the one who had asked for the water turned back to the window.

'You see—we are unarmed!'

He was a good-looking young man and his smile was boyish and candid.

Nadia did not return his smile, but she said, 'I will send water to you.'

She told the girl Randa to take a jug of iced water to them, and it was Marian who said, suddenly, 'Take it in one of the good crystal jugs and give them the crystal tumblers. Let us show them we are a civilized people! Butros would wish it. They are our guests.'

'They are the enemy,' Nadia protested.

'They have made themselves our guests, and they are friendly.'

Randa fetched the iced water in a crystal jug and set two cut-crystal glasses beside it on a silver tray and went on her bare feet down the wide marble staircase and across the tessellated entrance hall to the front door.

When she opened the door the two soldiers were sitting on the low balustrade of the porch. She indicated the tray, which she had placed on a table just inside the door, and the one who had asked for the water thanked her in Arabic.

The other one strolled over and said in a twanging English, 'Hullo, beautiful! Speak English?'

Randa who did in fact speak a little English, having learned it in the service of the Mansour family, shook her head.

The other said, 'He's a Lebanese-American. He doesn't know much Arabic.'

He poured a glass of water and gulped it down and poured another. The other soldier drank half a glass of water then dashed the glass to the floor and the splinters of crystal flew in all directions. He laughed, excitedly.

'We do that at Jewish weddings—it's symbolic!'

Randa did not understand what he said, but she shrank back, frightened by his tone and manner, and dismayed by the breaking of the precious glass. He reached out and grabbed her wrists.

'Come on, beautiful, let's have a wedding!'

The girl screamed and struggled violently, but there was a reception room opening off the hall and he pulled her into it and closed the door. The other soldier laughed, and poured himself some more water.

Randa's screams brought Nadia and Marian and other women to the top of the staircase.

Marian called out sharply, 'What is the matter? What is happening? Where is the maid?'

The soldier laughed.

'Losing her maidenhead by the sound of it!'

Marian had rushed down the stairs in a blind rage, and Nadia had followed her. The soldier waited at the bottom of the stairs and his arms closed round Nadia as she came down. He laughed triumphantly as she struggled and screamed and kicked. Her arms were pinioned to her sides, and his grip was intensely strong. He lifted her the few feet across the hall to the room, and with his hand on the handle of the door looked over his shoulder to say to Marian, 'It's all right, Mother, you can go!'

Then the door slammed in Marian's face and a key turned in the lock. Nadia's shouts and screams came above the sobbing of the girl.

Randa trudged along behind Nadia and the Englishwoman. With her were other servants from the Mansour house and estate and various people who had sheltered there the last few days and nights. At the end, and until the men were taken away, there were about a hundred people in that big old house, Darat el Kheir, House of Prosperity. The girl was suffering from shock and plodded along dazed, like a stunned animal, too sunk in misery to be aware even of heat or thirst; too engulfed in horror even to know fear.

The Englishwoman was similarly engulfed. As the mistress of the house she could have countermanded Nadia's order to Randa to take water to the two soldiers. She could have forbidden it and kept the house closed against them. Then, for certain, they would have shot their way in; but at least, then, even if Nadia and Randa had still been raped, at least she would not have been morally responsible.

Butros had returned from the mosque without Nasri and shattered by the news of the massacre at the Dahmash mosque and she had not yet told him about Nadia and the maid; nor had Farid been told. She was intensely worried about Butros; how could a man of his age, over sixty, unused to walking even on smooth pavements, and with a bad heart, possibly survive hours of stumbling over this savagely rough ground in this heat and without water? He walked blindly, as all the elderly ones did, placing one foot before the other, dully, automatically, because the alternative was to lie down among the grey boulders and the bleached scrub and die, as many were doing, unable to struggle on any longer, gasping in the hot scant shade of rocks, or in the occasional stony olive grove, moaning, 'Give me water! Give me water!'

For Butros the great thirst had begun before they had all been turned out into the wilderness, their only possessions the clothes they wore, and stripped of wrist-watches, fountain-pens, even wedding-rings. The thirst had begun at the mosque; there was water there at the cistern at which the faithful made their token ablutions before they prayed, but the Israeli guards had urinated into it, laughing, and calling to the Palestinians, 'Come and drink! It tastes good!'

When he got back to the house he found three soldiers, one of them a woman, standing beside his car at the top of the long avenue of date-palms and casuarina trees that led up to the house.

The woman was young, good-looking, in a hard-eyed way, and very sure of herself. She butted him in the back with a sten-gun and in a strong Germanic accent asked if he spoke English; when he said yes she demanded the keys of the car. He handed them over and all three got in. The woman leaned out of the window beside the driver's seat to say, 'You and your family had better get out, quick, or your lives won't be worth a *fils*!'[1]

Her companions laughed, and she amplified, 'Not even the price of a bullet!' She then spat at him and they drove off.

He had stood at the top of the steps of the porch his house watching the big white car driven off down the avenue of casuarina trees like a host speeding his guests. Then, heavily and wearily, he had gone into the house and the evacuation had begun. In the town it should be possible to get taxis into Ramallah. Or if they succeeded in getting only one car that party could go ahead and come back with transport from Ramallah.

But when they reached the town there was no transport of any kind; it had all been requisitioned by the Israeli military, and loud-speaker vans were parading the streets ordering the people to get out within half an hour. The streets were a milling confusion of people, and troops were everywhere, trigger-happy and drunk with victory. Happy uniformed boys and girls marched about with buckets full of wrist-watches, fountain-pens, jewellery. A soldier deliberately stopped in front of a party of veiled women huddled in a shop doorway, opened his flies and urinated, facing them. Other soldiers seeing him laughed and made obscene gestures in the direction of the women.

Butros standing on a street corner with Marian and Anton and other members of his household saw the incident and his right hand clenched on the silver head of the cane he always carried.

'They do everything to humiliate us!'

Marian laid a hand on his arm.

'They know no better. *Yalla!* Perhaps we will get a lift along the road.'

But there had been no lift and no road, only the wilderness, and the day already hotting up.

It was not until they were in the wilderness that the Palestinians realized the extent to which the usurpers of their land were determined to humiliate them. There this proud, generous people was

1. The smallest Jordanian coin.

stripped of even the human attributes. There are circumstances in which only the will to survive persists. Circumstances in which mothers will abandon their babies for the jackals to devour, unable to carry them further; in which the young leave the old to die; in which men and women drink their own urine. And that of their children. It was water; something with which to moisten the parched mouth, the cracking lips, round which white salty rims formed as the day progressed.

Once when Anton and Amin were resting in the scant shade of an olive grove, waiting for the rest of the family to catch up, the blind boy said, 'There are Roman cisterns in these parts and sometimes there is still water in them. If you come to any groups of rocks you should investigate. When I had sight I used to go with my father into the wilderness with our herds of goats, and we found such wells between Lydda and Ni'leen. There are carob trees, too—nice sweet carob pods! Don't you like them! And soon we'll reach the *wadi* and it will be easier for us—we can follow it all the way to the village. How do you feel?'

'My feet hurt terribly. And I don't know if I can go on carrying the jacket of my suit.'

'Why don't you throw it away?'

'It's my best suit. If I throw it away when I get to Ramallah I won't have anything to wear and it's cold there in the winter.'

'Your cousins will fix you up. Besides, who says we shall be there in the winter? The Iraqi army will join in with the Arab Legion to liberate Palestine and throw the Jews into the sea! *Insh'allah!*'

'*Insh'allah,*' Anton repeated, automatically, then remembering he was a Christian added piously in English, 'Please God!'

A crowd of people rested with them among the olive trees, lying stretched out on the stony earth, or sitting with their backs against the gnarled trunks of the trees, staring out at the vast monotonous landscape of red earth and grey boulder and white scrub, and always the range upon range of hills—the bare, rocky Palestine hills, and the undulating plain like an immobilized sea. There were a number of whimpering children, an old woman who moaned perpetually for water, a group of women who sat bolt upright, their faces veiled, not speaking, only their rough hands giving a

24

clue to their identity as country women, a young woman who sat with a dead baby at her breast, gazing down at it, blankly, her white head-dress half drawn across her face. No one heeded anyone else. The landscape teemed with people, thousands of them, as far as the eye could see, all moving slowly in one direction eastwards, facing towards Jordan.

Anton's parents and other members of the Mansour family came up at last to the group of olive trees and sank down in the hot shade. The boy looked anxiously at his mother. She was twenty years younger than his father and very much stronger, but his concern was for her. He had a feeling that in spite of his age and his bad heart his father was indestructible; Butrous Al-Mansour was of a distinguished Palestinian family, and, his son was convinced, a great man in his own right, and great men do not lie down and die; they may be insulted and humiliated and dispossessed by the enemy, and turned out into the wilderness, but to die would be to accept defeat, and for that they are too proud. Anton had this comforting conception of his Arab father, but his English mother could not, he felt, be expected to have such moral and physical stamina, and she had been in a very bad state when they had left the house—something to do with the Hagana soldiers getting hold of Cousin Nadia and the maid, Randa. He didn't know what it was all about, but there had been screams and a great commotion and everyone sobbing and crying, and when the two soldiers had left the house they had had to fight off the women clutching and clawing at them, and he had been terrified the soldiers would take up their guns and start shooting: at one point it had looked as though they would.

It had all been very frightening and upsetting, and when at last the soldiers had been allowed to get away his mother had col-lapsed and looked terrible. Cousin Nadia looked terrible, too, and Randa did nothing but cry. His mother complained of a dreadful headache after the soldiers had gone, and still with that headache next day she had set out to walk to Ramallah over land that no one except a shepherd would dream of setting foot on. She had plodded on in silence after a time, like most of them, not even coming to him when she saw that he was having another bout of nose-bleeding, but he didn't hold it against her; there was nothing she could do for him ; there was nothing anyone could do for anyone. It was each for himself—a degradation the Jews forced upon them when they turned them off the road to struggle and suffer like beasts in the wilderness. They want to make us suffer, he thought, they want to humiliate us; they can do this to us but they can't destroy us. The proud thought sustained him for a time, but then the small black planes came over, flying low, and there was only terror, the mortal fear of death; and as the day wore on it became clear that many people were being destroyed in the most horrible fashion, old people and little children, the helpless ones. And his mother looked terrible, and as though she too could be destroyed.

She sank down beside him now and for the first time since they had left the house gave him a small smile. Even in the last few terrifying nights when the town had been shelled and bombed as the Jewish troops closed in she had managed an occasional smile, to keep their spirits up. It had been terrifying, but there had not been that personal mortal fear of death that came with the news of the massacre at the small mosque, and with the relentless exposure of the wilderness with the sinister black planes flying in low, with that strange sound that was different from any other.

'We must be halfway to Ni'leen,' she said. 'Someone was saying they could see the *wadi* already. At least we'll know where we are then—it's the walking blindly that's so exhausting. Just walking to somewhere vaguely over there.'

She was a small thin dark-haired woman with good features and surprisingly blue eyes, which Anton had inherited; she could have passed for an Arab, and frequently did; there was nothing distinctively English, or even European, about her. Normally she looked younger than her forty-odd years; then she looked almost unrecognizably old, with dark shadows of mental and physical exhaustion under her eyes and her lips cracked and bleeding. Her thin cotton dress which had been crisp and fresh when she had started out had become a limp, sweat-soaked rag. She looked like a gypsy who had slept out in a ditch, she who was normally so neat and trim. Nadia, who sat beside her, was equally bedraggled,

26

and her pale beautiful face that of a sleepwalker. She stared into space and did not speak. Butros and his brother Farid sat a little apart, on a boulder, Butros leaning on his silver-headed cane, his fine head tilted a little back as he searched the landscape for the Wadi Al Malaki that came out below the village of Ni'leen, where they would pass the night—and slake their thirst even if there was nothing to eat. He had put on weight in recent years, but at sixty-two was still a handsome man, with a distinguished presence. There was both humour and sadness in his face, and an immense dignity. His brother Farid, some ten years younger, was like him, but less handsome, less distinguished, with a certain wry humour but without the underlying melancholy which was part of the older man's charm and sensibility. Marian liked and felt affection for her brother-in-law, but she could never have married anyone but Butros.

Farid's wife, Majdeh, a good-looking woman running to fat, sat on the grass beside Nadia, trying to soothe the two children, who whimpered from thirst and exhaustion. The older child, a little girl of four, lay on the rough ground crying with a persistent misery.

Majdeh looked despairingly across at her sister-in-law.

'I don't know how we shall get the children there.'

'It's only another two hours,' Marian comforted her. It would be three, at least, she knew, but two sounded so much less, and once two-thirds of the way was covered it would be possible to find the strength for the last lap. The heat of the day would be diminishing, too, which would help.

'Perhaps we'll come across a Roman cistern,' Anton said, hope-fully. 'Amin says there are some in these parts and there might be water in them.'

Marian wondered wrily how it was proposed to get the water up even if they found such a well; if there was water it would be deep down; but there was such eagerness in the boy's voice—so young an eagerness—that she had no heart to discourage him.

'We must watch out for them,' she said.

Sitting there under the olive trees it was possible to be human again, released from the destroying, dehumanizing effort and exhaustion of the trek. The raging thirst remained, but with the body no longer sweating and struggling it was a degree less frightful, and there was relief from the misery of broken blisters on the feet which made every step agonizing, something not to be borne, yet which had to be borne, as an alternative to lying down and dying of sunstroke and thirst. There was relief, too, from terror, for it was some time now since they had seen an Israeli soldier or plane. They were no longer being hounded into the wilderness, but they had been driven so far out into it that they were miles off their route. The stony course of the *wadi*, when at last they came to it, would be new torture for the bleeding and swollen feet, being nothing but a dried-up river-bed, but at least it would be a clearly defined track; they would be no longer walking blindly. They would know then, positively, that in one hour, two hours, they must come to the village; the village of Ni'leen, still in Arab hands.

People came and went; some rested out in the open, in the scant shade of rocks and boulders; the movement was ceaseless, the undulating landscape as crowded as the foreground in a street, with a vast teeming motley of people, tens of thousands of people, a *mélange* of men and boys in white shirts and trousers, and in the traditional Arab dress and head-dress, women and girls in European dresses, and in nun-like black *abbahs*, or the beautiful biblical Palestinian dresses, long and straight and heavily embroidered, with the veil-like white head-dresses flowing down the back, older women in long straight black or grey dresses, their heads tied with kerchiefs; village people and town people, poor people and well-to-do people, Christians and Moslems, and everywhere children, carried by their parents, dragging at their mothers' skirts, small, dark-haired, dark-eyed children, the rising generation of Palestinians, without a country, without homes, without a future, many of them destined to grow up in the squalor and misery of camps, many of them doomed to die there in the wilderness. . . .

Some, like the Mansours, had relatives in Ramallah; those were the lucky ones, and they were a small minority. A few had money or property in that part of Palestine which was now 'Israel'; the vast majority had nothing but the clothes they wore and their faith in God; they left behind them lands which their families had owned and worked for countless centuries. Dignified, hard-working men and women, struggling now for survival in the burning plain, toiling with bleeding feet in broken shoes over terrain in which not even the bedouin would attempt to walk, collapsing from sunstroke, exhaustion, thirst, but the great mass of them stumbling on, silently, doggedly, placing one foot before the other, like automatons; going on because the alternative was death and the will to live persists to the last parched gasp.

There wandered into the Englishwoman's mind the thought: If I hadn't married a Palestinian fourteen years ago I wouldn't be here now. The small flame of the thought flickered and went out before the impact of the counter-thought: I might have been in England during the war and been killed in the blitz.

She looked across to her husband. He sat leaning forward from the boulder, both hands on the head of his cane. His white shirt clung wetly to his body. There were bags under his eyes; he looked old and ill; yet there was still about him that distinction, that air of authority, which made men address him as *Bey*. . . .

He had suffered too much, she thought, how can he live? And if he doesn't how can I? As our days, so shall our strength be. Trite but true, my father used to say. O God, let it be true now! Give us strength to go on. Just a little longer. Just the few hours more it will take. Give Butros the strength. Butros especially. Anton and I will manage. . . . Only if Butros doesn't manage too there's no point in it. . . .

Butros did not speak to his wife or his son, or his brother, or anyone else, whilst they rested amongst the olive trees; he did not even turn his head to look at them. Not because he was indifferent to their sufferings and their capacity for survival, but because the whole tragedy which was being enacted, and of which he and his family were only a tiny fraction, was so major a human disaster, so monstrous a wrong done to an innocent people, that pity for individual suffering was engulfed in it. This ejection of thousands of men, women and children into the wilderness was no less a massacre than the slaughter by machine-gun and bayonet of the women and children of the village of Deir Yassin on the tenth of April, and the mowing down of three hundred men in the Dahmash mosque at Lydda three days ago; it was a massacre of the old and the babes in arms, and the little ones just learning to walk; a massacre of the innocents.

It was possible to bring an iron self-control to bear on physical suffering—and his was so intense that he was continually on the point of collapse, but doggedly refusing to die like an animal in the wilderness, and out of that stubborn pride always find a reserve of strength to keep going; somehow to keep going. But for the inner agony there were no reserves of strength. He had been confronted with too much horror in the last twenty-four hours, been called upon to endure too much. There had been the horror of the mosque, the unslaked thirst, day and night, the taunts of the soldiers as they polluted the cistern and mockingly invited them to drink, the lack of sanitary arrangements, so that as the hot hours passed and men began to relieve themselves against the walls and in any odd corner the stench became almost suffocating; and above all the fear and uncertainty—what was to happen to them, what might happen to their families in their absence, the meaning and whereabouts of the intermittent spurts of machine-gun fire in the town. At one point there was a long bout of it. When they were released in the morning they knew what it was—the massacre at the Dahmash mosque. The mosque to which Farid and the others had urged they should go. To which they had so nearly gone. The shock and horror . . . and then the order to get out, 'or your life will not be worth a *fils*!'

All his life he would remember the expression on the face of that woman soldier as she leaned out of the car—his car—to spit that venom at him. All his life he had loved and reverenced women, idealized them as gentle, tender, compassionate creatures, wives and mothers; and then in the end a woman had spat at him—not even the woman who had left him had done that. . . .

And then the trek into the wilderness in the heat of the sun—the terrible July sun, savage there in the coastal plain—and the small black planes flying in low, driving the people off the road, into the wilderness, and always deeper into the wilderness, into the mountains; the panic and the terror, the dehumanizing, the deliberate degradation imposed upon them . . . as though to take their country, their homes, their land, every material possession, was not enough, and they had to take from them their human dignity as well. And from many of them their lives.

He was as aware of the woman who sat near him under the olive trees with the dead baby at her breast as he had been of the woman who with a wild cry had flung her living baby into a gully, unable to carry it further—unable to go on being a human being, demented by suffering. He had been aware of the old people who finally collapsed and who lay where they fell and were left there to die, the crowds going past them and over them like the unheeding chariot wheels of some Roman circus. He had been dully, indifferently, aware of the people, both men and women, who cupped their hands to save their urine, and that of others, as precious water. He had been intensely aware of his wife limping painfully in her broken sandals, and of the misery in her face, but for all his love and caring there was nothing he could do for her, and that was part of his own agony. He had been aware of his son trudging along with the blind boy's hand locked in his, and it had seemed to him the only good thing in all that hell of suffering and each-for-himself struggle for survival. Whoever else perished his son Anton should be allowed to survive. Anguish made him dumb.

He got up and they went on again and this time Marian walked beside him.

'We shall soon come to the *wadi*,' she said, trying to hearten him. '*Insh'allah.*'

His gaze rested on her for a moment.

He said in English, 'I shall make it—don't worry. How are you?'
'I'm all right.'

After a few minutes she dropped behind to pick up one of Nadia's children. After that she stumbled, blindly, the child's weight almost insupportable. She was half fainting when someone came and took the child from her. It was Farid.

'There may be a Roman cistern in those rocks ahead of us,' he said, encouragingly.

'It's better not to hope.'

He made no comment, but heaved the whimpering child up on to his shoulders and trudged off. Marian fell back with the other women.

Majdeh said, 'If there's no water when we get to those rocks I shall die—I can't go on. Oh, for God's sake!' She raised a hand and slapped the child clinging to her across the face and then pushed him violently from her. The child fell to the ground sobbing.

'I can't carry him any more!' Majdeh cried, wildly, then burst into tears. 'I'm finished!' she sobbed. 'I can't go on!'

Marian lifted up the weeping child and tried to soothe him. To Majdeh she said, 'We're coming to water soon—the worst is over now. Take heart!'

She straddled the child across her back and they went on. They all went on, a vast straggling concourse of people slowly, painfully, moving eastward.

By the time the Mansour party reached the rocks a huge crowd was gathered round.

Anton and the blind boy edged their way into the crowd and persistently manœuvred their way to the front. The rocks were on slightly rising ground, and there was a well there, all right, a deep shaft with a glimmer of water at the bottom. People had knotted handkerchiefs and strips of their clothing together and were lowering them down the shaft; they came up muddy but wet; families divided portions of the wet material between them and sucked them; wet muddy handkerchiefs were claimed and eagerly sucked. Women were using their head-veils. The two boys conferred together and decided that even between them they could not make a rope long enough to reach the water, but if all the women in their party tore off strips of their dresses they could knot them together and make a long enough rope.

When they rejoined the others the servant girl Randa was carrying the child and Marian was supporting the still hysterical Majdeh.

'There's water in the well—very muddy,' Anton told them. 'People are lowering ropes of handkerchieves and strips of cloth. They come up black with mud, but wet. People are sucking them.'

'Who wants to suck mud?' Majdeh screamed. 'I'd sooner drink my own water!'

Marian, exhausted and frayed beyond endurance, had suddenly had enough; she struck her across the face. Majdeh staggered and fell down; then sat there crying quietly, utterly wretched but no longer hysterical. Marian dropped down beside her and began tearing at the hem of her dress; when she had ripped it off she began on Nadia's, assisted by Anton. The blind boy stayed with them whilst Anton went back to the rocks with the strips of cloth. He was sometime away, and when he returned he found that his father and uncle had joined the group. The women had one muddy strip of cloth and the men the other; they sucked on the strips and in the gratitude of their dry mouths for the precious moisture did not taste the mud.

There was no shade near the rocks and they did not stay long, and soon afterwards came in close to the desert hills and entered a broad shallow valley, and there at last was the *wadi*.

2

THE *wadi* seemed as intolerable as the wilderness itself, and it was so stony that some people preferred to walk at either side of it, picking their way among the rocks and boulders. But the *wadi* was a route, as clearly defined as a railway track, and the vast concourse of people gradually converged upon it, forming themselves into an endless procession, stretching away into the distance as far as the eye could see.

There were outcrops of prickly pear now, and clumps of pink-flowered oleander, breaking the red-earth, grey-boulder monotony of the wilderness, and then suddenly, astonishingly, there were little grey-green scatterings of carob trees—stunted little trees, but with the long brown seed-pods dangling from their branches.

Anton's hand tightened on the blind boy's.

'Carob trees!' he cried. '*Yalla!*'

'Where? Above the *wadi*?'

'Yes. Quite close. People are already swarming all over them like ants!'

'Go without me. It's easier. I'll wait here.'

Amin dropped down on to his haunches to squat, waiting; Anton, released from the drag of the blind boy's weight, scrambled up the side of the *wadi* and raced the few yards across to the nearest tree. Several men and boys had already climbed it, but he swarmed up and snatched at the nearest seed-pods, the precious locust beans. A youth in the branches immediately above him kicked at him and shouted at him, angrily, to find another tree, but he dodged the kicks and hung on, snatching at the seed-pods and stuffing them into his trouser-pocket and inside his sweat-soaked shirt. Then the youth above him kicked at his face, savagely, forcing him down. Thirst had diminished hunger, but there had been very little to eat in the last few days of bombardment, and those people who had had as much as a small cup of Turkish coffee and a few olives early that morning were lucky. Anton was hungry, and he knew that Amin was, and who knew if there would be anything to eat at Ni'leen when they reached there?

Amin was waiting where he had left him when he got back to the *wadi*, but his parents and the others were now far ahead, out of sight. He gave one of the pods to Amin and they trudged on again, munching the dry sweetness of the bean, like a dried date, and feeling sustained by it. They agreed to eat only one each, saving the rest for the others when they caught up with them.

The sun was lowering now and though they sweated as they stumbled along the stony track the heat no longer savaged them. Children still whimpered piteously, and old people still halted every few yards panting and gasping, but no one collapsed; all those who were going to collapse had done so hours ago; the people still on their feet in the *wadi* were going to reach Ramallah.

Ni'leen is a tiny village rising in tiers on the hillside above the valley threaded by the Wadi Lydd, the continuation of the Wadi Al Malaki. A road skirts the village and on the valley side there is a stone fountain from which the village people draw their water. There are a few fig trees in the vicinity, and where the land flows gently down to the valley there are some terraced olive groves.

Upon this hamlet there was the debouchment of a hundred thousand or so exhausted and thirst-crazed people. They inundated the one street in a vast tidal wave of sweating humanity. The crowd round the fountain was a solid mass of people blocking the street in all directions.

Anton said, 'It might be hours before we get near the fountain. Let's go up to the top of the village—we might find someone to give us a cup of water and something to eat.'

They made their way up narrow alleyways and between hedges of prickly pear; there were a few lean pariah dogs and scavenging cats, but no other sign of life. The villagers had had news of the fall of Lydda and had fled along the road to Ramallah.

There were a few open-fronted shops but stripped bare of everything. In the middle of the labyrinth of alleyways they came to a small dark bakery, little more than a cave. A smell of baking bread came from it. Had the baker stayed behind in the deserted village? Anton peered into the gloom of the interior and saw the red glow of the oven, and laid along the flat brickwork top a small pile of the flat round pancakes of peasant bread. He called out and waited, but there was no answer, and no one came. Whether the baker had gone for good or only temporarily, the freshly baked bread was there and Anton helped himself.

He said, as they left the bakery, 'The thing now is to get back and find the others.'

On the way down, moving slowly over the rough cobbles because of Amin, a small party of people overtook and passed them; they were carrying bundles and obviously evacuating. Anton had a sudden pang of guilt, wondering if one of them was the baker and if the pile of bread from which he had taken a few rounds had been placed there in readiness for these people. He thought it likely, but had no intention of offering to give the bread back; he and Amin had it hidden in their shirts, with the carob beans. He was frightened when one of the men stopped and spoke to him, asking him where they were from.

'Lydda,' Anton told him. 'My friend and I came up here to see if anyone would give us water, but we didn't find anyone.'

'Most people went this morning, when we got the news,' the man told him. 'My family decided to risk waiting till the evening and to walk through the night to Ramallah. There will be thousands on the road in the morning.'

'*Insh'allah*,' Amin murmured.

'We'll all be back in a few days,' the man said, cheerfully. 'When the Iraqi army moves up. *Insh'allah*.'

'*Insh'allah*,' the boys repeated, and then as the man hurried down to join his companions, who had not waited for him, '*Maa'alsalama*.'

'*Maa'alsalama*,' they said, relieved that he had gone and convinced that it was from him they had stolen.

Amin said, as they stumbled down the steep alleyways, 'Even if the Iraqi army liberates Palestine we shan't be back in a few days. It will take longer than that. Perhaps, even, we shall never go back.'

Anton offered no comment. The Jews were very highly organized, he had heard his father say, and the Arabs were not. All he could think of now was finding his parents and getting to the fountain. Also his hand, which had been for so many hours clenched with Amin's felt as though it would never open out flat again.

There was still a big crowd pressing round the fountain when they got back, but it had thinned to some extent because many people had realized the futility of all trying to get there at once and were sitting or lying under the olive trees, or on the ground with their backs against the walls of houses beside the road, waiting, thankful to be at least no longer placing one lacerated foot before the other. They were in Jordan now, in Arab territory; that part of Jordan that once was Palestine, like the land over there to the West, between the sea and the long lines of the bare hills. They sat staring at the hills, and the setting sun crimsoning the sky above them, and at the dark formlessness of the future. Some of them wept, from exhaustion and despair. Others—most of them—sat dully staring; the beginning of the vast refugee inertia.

Anton and the blind boy inched their way to the front of the crowd and came at last to the water, scooping it up in their hands and splashing it over their faces, sucking it down their parched throats with loud animal noises, and nudged and pushed all the time by people pressing on from behind and all around. It was beginning to grow dark and when they left the fountain Anton was worrying about his parents. He found a place under the olive trees for Amin and then went searching, going from tree to tree, sometimes tripping over prostrate bodies and being cursed for his clumsiness, peering in the gathering dusk into every group of people and sometimes being shooed away like a pariah dog. Fear leapt up in him that perhaps they had not reached Ni'leen; perhaps his father had collapsed and his mother was sitting beside him down there in the *wadi*; perhaps they were all still down there in the wilderness. He should never have run off to the carob tree; it was an unlucky tree, anyhow, supposed to be haunted by evil spirits.

The hard dry seed-pods pressed against his warm body, and the rounds of stolen bread. He began to sob, helplessly, blundering along the olive terraces, picking his way between prostrate bodies, going from group to group, all his courage ebbing away in exhaustion and anxiety.

When a strong hand suddenly grabbed him by the shoulder he cringed in terror, convinced that he was going to be flung down to the terrace below, with a curse; instead of which a familiar voice cried, 'Where do you think you're off to? We've been looking for you everywhere!' and with a kind of anguish of relief he looked up into the face of his uncle.

'Oh!' he gasped, and clung to his uncle's hand, then could say no more because his nose began bleeding again.

The night was warm and still, and full of the incessant sound of crickets. It was full also of the sound of people snoring heavily in the sleep of exhaustion, and of people talking, and children crying. Sometimes there was the horrible short quick barking of a jackal, and then a dog would start up dogs in all direction. There were those who slept as though they would never wake, and those who stared sleeplessly at the bodies huddled all round them on the terraced hillside and waited for the dawn.

Marian slept, lying flat on the stony ground, utterly spent. Majdeh slept heavily next to her, the two children curled up beside her. Nadia lay awake, weeping and worrying. Butros sat with his back to a gnarled old tree feeling as though he would never sleep again. Anton sat up beside him, afraid to lie down for fear of starting his nose bleeding again. Farid had tried to stay awake to keep his brother company, but had finally fallen asleep where he sat.

Butros stared at the shadowy outline of the hills, and said aloud, to no one in particular, 'They couldn't kill us. Only the very old and the very young. They turned us out into the wilderness to die like dogs, but we didn't die. We are still here—most of us. A people without a country!'

Anton said, 'Perhaps the Iraqi army will soon liberate our country and we can go back.'

Butros looked down at the pale glimmer of his son's face beside him.

'Perhaps,' he said, gently. '*Insh'allah,*' and then, 'Lie down, son, and try to sleep. We have to start walking again as soon as it's light.'

Anton slid down beside his father, his body crushing out a scent of wild thyme. He felt as though he still had Amin's hand clasped in his; he could still feel the pressure of their two hands pressed into the base of his shoulder.

He said in English, happily, 'We made it!' then on a small sigh of relaxation fell asleep.

The second day was less terrible than the first because although it was hot the refugees were no longer in the plain, and also they were on a road. The road was dusty and winding and endless, but it was a road, and blistered and swollen feet were spared the additional torture of picking a way through rocks and stones. There was also release, now, from fear, for they were in Arab-held territory. How long it remained in the hands of the Arabs was a matter for speculation, but there was no sign of Jewish planes or troops, and it was understood that the Arab Legion was in Ramallah.

People began going to the fountain before it was fully light, and by sunrise the crowd round it was dense. Many people, the Mansours among them, decided that it was better not to spend time trying to get to the water but to get going on the road before the day became hot. The crowd on the road quickly swelled into a mammoth procession. When it had been going about an hour-and-a-half two cars were sighted coming from Ramallah.

Butros, peering with narrowed eyes, murmured to Marian at his side, 'One of them could be for us—Khalil would have got the Lydda news last night and if he has petrol he would send out for us——'

The crowd fell back to the sides of the road as the cars approached, a large black Buick and a maroon-coloured Chevrolet. They drove slowly through the crowd and it was some time before they neared the Mansour party; then Butros gave a shout.

'Ahmad!' he cried. 'Khalil's driver!'

Farid recognized him at the same time and also shouted, excitedly, and the driver stopped. Marian, Majdeh, and Nadia piled in at the back, Butros and Farid in front beside the driver. Anton hung back.

'Quickly!' Marian commanded, 'or we'll have the mob trying to get in with us!'

'There's not room for Amin,' Anton protested. He was still gripping the blind boy's hand close to his shoulder.

Majdeh said, 'Amin must go on with the other servants. If we take him we've got to take them all!'

'We don't know where the others are,' Anton told her.

Majdeh had spoken in Arabic and Amin said, quickly, 'It's all right. Everyone is going to Ramallah—anyone will walk with me.'

He tried to disengage his hand from Anton's, but Anton gripped it the tighter.

'No,' he insisted. 'If you walk, so do I!'

'Oh, get *in*!' Marian cried, wildly, aware of the faces already crowding at the car windows. 'You can squeeze in between us and Amin can sit on the floor.'

The two boys climbed in, the car door slammed, and the driver continued to drive ahead, looking for a place to turn, a number of people shaking their fists after the car. The Chevrolet followed empty, the people it had been sent to pick up being a mile or more farther down the seemingly endless procession.

Butros asked the driver, 'How is it in Ramallah?'

'Terrible,' the driver told him. 'Thousands of refugees came in last night and there was nothing to feed them with. Bread is being distributed from the Legion depot this morning—Glubb Pasha ordered it, they say.'

'Is he there?'

'No, in Jerusalem. They telephoned him there. People were stoning the soldiers yesterday when we got the news that the Jews had taken Lydda and Ramleh.'

There was satisfaction in the driver's voice.

Butros offered no comment. Bitterness was understandable; everyone had believed that the three armoured cars which had engaged the Palmach, the spearhead of the Israeli troops, outside

Lydda, were the advance guard for its relief, but no supporting Legion troops had materialized and the fighting was confined to the outskirts of the town; the Palmach were there in force, and what were three armoured cars against it? He believed that when the history of the Arab-Israeli war came to be written the soldiers of the Arab Legion would be shown to have fought gallantly against overwhelming odds. That Arab soldiers should have been stoned by an infuriated civilian populace, who could obviously know nothing of military problems, he found deeply shocking, one more wound on the already cruelly lacerated Palestinian soul.

When the two cars turned and headed for Ramallah the crowd parted sullenly to make way for them.

They make us feel guilty for being so privileged, Marian thought, despairingly. But then our whole life is privileged. It was a relief when they met a few other cars coming out from Ramallah— though a whole fleet of them could only have taken up a handful of those exhausted, footsore, hungry and thirsty, sweating tens of thousands plodding along the winding road, through the deep dust, on that last lap to Ramallah.

3

EVEN before the arrival of the main body of refugees, from Lydda and Ramleh, the little hill town presented an astonishing sight, with the thousands of homeless milling in its narrow main street looking for food and shelter. Under every olive tree on the hillside terraces a family was camped out, and in every garden, and along every wall and fence of the pine-flanked avenues of the residential quarter, primitive tents of sacking, and even portions of clothing, were rigged up, sheltering men, women and children, providing them with an illusion of privacy and a home.

The Egyptian Red Crescent, the police, and the army, organized a distribution of food, blankets, tents. The vast exodus had not been forseen and no preparations had been made for such an influx; it had somehow been unthinkable that Lydda should fall; it had been the place to which people from outlying districts had gone for safety; it had a strong National Guard, and every able-bodied man had a gun. The noise of battle raged all round it, but Lydda itself was safe. Reinforcements would come and the Israelis be pushed back to the sea. Driven into the sea. Instead of which the Palestinians were driven eastwards into the wilderness. And Ramallah received the first impact of that major human disaster. It reeled under the impact, but recovered from the shock and began to organize; army lorries from Amman, far away on the arid hills at the other side of the great Jordan Valley, came rumbling in laden with sacks of flour. Loud-speakers in the streets directed the people to distribution centres. The big American Friends Boys' School was immediately turned into a temporary hospital and clinic for the sick and wounded of that terrible exodus. And for the babies born during it, and their exhausted mothers.

The people ravaged the olive groves and orchards and vineyards for wood for their fires, and the owners winced but brought traditional Arab hospitality to bear. '*Tfadalu*,' they said. 'Help yourselves!' How should the starving and destitute and homeless be denied? The nations of the world had voted away their country to the Jews, and the Jews had entered into possession of their homes and lands. God have mercy on their homelessness and hunger. Such as we have we give them. *Tfadalu*.

The big black Buick which Khalil Dahoud had sent out with his driver early that morning in the hope of picking up his brothers-in-law, Butros and Farid Mansour, and their wives and families, on the last lap of the trek, moved slowly down the overcrowded main street and out into the residential area where the pine trees were already being used as posts from which to string up some kind of shelter.

When the car drew up opposite the gates of the Dahoud villa, lying back from the road in a long garden full of flowering trees and shrubs, people squatting under awnings of sacking rigged from the fence regarded them sullenly. These, their looks said, were clearly the lucky ones, those who had made at least part of the exodus by car and had a home and family to come to. . . .

Khalil Dahoud was a tall, fair-skinned, handsome man of so aristocratic a presence and so formal a manner that those who did not know him believed him to be cold, whereas he was in fact a man of immense generosity and innate kindness. He was a landowner and very wealthy. His wife, Muna, had the Mansour good looks and charm—and something of her elder brother's irascibility. Khalil was a Moslem, and the elders of both families had been initially deeply affronted by the marriage—though not Butros, who was then in the position of a deserted husband, his wife having run off with a younger man, and not Farid, who was atheist and rebellious and married to a superstitiously religious wife. Khalil had been delighted when nearing fifty Butros had given the elders another shock by marrying an Englishwoman twenty years younger—a foreigner, that is to say, and old at that.

Anton was a little afraid of the Dahoud family—his haughty-seeming uncle Khalil, his aunt Muna with her smiles and sweetness and sudden rages, and the four girl cousins, the youngest near to his own age, the eldest a big girl of sixteen with horn-rimmed spectacles and the appearance and manner of who one knows all the answers and cannot be bothered with anyone who doesn't. . . .

Marian liked her brother-in-law but found Muna tiresome, and the girls singularly unattractive, considering how good-looking their parents were. They would pass as English, she thought, with their fair complexions and offhand manners and gaucherie. Butros loved Muna and forgave her her tantrums, recognizing in her a female version of himself; Khalil he made no attempt to understand, but was bound to respect because he was rich, aristo-cratic—he believed profoundly in good families—and his sister's husband.

Muna came running now in her impulsive way to greet them, with Khalil following her, stiff and stately, but embracing his brothers-in-law on both cheeks, and kissing the hands of the women, and affectionately lightly slapping Anton's cheeks—a Moslem custom which Butros always found irritating and tried not to notice. There were exclamations, commiserations, questions, and a procession under a pergola festooned with wine-coloured Bougainvillea to the white villa, which was similarly festooned. A flight of white steps led up to a wide terrace where tables and chairs were set out. The Mansour party sank into chairs and cold drinks were brought. A servant took away Nadia's children and wanted to include Amin, but Anton insisted that he stay with them.

'He is my friend,' he explained.

'Where are his family?' Muna demanded.

Marian said quickly, 'They will arrive later—they know where to come. They are in our employ. Let him stay with Anton now—they have walked together all the way.'

Khalil laid a hand on the blind boy's arm.

He said gently, 'You are welcome. This is your home.'

'We all need baths,' Marian said, and then suddenly, for no reason, burst into tears.

Of all the inmates of the Dahoud house that night only Butros, exhausted by the trek and by his vigil on the hillside below Ni'leen the previous night, slept soundly. He slept so soundly that his deep, resonant snores penetrated to Marian lying insomniac in the adjoining room.

Nadia, in a room with her two children, lay wondering when Nasri woud be released by the Israelis and how soon he would get to Ramallah, and whether in his shame and anger he would kill her when he knew what had happened, or whether she should kill herself before his return. These thoughts alternated with spurts of hopefulness, in which Nasri's return was delayed until in the course of time it had been revealed that she was not pregnant as a result of the dreadful thing that had happened to her, and Nasri need be told nothing about it.... But fear always clouded over this glimmer of hope. Her mother and Marian had tried to comfort her by telling her that if she was found to be pregnant Nasri and her father should go together to a Palestinian doctor and tell him what had happened and ask him for an abortion; no Palestinian doctor would refuse. When she closed her eyes she saw again the triumphantly laughing face of the young Lebanese-American and she rolled her head from side to side on the pillow moaning in mental anguish.

In the room next to her lay her parents. They, too, were wide awake, Majdeh having broken the shocking news to Farid after they had retired to their room.

'If only Nasri doesn't arrive here too soon Nadia might find everything is all right and he need never know,' Majdeh urged. 'Why make him suffer unnecessarily? In about ten days' time she will know.'

Farid said grimly, 'You had better pray hard that he doesn't return before Nadia is ready for him and that all is well. But if he gets back before it's known whether she's pregnant or not Khalil had better tell him.'

'Why Khalil? Why not Butros, as the head of the family?'

'Butros would find it too upsetting. Khalil is cool and calm—as a lawyer or a doctor might be. Nasri would take it better from him....'

They lay flat on their backs in the wide bed, their arms along their sides, relaxed in the blessedness of having their swollen feet off the ground, and of lying in a bed instead of on the stony hillside. Just to lie flat was so blessed. If only they hadn't the worry about Nadia nagging at them they could have slipped easily into sleep, but worry kept them staring at the darkness. Farid did fall asleep eventually, but Majdeh every time she dozed would wake with a start thinking she heard Nadia sobbing in the next room.

At the back of the house, in a room which looked from the first floor down into a garden where there was a fountain and some small orange trees, Khalil lay in bed with his hands clasped under his head and his face turned towards the moonlight outside. Jasmine cascaded round the window and the warm still night was full of its scent, and of a tumult of cicadas. Muna sat beside him, propped up with pillows and smoking a cigarette. She, also, turned her face to the window and the moonlight. They had discussed the Nadia disaster already, with the rest of the family, and privately; there was no more to be said about it. If the worst happened Khalil had a Palestinian doctor friend whom he was quite confident would terminate the pregnancy. Khalil would talk to Nasri when he arrived, and he would surely have nothing but pity for his wretched wife. They had been shocked and concerned, but more important was the question as to whether the Jews were likely to break through to Latrun, now that they occupied Lydda and Ramleh. Latrun was at the cross-roads, one way to Ramallah, the other to Jerusalem. There were said to be still Arab Legion forces in Latrun, but it was becoming clear that the Arabs were outnumbered everywhere. If Latrun fell the road was opened to Ramallah. And Ramallah now was stuffed to bursting point with refugees. Would there be another exodus—this time down to Jericho, twelve hundred feet below sea-level, and sweltering in the unbelievable July heat? Ought they, the Dahouds and the Mansours, to get out now, whilst the road was still open? Butros had a house there, big enough for them all. Muna was nervous, harrowed by the stories of the trek from Lydda, and worried about the four girls. Butros thought they should go; he intended going down with Marian and Anton tomorrow if they were all sufficiently rested.

Khalil made a gesture of impatience.

'Butros is old, and he has been unnerved by his experiences. Lydda and Ramleh fell because they weren't defended. In the Latrun area the Legion is present in force. It will be time enough to go down to Jericho if Latrun falls, but I don't believe it will.'

He turned his head and because the moonlight fell directly across their pillows she could see that he smiled his small quizzical smile.

'Why do you worry so much? You profess belief in God—why don't you trust in your God? God is good or he is not God. Isn't that so?'

He reached out a hand to her.

'Why don't we sleep?'

She stubbed out her cigarette and slid down beside him.

She mocked him, 'Who is the unbeliever?'

She laid her head on his shoulder and an arm across his body. He did not speak or move and soon he was asleep.

She envied him the quality of stillness, in his mind and in his body. She thought: We Mansours are so restless and nervous. We pride ourselves on being Christian as though some special virtue attached to it, instead of it being an accident of birth. Perhaps if you're an Arab it's better to be Moslem—it fits better; the difference between the ready-made coat and the made-to-measure. Islam was made-to-measure by the Prophet for the Arabs.

But Khalil is an unbeliever and prefers to wear a coat of his own making. Perhaps he is right and one day there maybe an end of all religions and people will be free. When a Jew abandons his religion he ceases to be a Jew. But he can still be an Israeli.

In her drowsy state the reflection seemed both witty and profound. She resolved to remember it and repeat it to Khalil in the morning. But when she wakened in the morning Khalil, who got up most mornings as soon as it was light, had gone.

She rang a bell and a servant brought Turkish coffee, and before she had finished drinking it Marian was standing beside her bed, looking astonishingly cool and fresh, her dress having been laundered overnight, and saying that Butros insisted on going down to Jericho; he had telephoned the house, and Khalil had arranged for Ahmad to drive them down. . . .

4

TO GO from two thousand feet above sea-level down to Jericho twelve hundred feet below sea-level, in the heat of mid-July, was as everyone protested—everyone except Marian—crazy. Why should anyone in their right mind wish to go from the coolness of the hills down, down, down to the burning desert?

Marian counter-insisted that to seek peace of mind was not crazy, and there was none for Butros in Ramallah, on the direct road from threatened Latrun and its streets milling with refugees. He had suffered enough, Marian declared, almost in tears from her own physical and nervous exhaustion, and if Jericho in the blistering heat was where he longed to be, as he did, it made sense that he should go there, and that his wife and son should go with him.

But it was, she knew, not only that in his exhausted state he felt insecure in Ramallah and shrank from even the possibility of another ordeal at the hands of the Israelis, and that the atmosphere of Ramallah, in all its refugee confusion and wretchedness, got on his nerves; all that was real enough, but there was also the deep need to escape from people.

For weeks past at home in Lydda they had been living night and day surrounded by worried and frightened people, relatives and friends, and complete strangers who had sought refuge at the big house; they had lived in fear, too close to each other, and under constant strain. The Israelis were closing in during those last few days, and the horror of what had happened at Deir Yassin only a few months ago, when the entire village had been massacred in the most horrible fashion, was actively in all their minds. What happened a few miles from Jerusalem could happen in undefended

Lydda. The strain of the last few days had been almost unendurable, between the dread of massacre and the constant shelling and the bursts of gunfire. And all the time life lived at too close quarters, no privacy in which to weep or pray or make love, and for some the total lack of privacy was worse than for others, and Butros was among those for whom it had been intolerable.

At Khalil's house although the company was less than a dozen, and consisted of the immediate family circle, for Butros there were still too many people—and too many tensions. Between him and his brother-in-law there had never been much communication, and the four giggling schoolgirl daughters got on his nerves. Everyone and everything got on his nerves—except his wife and son—and he wanted, needed, to be alone with them. The physical discomfort of the Jericho heat would be negligible for him; Jericho was safe; Jericho was not milling with tragic, destitute displaced people—that was to come. In Jericho it would be possible to be quiet and alone with the only two people in the world who deeply mattered.

All this Marian understood, and it similarly spoke to her own nervously exhausted condition. The heat in Jericho, she knew, would be relentless; but they would feel safe, Butros would relax—and they would be blessedly alone.

Anton was relieved that they were not to stay in Ramallah. He, also, did not feel safe there; and apart from not feeling at ease with his Dahoud relatives the Jericho house was a second home. Amin and his parents would go down with them, as servants, and he and Amin would be together. School would not re-start for either of them till late in September—and by that time, who knows, they might be back home in Lydda; they and all of them. . . .

Butros was determined on the valley route to Jericho. It was a second-class road, rough, narrow, and in places stony; also because it was very winding it took longer; but the good main road led through the centre of Jerusalem, and there was fighting in the Old City, with the Jews lobbing over heavy mortar bombs. Nothing would have induced him to go through Jerusalem, though Farid, who was remaining in Ramallah, urged that with the Arab Legion there they would have more protection than driving out into the countryside. The Jericho road was still open; out in the valley anything might happen.

Anything might happen anywhere, Butros countered, but by all reports Jerusalem was continuously shelled, and the Jews were in Notre Dame, with machine-guns at the windows. It would be a pity to have survived the exodus from Lydda only to be killed by a machine-gun or a shell in Jerusalem. In the valley they were unlikely to meet anyone but Bedouin refugees.

Khalil prophesied that they would be driving back through Ramallah in a week or two on their way back to Lydda.

'We shall have thrown the Jews into the sea,' he declared, nonchalantly.

Butros smiled the small half-sad, half-rueful smile characteristic of him.

'You talk as though we have powerful armies to dispose of! We hadn't even enough to send troops to hold Lydda and Ramleh!'

'The Legion hadn't, but the Iraqis haven't yet come into the area.'

Butros said, wrily amused, 'I hope they arrive in time!'

Muna was angry. Butros seemed always to make a point of disagreeing with Khalil.

'A defeatist attitude doesn't help!' she said, sharply.

'It always helps to be realistic,' her brother told her, smiling.

Marian cried, desperately trying to be neutral, as a good guest, 'How do any of us know? Only the military know where the troops are and what they're capable of!'

It was a relief to get away: from the Dahoud house, and from teeming Ramallah itself.

When the road was clear of the town and running along the top of the deep gorge between the high hills it was possible to relax a little. The hills and valley here were green, with patches of cultivation in the valley, and cattle grazing the bright green of alfafa, and neat squares of apple and orange orchards, and precious streams of water. The valley sang with its green fertility, but the song ended with the valley. The road wound round and down and the land broadened out into desert, flanked by low bare brown hills. Now there was neither water nor cultivation, and after a solitary small bedouin camp of low black hair tents, hugging the sand, no sign of life. There was a crackling in the ear-drums from the steep descent and Anton asked, 'Are we down to sea-level yet?'

His father told him no, it was a long way down to Jericho yet. Butros felt the pressure of the descent, but his spirits were lifting. He wound the car window lower down. The heat was now very pronounced. He gazed out of the window at the hot golden-brown waste, then turned to Marian, smiling.

'No people,' he said, happily.

She returned his smile, and laid a hand momentarily on his clasped on the silver knob of his cane.

'We were right to come.'

'It won't be any hotter than Lydda.'

'Only more airless—no sea-breezes.'

They both fell silent then, thinking of the long stretch of Mediterranean coast, from Acre down to Jaffa, the Palestinian coastline, from which the plain, with all its orange groves flowed away to the Judaean hills, crowned by Jerusalem. Now there was no Palestine, and the coastline was the coastline of the new country carved out of the ancient one: the new country called 'Israel'. There was no going to the coast now in the heat of summer if you were a Palestinian. For the Palestinians there was only the bitter-salt lake of the Dead Sea, the pool left when the sea went out millenia ago.

It came into view, heat-drained of colour, like the sky, across a surrealist landscape of strange shapes carved out of solidified sand, the landscape of a dream, the bottom of the sea. It lay there, a still, shimmering lake, between the dun-coloured Mountains of Moab and the folds of the Judaean hills.

Butros regarded it with satisfaction, because the sight of it meant they were now not far from Jericho, and Jericho was where he longed to be; Marian with affection, because it was associated with the brief romantic phase of her life, the memory of which she cherished; Anton with pleasure, in the thought of camping beside it with Amin, and floating in it on moonlight nights. He leaned over the back of the seat to tell the blind boy their whereabouts.

51

'We'll have some good times!' he cried happily. 'At least the Dead Sea is ours!'

'Only this end of it and the east shore,' his father corrected him.

Amin's father grumbled, 'Who wants that stinking sea? We should have stayed in Ramallah.'

Marian said, without looking round, 'You are always grumbling, Yusuf. No one compelled you to come down to Jericho with us!'

She had never liked him and always wondered why Butros tolerated him.

With great dignity Yusuf replied, 'I am at my master's service!'

Butros smiled faintly, but kept silent. It was Yusuf's privilege to complain; he was a good servant and they understood each other. He knew that if Marian had had her way she would have dismissed him long ago, but Marian did not appreciate good cooking as he did, and Yusuf in addition to being a competent driver was also a very good cook. A misdemeanour has to be major before you sack so valuable a servant, and Yusuf never did more than grumble.

Yusuf's wife drew her head veil closer round her face, excluding herself from these wrangles; she also would have preferred to remain in Ramallah; there was no life down here in Jericho; it was as dead as the Dead Sea; she could have remained behind at the Dahoud house, with her parents and her other children, until it was time to return to Lydda, but just as Yusuf owed allegiance to the master, so she owed allegiance to her husband. Amin was the youngest of her eight children, and she had several grandchildren —from whom she minded being parted more than from her own children. Of her own, Amin was the dearest to her, because of his affliction, and because, too, he was curiously different from the others, of much higher intelligence, so that the Master took a special interest in him and intended that he should be properly educated at a special school for the blind, and he and the Master's son were like brothers.

Ahead of them rose the massif of the Judaean hills, heat-hazed in the distance and crowned by the spires of Jerusalem. In the foreground the Mount of Temptation rose flat-topped above a foreground of tall cypresses. At the Greek Orthodox monastery half-way up, Marian found herself thinking, the monks would be cool in their rooms carved out of the rock; and among the ruins at the top the wild marigolds would be burnished gold in the hot sun. She and Butros had once made the ascent together. They had been married in Jerusalem, and at her wish gone down to Jericho for their honeymoon. She had had a great desire to spend the first few weeks of her married life in that house, Dar el-Salam, House of Peace, to which she had first gone with her father, and where Butros had first seen her—as she had, so intensely, willed that he should—as the woman who loved him and wished to marry him, and whom, astonishingly, as it had seemed to him, after all his years in the emotional wilderness since Siriya had left him, he could take as his second wife—the daughter of his English friend, Robert Melby.

Her mother had been not quite happy about the marriage, not because Butros Al-Mansour was a Palestinian, but because he was twenty years older than Marian, and divorced. But Marian, at thirty, had almost consciously married her father, for she loved Butros for the qualities she loved in her father. Robert Melby had been at that time, before World War II, Principal of a school for blind boys of all faiths in Jaffa. The school was organized by a Society for Blind Welfare in Palestine, with its headquarters in London. Butros, in his role of distinguished local landowner, had been on the committee and took an active interest in the running and financing of the school. Mutual liking and respect had developed a strong friendship between the two men. It seemed to Marian that despite their totally different backgrounds they had much in common—a comparable integrity and distinction of personality. Marian, who worked at the school for five years before her marriage, was attracted to Butros Mansour initially because he was her father's friend and in many respects like her father, because she recognized his integrity, because of a quality of warmth and charm which forgave all his bursts of irascibility, and because she was aware of his loneliness. He was a Christian of the Eastern Orthodox Church and had had to wait seven years for his divorce, but was already divorced when they met. There were no children of that first marriage, a fact which was part of his loneliness, and for which at first Marian had pitied him, but of which later she was glad, for it left the way clear for her to absorb him completely.

They were married in 1934 and lived first on the estate at Jaffa, among the orange groves, and later moved into Lydda. Their son, whom they named Anton after his paternal grandfather, was born in the following year.

Butros was an ardent nationalist in those years of the thirties, of the 'sub-war' of the Palestinian struggle for independence, and his friend Robert Melby was very sympathetic to those aspirations—so much so, indeed, that he seemed to his superiors at his Society's H.Q. in London to be becoming too much involved in politics. After a little correspondence between London and Jaffa the Society had decided to recall him, his intransigence adding to their embarrassment. He didn't blame them, but had been unable to act otherwise—feeling as he did on the Palestinian question. There was a sense, too, Marian knew, in which he had been glad to leave Palestine, deeply as he loved it, for more than one Arab friend had been hanged for his activities, in accordance with British policy at the time, and the situation had begun to be intolerable for him. He had returned to England in 1938. Marian remained with her husband and child in Lydda, not materially much affected by the war when it came, but filled with anxiety—there was a British military base not far away at Sarafand; enemy planes came over and there were air-raid warnings and stampedes to public air-raid shelters. But the Mansours and their servants stayed fatalistically in their house. In the summer they went up to Ramallah, to a rented house, and sometimes in the winter down to Jericho. Anton went to school in Lydda, and it was always understood that eventually he would go to the American Friends' School in Ramallah, reputedly the best school in Palestine.

But when the time came it was 1948. The spring of 1948. The sultry month of May, and the battle for Jerusalem was joined.

There were no signs of war in the little town of Jericho. In the narrow winding main street, flanked by small ferny-leafed golmohur trees, men sat on low stools on the pavement outside openfronted cafés, radios blared from open-fronted shops, men beat over-loaded donkeys along the gutter as usual, lounged in shop doorways, told their beads; women went by balancing cans of water on their heads, small children clinging to their skirts.

The black Buick moved slowly down the main street, cleaving a way through people and donkeys, barrows and carts and prowling pariah dogs, and came to where the road forks and narrow lanes plunge through a lushness of date-palms and wine-coloured Bougainvillea cascading over garden walls. There was a new angle now on the Mount of Temptation and it was much closer. The car drew up at wrought-iron gates and a shabby man emerged from a shack almost smothered by the huge fronds of banana leaves, saluted and opened the gates and the car passed up a drive of crowded date-palms, cypresses and casuarina trees to a square white-shuttered house, with a broad first-floor balcony at the side facing the mountain. There was an orange grove at one side of the drive and at the other a tangle of overgrown rose-beds and flowering shrubs.

Shallow steps led up to a colonaded terrace where a glass door led into the house. A dark-skinned, barefooted man in a crumpled white linen suit was laying a table on the terrace. At the sight of the car he straightened up and stood to attention. When his master emerged from the car he saluted; then Butros greeted him by name and he relaxed, smiled, and bade the family welcome home. Then he asked how had it been in Lydda? They had heard terrible stories. He drew up wicker chairs, and a few moments later had placed soft drinks, ice, and whisky on a table beside them.

The Mansours were at home.

It was very hot. Yusuf, immediately useful, brought out a fan and stood it on a table near where they sat. It churned up hot air, but the churned-up air was easier to breathe than the hot steady pressure of the motionless air. They sat with their swollen and blistered feet up on stools and let relaxation seep through their limbs.

Anton longed to explore the wild jungle of the garden, which he always did when he first arrived, but his feet were too painful. He lay back in the wicker chair wondering, restlessly, how soon it would be possible to get to the Dead Sea. He could borrow one of the servants' bicycles, but there was the problem of Amin. It was not too far to walk if you took short cuts across the desert, but at this time of the year you had to watch out for snakes and scorpions, whose stings were poisonous. It made it exciting.

'Shall we go back to Ramallah when it's safe?' he asked, suddenly anxious.

'You will go to school there in the autumn, all being well,' his father told him. 'Your mother and I will stay here.'

He did not add, 'Until we can return to Lydda,' because he did not believe in the return to Lydda. What the Jews had they held. And who was going to push them back and throw them into the sea? Where was the great army of liberation? He did not believe in it.

'Can Amin and I go camping when our feet are better?'

'We must wait and see what happens at Latrun, and in Jerusalem. If the Jews capture Jerusalem there will be nothing to stop them pouring down south. We have to wait. . . .'

5

IT WAS very much longer than anyone had expected before Nadia's husband, Nasri Dajani, returned to Ramallah. He was released from the concentration camp, with other men of military age in the Lydda-Ramleh area rounded up at the same time, late in October. In the three months since the round-up, and the mass exodus from Lydda, many things had happened.

Six days after the fall of Lydda the Jewish advance across the coastal plain to Latrun had been repulsed by a single gun mounted on the roof of the police post and manned by the 2nd Regiment of the Arab Legion. The Jews had five tanks in the field and infantry massed for attack, but, incredibly, the single gun knocked out the five tanks and the infantry never advanced.[1]

In the late afternoon of that memorable day the Security Council truce was officially in operation, to become known as the 'shooting truce', because it was punctuated by bursts of Israeli machine-gun fire and incidents created by Israeli snipers. Count Bernadotte went to Jerusalem to discuss ways and means of making the truce effective.

At that time the Egyptian army held the Gaza sector, and the Iraqi army was in the north of Jordan.

By August some forty thousand refugees had pitched their tents, under the supervision of the Trans-Jordan police, on the hillsides around Jericho, close to a stream.

In September Count Bernadotte was assassinated in Jerusalem by Jewish terrorists of the Stern Gang.

In October the Israelis with their brand-new aircraft smuggled in

1. Glubb gives an account of this in his book, *A Soldier with the Arabs* (Hodder & Stoughton, London 1957).

from Czechoslovakia bombed the Egyptian bases in the Gaza area, and their ground forces broke through the Egyptian lines and took Huleiqat to the west and Beersheba to the south, and Beit Hanun south of Huleiqat. An Egyptian garrison of some 2,500 men was besieged at Falluja. In charge of a contingent of infantry there was a young officer called Abdul Gamal Nasser. . . .

On October 22nd, the day after the fall of Beersheba, there was officially a cease-fire. Meawhile Israeli troops moved down from Artuf, south of Latrun towards Hebron, south of Jericho. Arab Legion forces also moved south. Hebron was saved by an Arab Legion reconnaissance force of seven armoured cars ambushing an Israeli column of some thirty or so. The Arab Legion then set up defence posts below the village of Dahiriya, a little south of Hebron, on the road to Beersheba.

On October 31st U.N.O. Observers reported a massacre by the Israelis of thirty Arab women and children at the village of Dawaima, west of Hebron.

It was after all Nadia who broke the news to Nasri about the Israeli soldier. She was three months pregnant, and very unwell. She was also near breaking point with nervous strain. The doctor to whom her father had taken her had verified that she was pregnant but refused to consider terminating the pregnancy without authority from the husband, since it did not follow, he pointed out, that she was pregnant by the Jew. It was useless for her to insist that Nasri would never wish her to go through with a pregnancy to bear a child that might not be his; the doctor equally vehemently insisted that he must be assured of this by Nasri himself.

'But who knows when he will be back?' Nadia cried, wildly.

'We dare not wait till he comes—it might be too late to do anything by then,' Farid pleaded.

The doctor remained adamant.

'There is still time,' he declared, but added, 'If he is not back in a month's time we will reconsider.'

But in a month's time Nasri was home.

The doctor in the meantime had relieved the girl, Randa, of her pregnancy, and two other Palestinian refugee girls brought to him by their distraught parents, one of whom had been raped in her father's presence. He was not the only Palestinian doctor to defy the law in this way at that time.

Nadia continued to suffer from morning-sickness, and to long for and yet dread her husband's return. Then, suddenly, without warning, he was back; he arrived dirty, dishevelled and exhausted, having walked most of the way from Lydda; he was also haggard and had lost weight, and his manner was strained.

Nasri Dajani was a young man upon whom, until the carving up of his country, life had sat lightly. He had a wealthy and indulgent father, a beautiful young wife, two children to whom he was devoted, and with them he had lived a pleasant and easy life in the family mansion in Jaffa. When the fighting began in that area in May they had fled from Jaffa to the Mansour house in Lydda. It was the end of his youthful insouciance, but the young man who had been marched off by the Israeli soldiers in mid-July had still a certain jauntiness of manner and outlook, whereas the Nasri Dajana who limped into Ramallah at the end of October looked very much older than his years, and there was a new tightness about his lips.

He was one of the fortunate ones in that he knew where to look for his family after the evacuation of Lydda; it was always understood that if they had to leave they would go to the Dahoud house in Ramallah; what he had, tormentingly, not known was how many of them had survived the ordeal of the exodus, what had happened to his wife and children, his parents, and the rest of his family. All the way from Lydda he had been agonized by the speculation as to what he might find when he reached Ramallah. The swarms of refugees encamped everywhere he had expected, yet their density appalled him as much as their wretchedness.

The street of pine trees, which was often called the Lovers' Street—because the pines made it dark in the evenings—was now the Street of the Refugees, and the tide of human misery flowed up to the gates of the Dahoud house and even into the garden itself.

He could see his children playing up near the house as he turned in, in charge of the servant-girl, Randa. He gave a shout and they all turned; then the children came running with excited cries, and the girl, startled, turned and ran up the steps and across the terrace and into the house.

In a moment she was back with Nadia, followed by Nadia's parents; he was aware of Majdeh and Farid but could see only his wife, in a white dress with a scarlet belt; Nadia running down the steps towards him. . . .

After the confusion of embraces, exclamations, questions, reassurances about his parents, who were at their house in Jerusalem, Nasri's first need was for a bath and a change of clothes; his second to be blessedly alone with his wife.

The bath was prepared and Khalil provided him with clothes. Majdeh, agitatedly, took Nadia aside whilst Nasri was in the bathroom.

'When he comes out of the bath you will have to go to him in the bedroom—what are you going to do? What are you going to tell him?'

'The truth, of course. Now that he's back I'm not afraid any more. He's had experience of the Jews himself now. He will understand. He will go with me to the doctor.'

'How can you be sure? He might be afraid it's his own child.'

'He won't take a chance. He dare not.'

'You can't tell. Men are strange. It might turn him against you. What will you do then?'

'Wait!' Nadia said, bitterly. 'Isn't that what we Palestinians have got to learn to be good at?'

Majdeh sighed and got up.

'God help you,' she said. 'I'll pray for you.'

The conversation had taken place outside on the terrace. Nadia also got up and followed her mother into the house. Majdeh went on through to the kitchen, and Nadia went upstairs. Nasri, wearing a silk dressing-gown of Khalil's, came out of the bathroom as she reached the landing. Now that he was shaved he looked less haggard, and all over again she thought how good-looking he was, and her heart contracted.

'I'm a new man,' he assured her, smiling.

They went into the bedroom together and he turned the key in the door, then took her in his arms.

'I've longed for you,' he said simply. 'You can't believe how much! When you came running down the path to meet me I thought you looked lovelier than ever!'

They kissed and she heard his heart pounding; when the kiss had spent itself he made to lead her to the bed but she drew away. She had become very pale.

'Nasri, I have to tell you something. Something terrible.'

Now the pounding she heard was from her own heart.

He stared at her, waiting; then, as she did not speak, 'What is it?' he asked, and was suddenly afraid.

She said, painfully, 'When all the men had gone away, that day, two Jewish soldiers came to the house, asking for water. They said they were Hagana. Randa took it to them and one of them grabbed her.'

She paused, her mind groping for words for the rest. For a moment they stood looking at each other, then she looked away and found strength to go on.

'They dragged her into a room. We heard her scream and Marian and I ran down the stairs to her. Then—then the other soldier got hold of me.'

She looked at him again, then, desperately.

'I fought and struggled, but he was young, and very strong.' She added, irrelevantly, 'He was a Lebanese American.'

He continued to stare at her without speaking and suddenly she broke.

'Don't look at me like that!' she screamed at him. 'It wasn't my fault! Don't you believe me? I'm three months' pregnant and nearly out of my mind with worry! We've got to do something about it—there's a doctor who will, if you agree—if you will come with me to him——'

She staggered over to the bed and collapsed there, sobbing hysterically.

Nasri continued to stand staring at her. He suddenly felt very cold, though the day was warm. He shivered and wrapped Khalil's dressing-gown closer round him, and the act released him from the trance. He went over to the bed and sat down on it beside her, but did not touch her.

'I've always said I didn't believe a woman could be raped. How can a man have a woman if she kicks and struggles? I couldn't do it. Why should this Jew be able to?'

She lifted her head and stared at him, aghast.

'You don't believe me? You think I'd go with a Jewish soldier like that of my own free will? Randa was in the room at the time. You can ask her. Ring the bell! Send for her!'

Then as he made no move she attempted to struggle off the bed to reach the bell by the door. He caught her wrists then.

'No! I believe you. Of course I believe you! Only it's so horrible! My wife with any man—but my wife with a Jew! O my God!'

He buried his face in his hands, then looked at her, piteously.

'That last night before I went away—we took a chance. You could be pregnant by me.'

'But we can't know—we can't be sure. We must go to the doctor. Soon! It's three months already!'

She reached out a hand and touched his haggard young face.

'Oh, Nasri—I so longed for you! I so longed for us to be together again——'

He took her hand and pressed it against his cheek.

'I longed for it too. Probably more than you.'

He kissed the palm of her hand, then abruptly got up, suddenly raging.

'Haven't the Jews done enough to us—taking our country and our homes and lands? Have they got to take our women too?'

He went over to the dressing-table and opened a box of cigarettes, extracted one and lit it.

'All right, we will go to the doctor and you will have an abortion. When you are recovered I shall go to Amman and join the Legion —they need men, and with any luck, I'll kill a few Jews before it's all over! What happened to Randa?'

'The doctor gave her an abortion. But the young man she was going to marry says it's now impossible, as she's no longer a virgin —his family are very orthodox Moslems and when he marries he has to show the handkerchief in the morning!'

'It should be easy enough to cheat—there are more ways than one of getting blood on to a handkerchief!'

'I think he doesn't want to marry her now—he would always remember that a Jew had had her first!'

Nasri said nothing. He felt cold again, and shivered.

'I'd better get dressed,' he said. 'I feel cold after the hot bath.'

Nadia got up from the bed and went over to the dressing-table and ran a comb through her hair.

'Yes,' she said, dully. 'You musn't catch cold. I will go along to the kitchen and see what's happening about lunch....'

Nadia's mother asked anxiously, when she could get her daughter alone, 'Is everything all right?'

'Yes. We are going together to see the doctor.'

'But in other ways—it hasn't turned him against you?'

'No,' Nadia said. 'Not at all!'

She even managed a small reassuring smile.

'Thank God!' Majdeh murmured. 'God is good. I always say so, but your father will never believe....'

A special meal was prepared that evening in celebration of Nasri's return, not as splendid as in the old days, for there were certain shortages, but nevertheless with the traditional lamb roasted whole and served, complete with its head, on a huge bed of rice. Muna telephoned to Dar el-Salam to invite Butros and Marian, but Butros was not feeling well—his old heart trouble he explained.

Khalil drove into Jerusalem to fetch Nasri's parents and other relatives living on the outskirts. He did not share his brother-in-law's nervousness about entering the Holy City.

The red and white check head-dress of the soldiers of the Arab Legion stood out against the grey battlements of the sixteenth-century walls of the Old City. It was necessary to avoid passing the Damascus Gate because Notre Dame across from it, hollow-eyed from battle, was still in the hands of Israeli troops, who had machine-guns trained on the Gate from there; it was also a favourite spot with snipers, who, to relieve their boredom, or remind the Arabs that they were still there, would take pot-shots at people in the open space in front of the Gate . . . in spite of the truce.

Khalil took the road up past the Museum to the Shaikh Jarrah quarter to the north and switched on the radio to the Israeli station, to which, with a painful interest, he listened a number of times every day. A smooth masculine voice speaking good Arabic was declaring the necessity for capturing Aqaba, the port at the head of the Red Sea, at the southernmost point of the Negev, which had been given to the Jews in the U.N.O. partition scheme. Khalil switched off, angrily. Aqaba was Trans-Jordan's remaining outlet to the sea now that she was robbed of the Mediterranean ports. He drove out along the Ramallah road and halted at an ornate modern villa, where Nasri's parents were staying with some near relatives.

The sun was setting in crimson splendour over the domes and spires of the Jerusalem skyline.

Muna resented Butros excusing himself from coming up to Ramallah, just as she had resented his departure for Jericho the day after the arrival from Lydda. She was convinced that he did not come because he did not want to, not because he was unwell. He had never liked Khalil, and now he resented him because he had not suffered in the Palestine tragedy. Farid's assurances that since the Lydda trek Butros really was very unwell did not mollify her; Butros could always be unwell when it suited him. His heart was not so bad that he could not survive the trek through the wilderness from Lydda to Ramallah in the heat of the day. He could always do what he wanted to do. She was angry with him because she loved him and he had hurt her.

But Farid was concerned about his brother's unwellness and resolved that when Nadia was over her trouble he would go and see him. Perhaps he would go down at the weekend with Anton, who since September had been attending the Friends' School, and who was living with them in Ramallah.

Nasri was happy to see his parents, but other than that he was quite indifferent as to whether Butros Mansour or anyone else was there or not; in the circumstances he would have preferred that no welcome-home party should have been arranged. He was home again after the long absence, restored to his wife and children, but the dream by which he had lived the last three months had turned into a nightmare and he longed to break out of it and be away again—away in Amman, training in the Arab Legion, and then off to wherever he was sent, anywhere where he could fight the enemy; fight and kill.

Nadia was so pretty, with her thick dark hair and her pale oval face and huge eyes; pretty and sweet; yet now whenever he looked at her he thought of a young Jewish soldier feeling her body, lying on top of her, possessing her; and he wanted to go out and kill. He told himself that she had suffered, that she had had this most terrible experience, and that he should pity her, be filled with love and tenderness for her; but all such feeling was dead in him and he could not feel anything except this savage jealousy, and in his body a cold deadness. He wanted the party to be over, because he had no heart in it, yet dreaded the night, when he must lie down in impotence beside the beautiful young woman who was his wife, and the mother of his children, who loved him, and whom he loved, but who had known another man—and that man the enemy.

Anton was excited at seeing Nasri again. Cousin Nadia's husband was a romantic, heroic figure in his eyes; he had been taken off to a camp by the Israelis and survived it and come back to tell the tale, and now he was going off to join the Arab Legion and help to throw the Jews into the sea . . . because in spite of what his father said he still believed—as most of them still did—that somehow that was going to happen. He had always liked Nasri, and Nasri had liked him, but this Nasri who had come to Ramallah was different; he no longer laughed and joked and fooled about; he did not even smile, and he spoke only when spoken to, and then only muttered a few words. He even looked different—thinner, and older; much older. Anton decided that it was because he had had a bad time with the Israelis; they had probably tortured him. He would be all right when he had been home a little while with Nadia and the children. Cousin Nadia, too, had been different since they had come to Ramallah; she, also, didn't laugh or joke any more, or even play with the children. She wasn't well, his Aunt Muna had said, and might have to have an operation, but they were waiting for Nasri to return.

Then, suddenly, Nasri was back, and his aunts set to work ordering the servants around, and even working themselves in the kitchen, to prepare a great feast, and all relatives and friends within reach were sent the good news and invited, and it was like Christmas. He was intensely disappointed that his parents couldn't come, and worried about his father, who had not been well since they had left Lydda, but when he said this to his Aunt Muna she had demanded, almost angrily, 'What can you expect—sitting down there in Jericho all through the summer?' adding, 'They must be crazy—both of them!'

But they weren't crazy, the boy thought, sadly, only unhappy—heartbroken—and when you are that you want to be in your own home, and Dar el-Salam was that, and no matter how much Uncle Khalil insisted, 'My house is yours!', with true Arab hospitality, the fact remained that it belonged to the Dahoud family and not to the Mansours; and Butros Mansour, his son knew, was a man used to ordering his own house and servants in his own way. He could never feel himself more than a guest in any other house—not even in the house of his sister's husband. Anton could understand that it had been easier for his parents to stay down in Jericho in spite of the fearful summer heat.

For himself he liked being in Ramallah now that he had recovered from his fear of the Jews breaking through. He liked the American Friends' School and was proud of the fact that it was said to be the best school in Palestine. He settled down quickly there, but since Amin had been sent away to a blind school in Bethlehem—Butros had arranged this—he was for the time being friendless. He got along with his girl cousins, once the initial shyness on both sides had abated, but even with the one of his own age he couldn't think in terms of friendship. You couldn't go camping and swimming and cycling with a girl, or share an interest in football. Between himself and the Dahoud girls there was an easygoing mutual toleration—they didn't mind him, and he didn't mind them; the question of friendship didn't come into it; they had their own girls' world, remote from his. For all practical purposes they were as much apart as they were in the segregation of the sexes in church on Sundays.

At the supper party the girls sat with their Aunt Majdeh, and a few other girls and women, at a small table in an annexe of the dining room; there was not room for everyone at the big table and the party seemed to divide naturally into this grouping, though Khalil thought privately that it was ancient Eastern tradition asserting itself—even, he thought sardonically, among the Christians. Nadia sat next to Nasri at the big table, and Muna and Khalil sat together in the middle. Anton was happy because he had Nasri on one side, and his Uncle Farid, the next best thing to his father, on the other. Everyone said what a pity Butros and Marian weren't there.

Before they had been invited to seat themselves at table Anton's eldest cousin had brought a girl over to him, holding her by the hand. 'This is my friend, Soraya,' she said. 'We're at the same school. Her father is Dr. Saba and he knows your father quite well.'

Being introduced to anyone, particularly females, was always an ordeal for Anton, but he forced himself to look at the girl and to murmur something polite. She seemed to him a very ordinary sort of girl, of no special interest, except that her father knew his.

He asked, politely, 'Are you from Lydda?'

'I was born there, but my family moved to here soon after. My father came over to see Butros Bey as soon as we heard you were here, but you'd already gone down to Jericho.'

'Is your father here tonight?'

'No. He's in America attending a medical conference.'

'Soraya's going to study medicine,' his cousin told him, proudly.

The girl laughed, self-consciously, exposing big irregular teeth, and Anton suddenly thought her rather ugly.

'I'd like to, but I don't know if I'll be any good.'

'Of course you will!' her friend said, loyally. 'You have to believe in yourself. You tell her, Anton!'

Anton said, confusedly, 'Yes, that's right,' and then to his intense relief it was announced that they should take their places at table.

Several times during the meal the girl looked across at Anton but never managed to catch his eye.

Khalil served arak and the men gradually became talkative and argumentative. Everyone except Nasri, who drank very little and remained silent, though in the old days the very sight of a glass of arak would bring a sparkle to his eye and he would seem to grow tipsily gay on the very smell of it. Toasts were drunk to him, wishing him return to his normal health and spirits, welcoming him back, wishing him luck in the Arab Legion, and a speedy return to Jaffa. . . .

'*Shukran*,' he said. 'Thank you,' each time, bowing slightly, his manner vaguely startled, like that of someone who has been dozing and jolted awake.

The meal, with its numerous dishes, all placed on the table at the same time, came to an end at last and they all adjourned to a large room in which peacock-blue plush armchairs and settees were ranged along the walls; the guests disposed themselves, in an involuntary segregation of the sexes, and Turkish coffee, fragrant with cardomom seeds, was served in tiny cups, and nargilehs were placed beside those of the male guests who wanted them. The water bubbled in the hubble-bubbles and conversation was fitful and flagging, punctuated by over-hearty bursts of laughter filling in the silences. The tension of which they were aware in the young man they were there to honour affected them all, making them ill-at-ease. The men wanted to discuss the one thing which interested them—and that intensely—the war situation; the possibilities of extricating the Egyptian forces besieged in Falluja since the Israeli break-through in the area; what had happened to the Syrian army; what should have been done, what ought now to be done, who was to blame, what could be expected to happen next. . . .

It was a very familiar conversation; it was the usual conversation when two or three were gathered together; it went round in circles, never reaching any conclusions because nobody really knew anything, but it was an outlet, and even a kind of comfort, because blame could be apportioned—if the Iraqis had done this, the Egyptians that, the Arab Legion the other—and a successful campaign worked out by armchair strategy. They looked to Nasri, who was young and had had direct contact with the enemy and was now going off to fight—if there was any more fighting to do—to take a leading part in the debate. But Nasri had nothing to say, and his silence oppressed them. They looked to him for inspiration and found in him only the embodiment of defeat.

Randa brought in a tray laden with small glasses of sweet milk-less tea, and under cover of the mild diversion caused Nasri took the opportunity to escape from the room. To the people round about who saw him go Nadia explained that he was in a bad nervous condition as a result of his internment. Everyone was very sympa-thetic; conversation was set in motion again among the women and spread to the men; it was an easy transition from sympathy for Nasri to discussion of the truce, Israeli abuses of it, and the situation in general.

To Nadia, worried about her husband, and filled with her own particular tension, created by her condition and his attitude, the evening seemed interminable. Her mother-in-law buttonholed her to insist to her that she must dissuade Nasri from joining the Arab Legion; he needed a rest, to recuperate, and anyhow who cared about the Legion now? Nadia replied that Nasri would do what he wanted to do—as he always had; then excused herself on the pre-text of looking to the children, who, she declared, usually wakened at about that time.

She did in fact peep in the children's room, but found them as she had expected sound asleep; she then went to her bedroom, her heart quickening with the fear of finding Nasri there and the dread of him not being there. She opened the door, fearfully; by the dim glow of a red-shaded lamp by the bed she made out the figure of Nasri lying fully dressed on the bed, his hands clasped under his head. There was a strong smell of cigarettes in the room.

She said, nervously, 'I wondered if you'd gone to bed.'

'I had to be alone. I couldn't stand it any longer.'

'They all came specially to see you—your parents and all of them.'

'I know, but I'm not ready to meet people. I have too much on my mind.'

She stood looking down at him, hesitating, then after a moment said, 'I have made an appointment for us to go to the doctor at ten tomorrow. To your old friend, Harid. He was glad to hear you were home again. He sent you his best wishes.'

He made no comment, and she added, 'He would like me to stay in his clinic for twenty-four hours.'

'He will do it tomorrow?'

'Yes—if you tell him to.'

He said, bitterly, 'I'll tell him. I haven't any choice, have I?'

'We neither of us have.' Her voice was not quite steady. She felt that if she could sink down beside him weeping all the tensions would be released, but the tone of his voice prohibited it.

She turned away from the bed.

'I must go and say good night to various people. I'll make your excuses to them—they'll understand. You'll see your parents in the morning—they're staying the night here.'

She returned to the party and when she rejoined him he had undressed and got into the bed and switched off the light. He did not speak when she entered the room.

She asked, softly, 'Are you asleep?'

'No. Did you expect me to be?'

She was aware of the edge to his voice.

'No,' she said. 'No. Not really.'

She wanted to ask him to switch on the light but was afraid. She undressed in the dark, put on her nightgown, ran a comb through her hair, and got in beside him.

He did not move; he was lying on his back and did not turn his head. After a few moments she reached up a hand and touched his cheek, softly.

'Nasri,' she pleaded, 'how can anything come between us when we love each other?'

He took her hand and held it.

'Because we're human, I suppose.'

'I've never changed towards you since the day we were married. I've never wanted anyone else—never for a moment. Please believe me!'

'I do believe you. But all the time I see—you know what I see. I

70

can't get it out of my mind. I can't think of loving any more. Only of going out and killing.'

His hand tightened on hers so strongly that she could have cried out with the pain.

'Try to understand,' he insisted.

'I do try,' and then, weakly, 'You're hurting me.'

He relaxed his grip.

'I'm sorry.'

He turned on his side, facing her.

'Shall we try to sleep?'

'Won't you even kiss me?'

He kissed her forehead.

'That doesn't count!'

'I know. It's why I didn't do it.'

She asked, sadly, 'Is it the best you can do?'

'For the present—yes.'

'Is it going to be better—later on—do you think?'

'I hope so. I'm sure I hope so!'

He drew her close to him, buried his face in her shoulder, and wept.

Later, holding her close to him, sleepless, he told her: 'I didn't know until I fell into the hands of the Jews that you could torture people without laying a finger on them. None of us were beaten or had our fingernails torn out. There were stories of it happening and we were frightened, but it didn't happen to us. None of us in the room I was in, anyhow. There were twenty of us. It was a fairly big building. We thought perhaps it had been a school, but we couldn't tell, because we had no idea where we were, and when we got to the building there was nothing to indicate, except that there was a yard with a high wall round that might have been the playground of a school. The room was stripped of everything except an open bucket in each corner. We were taken there in a closed truck, the kind they use for cattle. Only they couldn't pack cattle in as they packed us for they wouldn't arrive alive. We were several hours in the truck, and you know how hot it was. We suffered agonies of thirst. Also from the need to relieve ourselves as the hours wore on. The truck stopped several times, but we were none of us allowed out. There were two other soldiers up in front with the driver, but they none of them spoke Arabic. One of them spoke English, however, so we used that. We told him some of us were bursting our bladders and asked to be allowed out. He laughed and said not to waste it; we could drink it if we were thirsty.'

She asked him, 'Was it the same coming back?'

'No. The journey wasn't so long. They just dumped us at a check-post and Israeli guards escorted us to the Jordan side. At the building, whatever it was, our guards were as bored with nothing to do as we were, so they had fun with us. We were after all only a lot of Arab scum—sub-human. There would be sudden screams and groans in the night, blood-curdling, and we'd think of all the stories we'd heard about fingernails being torn out. Then a guard would unlock our door and stand there, grinning. "Who's next?" he'd say, and then read out some names. Those of us on the list would be taken out into the passage and the guards waiting there with their guns would tie our hands behind our backs, then we would be marched off and down the stairs and out into the yard and stood with our faces to the wall. Then one of them would say, 'Any of you wanting to pray had better get it over with, quick,' or something like that. Some of the men did pray, Christians and Moslems, both.'

'Did you pray?'

'I didn't pray, no. Except in my heart, that my son would grow up to avenge his father. They left us there for a couple of hours, with the guards marching up and down behind us, waiting for the firing squad that never came, the death that never came. When they'd had enough of it they took us back to our room. A few nights later they'd take another party from another room and we'd watch from the windows, sick with dread, wondering if this time they were just playing or really meant it, and we knew that the men down there believed it was their last hour, just as we had. They didn't lay a finger on us, as I said. They only terrorized us and humiliated us—and starved us.'

'What did they give you to eat?'

'Black bread and some kind of watery soup, mostly. I don't think they even hated us. They didn't have to. They were the victors. I think they merely despised us . . .'

He lay still, clutching her, staring into the darkness.

She brushed his sweating forehead with her lips.

'Try to sleep,' she urged, gently.

'I can't. If I close my eyes I think I'm back there in that room, and that in a moment I'll hear a scream, and then steps coming down the passage and the door being unlocked, and there'll be an Israeli guard grinning and saying, "Who's next?" Then he'll read names from a list and mine will be on it. . . .'

'You're safe now. It's all over now. This is Ramallah, Khalil's house, and we're together again.'

His grip on her, with all his tension behind it, was hardly to be borne.

'It's like a nightmare. I fight against it but I can't break free of it. It's still there.'

'It will go,' she soothed him. 'Tomorrow we'll ask the doctor for sleeping pills for you, and when you've had a few nights' sleep you'll feel different—it will all go.'

What did we either of us ever do to any Jew that they should do this to us? she thought bitterly. What did any of us Arabs ever do that they should do what they have done to us all?

6

BUTROS and Marian, sitting it out in the blistering summer heat in Jericho, had no visitors except for a few formal courtesy calls when they first arrived from local notables to welcome them back to Dar el-Salam and commiserate with them over the loss of their home, land and capital in Lydda. They had no social life whatsoever until Anton started going to school late in September, then they saw Farid every few weeks when he brought the boy down for the weekend in Khalil's car. Petrol rationing made the journey impossible oftener. He and Anton would travel back to Ramallah shortly after sunrise on the Monday morning. During the Christmas holidays he came with Majdeh and Nadia and the children and stayed until it was time to take Anton back to school at the end of January.

Nadia missed Nasri, who was away in Amman training with the Arab Legion, but she was innerly happy; she could forget the hideous thing which had happened to her in Lydda because she was now pregnant by Nasri. Once the operation was over it had been possible for him also to forget; there had been a gradual recovery from the mental and emotional shock, and a return to normal. The day before he left for Amman another party had been given for him, and this time, it was generally agreed, it was like a wedding party. Again the Mansours were not there, because Butros was not well, but Farid, driving Nasri to Amman in the morning, broke the journey in Jericho so that the young man might receive his uncle's blessing.

Nasri, who had not seen Butros for four months, was shocked by his appearance. He looked old and ill, Nasri thought, almost as though death had already touched him.

Butros's health had in fact considerably deteriorated since the Lydda trek; the heart condition from which he had suffered for years had worsened, and he had developed an arthritic hip, so that the little moving about he did was now done painfully and limpingly. There was all that on the physical side, and on the other a grief and despair and bitterness which added up to heartbreak. He wanted not to think of his house and lands and wealth in Lydda in the hands of the people who now called themselves Israelis, but he thought of it every day, and for a good part of every day, and it ate into his spirit, like cancer into the flesh. Palestine would not be liberated in his time; Anton might live to see it, in perhaps fifty years' time, when he was as old as his father was now: the Jewish state imposed on the heart of the Arab homeland would come to an end in the normal course of history, because eventually injustice did end and right prevail, but he did not believe it was going to end in any spectacular dramatic fashion through any Army of Liberation; for the present there would be an armistice, and frontiers would be drawn, and the Jews would consolidate their gains and successes into one massive victory.

As soon as it began to be cold in the hills still more refugees came pouring down from Ramallah, through the valley and out on to the Jericho road, heading for the warm bottom-of-the-basin of the Judaean wilderness. They camped out in caves on the bare hillsides, and in improvised tents; thousands of them, men, women and children, from Lydda and Ramleh and the villages and hamlets of the surrounding countryside, a ragged, destitute multitude of the displaced and dispossessed, yet only a part of the vast tragic Palestinian exodus, dependent on precariously organized charity for their mere existence.

From the first-floor balcony of the Mansour house could be seen, beyond the Mount of Temptation, in the foothills, the tent shanty-town which was the nucleus of what was to become one of the biggest refugee camps in Jordan. Butros and Marian would sit together on the balcony looking at it through the tall cypresses of their garden, but sometimes gazing at it spread monstrously over the hillsides they did not see it, but only their own house at Lydda, with the avenue of casuarina trees and date-palms, and always into

Butros's vision came the face of the Israeli woman soldier who had spat at him the warning that if he didn't get out his life wouldn't be worth a *fils*.

Marian, looking at him, knew that he suffered not merely for the loss of his home and lands and money and material possessions, and more than physically as a result of the trek; she knew that he suffered in the affront to his pride, and in the mass humiliation of the entire Palestinian people. Their lives had not been worth a *fils*—any of them.

Then on the first of December the West Bank of Jordan, all that was left of Arab Palestine, with the exception of the Gaza strip, was voted by the Jordanian government into Trans-Jordan, and Trans-Jordan ceased, like Palestine, to exist, and the new Hashemite Kingdom of Jordan closed like a sea over the wreck of Palestine. The last vestige of the Palestine nationalist dream was finally engulfed.

Marian thought of her father. She did not need his discreetly worded letters to know what he thought and felt. 'Why don't you both come to England, with Anton? Send Anton to school here?' he wrote, and she knew what he meant: How can you bear it?

She wrote to him, 'Butros will never leave Jericho—except to return to Lydda. Which means, of course, he will never leave Jericho.'

Then it was Christmas and Butros announced his intention of attending the service at the Greek Orthodox Church in Jericho, since he did not feel inclined to go up to Jerusalem. Anton went with him as a matter of course, and Marian because she wanted to be with them.

It was a warm sunny day, of cloudless blue sky, with flowers everywhere, crowding over old walls, festooning trellises, garlanding houses, wine-coloured and purple, scarlet and crimson, and white and gold, a lush tropical confusion. As always when entering the little town Marian felt, intensely, its sleepy backwater charm, but now the main street, with its little twisted golmohur trees, was crowded with listlessly wandering people, women wearing the long embroidered dresses of the Palestinian villages, men wearing shabby European jackets over long white or striped garments reaching to their ankles, and both men and women trailing little children by the hand as they wandered along, aimlessly, passing the time, the endless refugee time, their hearts as hungry as their bellies.

Marian looked at her husband's set face as they drove past in the station-waggon, with Yusuf at the wheel. She knew that the same thought was in his mind: These are the people we did the trek with, only we are luckier; we had a place to go to, another home; they had only the wilderness. In him, too, the same anger and pity and pain.

Then the cool darkness of the little church, full of the smell of incense, and above them the seven-candled candelabrum, the lighted candles shining like stars, symbolizing the Lord's illumination of the world with the light of spiritual truth.

Butros, for the most part, being unequal to standing for long, sat bolt upright in his seat, his hands clasped on the head of his cane, occasionally making a gesture of crossing himself, conforming the minimum, but following the priestly ritual with close attention and the approval with which he would have watched a well-acted play. He did not particularly believe, but going to church on Christmas Day was a thing you did, like giving alms to the poor, shouting at servants, serving arak with tabouli. For the greater part of the year he was agnostic, but at Christmas, and again at Easter, he gave unbelief the benefit of the doubt. Then he entered the church, as autocratic and imperious as in his own home, but present—a kind of courtesy genuflection.

'Why do you go to church when you don't really believe?' Marian had asked him once, early on.

He had smiled his deprecating smile and said, 'Because twice a year I am never quite sure to what extent I don't believe!'

But Anton had no doubts at all; he deeply believed, and standing beside his father followed everything at the altar with a rapt concentration. He was filled with awe at the holy mystery being enacted—the awful solemnity of the propitiation of very God, by Christ present at the heart of the Eucharist. At the time of the consecration of the sacrament he bowed his head in profound prayer, because at that time when Christ himself was being offered up to God, was the time when prayer was most potent. He had always prayed that he might be helped to live a good life, and that his parents might be protected from all harm, physical and spiritual, but that first Christmas of the Palestinian diaspora his prayer was all for his father's people, with whom he identified himself, that, of God's infinite mercy, they might be allowed to return home; that good might overcome evil, and justice prevail.

7

THERE was a prayer with which it had seemed presumptuous to trouble God, but which, unexpressed, persisted all the time in Anton after the first few weeks in Ramallah, and that was the longing for a friend to replace Amin. His affection for the blind boy remained unchanged, but he was no longer there, and visiting him at his school in Bethlehem had proved unsatisfactory. He had had a dream, which Amin had shared, that they could spend the school holidays together in Jericho, but Amin's mother had other ideas—with her other children and her grand-children in Ramallah the school holidays were a time for family reunion there. It would not have solved Anton's problem, anyhow, for his need was for a friend for every day, as he had had Amin in Lydda, and for a short time in Jericho.

He needed a friend at school, and all that first term there was no one. There were boys he liked and who liked him, but no one to whom he felt specially drawn, with whom it was possible to feel close, as with Amin—no one of whom he could say, in a special and proprietary way, 'my friend', proudly and confidently.

The weekends when he did not go to Jericho he would cycle about in the winding roads outside Ramallah, with their vast vistas of endless hills and their stony foregrounds holding no more than an occasional lonely shepherd minding a few black sheep. There would be outcrops of prickly-pear, and a solitary carob tree, and he would be reminded of the trek from Lydda and lose all pleasure in the ride and head back for Ramallah, depressed.

Then, like an answer to his unspoken prayer, in the new term after Christmas a boy called Walid Hussein turned up, a tall, dark boy of quite striking good looks, but who gave no indication of being aware of them. He was a little older than Anton and they were not in the same form; their first encounter was at the edge of the football field, when both were watching the game. Anton noticed him because at half-time when the other boys dispersed in groups, streaming away in the direction of the school buildings, he merely scrambled up among the small twisted pines on the rough ground above the playing field and sat down at the foot of a tree.

Anton, who was also alone, followed him up into the thin wood and strolled over to him.

'It doesn't look as if we're going to win,' he observed.

The dark boy looked up with a smile.

'We still have a chance.'

'Do you like it here?' Anton asked.

'I think I will when I get used to it. I never wanted to go to an American school. I wanted to go to the secondary school in Salt, but they wouldn't take me because I am a refugee. Then my banker uncle arranged for me here.'

'Where are you from?'

'Beersheba. My father was a schoolmaster there. We got out before the Jews came in and went to Dahiriya, to my father's people. It's a border village. Do you know it?'

Anton shook his head.

'I'm from Lydda. I came here with my family last summer. My name is Anton Mansour.'

'You're a Christian?'

'Yes. My mother is English.' He added, quickly, to dispel any prejudice, 'But she calls herself a Palestinian.'

The other boy laughed and flicked a pine cone through the trees.

'What do you call yourself?'

'Arab, of course.'

He seated himself at the foot of the tree.

'What is your name?'

'Hussein. Walid Hussein.'

'I have a Moslem uncle. He married my father's sister. I wish I'd been born a Moslem.'

'What difference does it make? We all believe in the same God.'

'If you're Arab it makes a difference. I can't explain.'

Hussein, leaning back against the trunk of the tree, regarded the younger boy with a good-natured amusement.

'Your father is a Palestinian, and Mansour is a good Arab name. Isn't that enough?'

Anton smiled uncertainly. He wanted to say, 'I want to feel wholly Arab,' but it would have been disloyal to his mother, who was after all a good Arab nationalist. He plucked at the thin grass where they sat, and Hussein asked, after a moment's silence, 'What did your father do in Lydda?'

'He was a landowner. One of the biggest. We have a house in Jericho and some orange groves, but we're not rich any more.'

Hussein laughed.

'But not poor either! My family are poor. Very poor. My father has now a teaching job in Salt—and many mouths to feed. We are a big family. I am the eldest, and my uncle's favourite.' He laughed again, his warm amused laugh. 'He tells everyone he has adopted me because I am the son he never had! But if my family hadn't had to leave Beersheba he would have done nothing for me. He used to despise my father because although he was the clever one of the family he never made any money. He always wanted to teach. He was never interested in money, only in knowledge. Then we became refugees and my uncle was able to have power as well as money. I've disappointed him by not being grateful. Why should I be grateful? He is only doing his duty. He is the rich member of the family, and has the good fortune not to be a refugee! I shall disappoint him still more when he knows that I don't intend to enter commerce and make money but become a teacher like my father. What do you intend to do?'

'I don't know,' Anton faltered. 'When we were in Lydda it was always taken for granted I would help my father run his estates. Now I don't know. But I know I don't want to go into commerce, and I don't think I could teach. I'm not clever like you——'

'Who said I was clever?'

'I just think it. I wish—I mean I only came here last term and I didn't make friends with anyone. I wish we could be friends——'

Hussein flicked another cone in the direction of the playing ground.

'Why not?' he said, carelessly.

Anton was not interested to visit at the house of Hussein's uncle, or to take him to the Dahoud house—all those bashful girl cousins, he thought—but it was of intense importance to take him to Jericho, not so much to present him to his parents as to make him part of his life there—part of all that was most important in his life. If his parents liked Walid and he liked them it would be good, but all that was of secondary importance; they had to be in Jericho together because Jericho was his place—as once Lydda had been.

Walid did not know Jericho; he had only passed through it, in a ramshackle bus, on his way from Hebron to Salt, and then again going in his uncle's car from Salt to Ramallah. He found it now exciting to go there with Anton, in a smart car owned by Anton's Moslem Uncle Khalil, though it was his Christian Uncle Farid, brother of Anton's father, who took them. He thought the Mansour house, set among its date-palms and orange groves, very fine—though no finer than his uncle's house at Ramallah—and could hardly wait to climb the Mount of Temptation with Anton. He liked Anton's parents and was impressed by the excellence of the Arabic spoken by Anton's English mother. He paid her what was for him the highest compliment possible by declaring that he would never have known she was English. . . .

Butros and Marian found him intelligent and well-mannered, and apparently completely unaware of his good looks. They were very happy that Anton had found such a friend, knowing how much he had missed Amin, but Marian had the feeling that the friendship meant more to Anton than it did to Walid. If she was right she hoped it didn't mean that eventually Anton would get hurt. She recognized at once that Walid was more intelligent than Anton, and possessed of much more mental drive and energy. He would always lead, she thought, and Anton would always follow—or try to. Walid, in time, might become impatient of the younger boy's hero-worshipping devotion.

In the meantime Anton was happier than he had been since he

left Lydda, for although he loved Amin the friendship had been handicapped by the fact that he had had to be Amin's eyes, whereas now he saw things through Walid's eyes; when Walid thought something ugly or beautiful, good or bad, he tried to see it like that, trusting his friend's judgment and mistrusting his own.

Walid very soon began to develop a plan for the Easter holidays. It would need permits, but his uncle should be able to arrange that for them. They would go first to stay with his relatives in Hebron, humble people who kept a shop where they sold the famous Hebron glass and other things, and from there, if they got the permits, they would go to Dahirya, to his father's people, who scratched a living from a few acres of stony soil, and there they could look along the Beersheba road, and across a valley into Occupied Territory. And one day they would infiltrate.

'How can we?' Anton protested.

'It's being done all the time,' Walid assured him.

'Those who do it either get shot by the Jews or caught by the Jordanian guard and sent to prison!'

'Some of them, but not all. Not all by any means!'

'Why do you want to do it?'

'Because I come from Beersheba and have the right to go back!'

Something quickened in Anton and he longed for the spring, which then seemed infinitely remote, for it was very cold in the hills that winter, the snow coming early. There was also the astonishing phenomenon of snow in Jericho. True it remained on the ground only a few hours, but that it should have been as cold as that down there below sea-level was most remarkable; it was also most terrible, because of that great army of the dispossessed and destitute encamped in their flimsy tents on the bare hillsides of the Judaean wilderness, with only such heating as small fires of a few sticks and a bundle of scrub gathered in the desert would provide. As on the trek, those who suffered most were the very old and the very young, and many died.

8

FEBRUARY, cold and grey still, but small pink clouds of almond blossom everywhere on the hillsides below Jerusalem, lighting the grey of the olive trees, terrace upon terrace; and among the stones and boulders and coarse grey grasses of the wasteland the crimson and purple of anemones, and pale gentle drifts of cyclamen, and small sweet-scented narcissus. In a Greek island in the Aegean Sea, where spring also broke in a wave of wild flowers and blossoms, Egyptian and Israeli military representatives met together to negotiate an armistice, and when it was accomplished, on the 24th of the month, to establish a Demarcation Line.

On the third day of April Jordan signed a similar agreement at Rhodes, and a Demarcation Line was drawn with a thick blue pencil which rode roughshod through towns and villages and agricultural lands, so that villages became separated from their lands, and sometimes houses themselves would be cut it half, with the front rooms in Jordan and the back rooms in the new Jewish state. Two hundred and eleven villages were mutilated in this way, depriving the villagers of their livelihood. The American mediator, Dr. Ralph Bunche, who supervised all this, was subsequently awarded the Nobel Peace Prize.

In March, at the height of the negotiations, Israeli forces marched on Aqaba in the south, and troops advanced between the Arab Legion posts in the Hebron area.

Butros listened to the news on the radio, and read the newspapers brought to him, and made very little comment. Since the final disappearance of Palestine as a separate entity, with the absorption of all that was left of it into Jordan, he had felt the disaster complete, and anything else that could happen of very little consequence. When Farid visited him it amazed him that his brother could still feel indignation, could still excitedly discuss what had long gone beyond discussion. He would smile a sad deprecatory smile whilst his brother fulminated.

'My dear,' he would say, gently, 'why do you insist on talking politics? For us Palestinians they don't exist any more. We ourselves barely exist. We no longer have a national existence. For the Jews it is the in-gathering; for us the diaspora. We have to accept it.'

Farid cried wildly that he didn't accept it; Palestine would be liberated.

The smile his brother turned upon him then was full and rich and warm.

'My dear!' he protested. 'My dear!'

Then signalled Yusuf lingering, listening, at the back of the verandah, to bring whisky, glasses, ice.

'Your faith does you much credit, Farid,' Butros continued, still smiling, 'but it does nothing for you. Whisky does.'

Farid said, shortly, 'You drink too much these days. Especially for someone with a bad heart.'

'Probably, Farid. Probably. Ah, Marian!'

Both men got to their feet as Marian came out on to the verandah. She greeted Farid, and Butros, pulling a chair forward for her, said, 'I have been trying to persuade Farid of the futility of talking politics. His reply is that I drink too much.'

She smiled at him.

'You drink more than is good for your heart.'

'But then I suffer more than is good for my heart, so it evens out!'

He moved across to the table where Yusuf had set down the decanter and glasses.

He said, smiling, and pouring whisky lavishly over the ice in each of the three glasses, 'Here is the only thing left worth discussing.'

Both smiled politely, Farid masking disapproval, Marian sadness.

Butros was not in fact entirely serious; with Marian he discussed a number of things—their son was one of them—and his mocking line with his brother was purely defensive, so wearisome and futile did he find all the political bickers and arguments and dissensions, and all the brave talk of liberation in the face of crushing defeat merely sickened him. He complained to Marian that he couldn't go into Jericho to get his hair cut without being subjected to the Palestine theme, from one angle or another, and from whatever angle ill-informed and unrealistic. He was impatient of it all, not from cynicism, as Farid was inclined to think, but because he deeply cared, and had suffered, not only personally, materially and physically, mentally and emotionally, in his pride and dignity as a human being, but in his national consciousness. Farid had similarly suffered, but he was a younger man, of a more volatile temperament—and a good deal less intelligent.

Anton had obtained his parents' permission to spend a few days of the Easter holidays in Hebron, but Walid had made him promise to say nothing about going also to Dahiriya, for fear that as it was so close to the Demarcation Line they might forbid it, 'and then,' said Walid, 'you might feel guilty about going.'

'I'll feel guilty, anyhow,' Anton told him, ruefully.

Walid was impatient; parents always worried about their children for no reason, and if one told them everything one would never do anything or go anywhere. Anton could tell his parents, about Dahiriya when they got back; that would undo the deception, wouldn't it? Anton didn't think so but felt it useless to try to explain to Walid. They looked at things differently, he knew, not because they were of different religions, but because of different temperaments. He was quite sure that Walid would lie and deceive to the utmost in order to gain his own way if he thought it important that he should, and he admired this quality of ruthlessness in his friend, as a mental toughness in which he felt himself regrettably lacking. He thought it very probable that his father, at least, would wish him not to go so close to the Demarcation Line, and it made him feel guilty. He comforted himself by reflecting that what his parents didn't know they couldn't worry about. He would find Hebron an interesting old town, his father told him; he should visit a glass factory and see the famous glass, made from all manner of oddments of waste glass, being blown; and there was a fine mosque, which had been a Crusader church, which he should get Walid to take him to.

Yusuf would drive them to Hebron in the station-waggon and come back for them on the appointed day.

They set out in the early morning for the long climb up through the bare hills of rock and sand to Jerusalem on its hills above the deep valley. Walid was excited at going there, not having been there since the previous October, and in the knowledge of all that had happened there in that time, but Yusuf was nervous of Jewish snipers as they drove along the edge of No Man's Land with its shelled houses, and gardens and olive groves gone wild and desolate; he wanted only to be safely through the city and heading south for Hebron.

When Jerusalem was behind them Walid began to talk in English, to exclude Yusuf. Tomorrow they would go to Dahiriya, to his grandparents; they would borrow bicycles in Hebron; it was only a matter of about ten kilometres. There was a military check-post there; the road went straight on, winding away through the hills, to Beersheba, but of course you couldn't go along it; a few miles along the road you came to the white stones and a notice in Hebrew which announced the demarcation point, and the Israeli guards were on the hilltops above the road at each side, bored with nothing to do and only too glad of an excuse to shoot. So you didn't go beyond the check-post, though your hometown was only a few kilometres farther on, down that road, the old road to Beersheba where now nobody went. . . .

Walid spoke in low tense tones and it came to Anton that this was not a schoolboy planning a lark, but a young Palestinian in deadly earnest. It made him feel juvenile and inadequate.

'My grandparents, my father's people, at Dahiriya are poor farming people, as I told you. One of their sons, my Uncle Munir, lives with them now—he came with us from Beersheba. He lived outside Beersheba and had enough land to make a comfortable living, with market-gardens and a small orange grove. He used to bring what he grew into the town on market days, with eggs, and live chickens. Now all his land is the other side of the Demarcation

Line. There is a place near where my grandfather's last field is where you can stand and look across the valley and see some of my uncle's olive trees.

'My uncle says it's important Palestinians should infiltrate across the Demarcation Line everywhere, not in the way they have been doing, to pick a few of their own oranges, or plant a piece of their own land in what is now called No Man's Land. He says it's not worth risking getting shot or going to prison for a few oranges or for a crop you may never get the chance to harvest, but it's worth everything, he says, to get back to where you came from and contact the Palestinians still there and start a resistance movement. He says the time to do it isn't yet—things are too unsettled. Palestinians are still being expelled. But in a few years' time, when things have settled down, and the Israelis begin to feel safe, then something could be started. We are always being told that it's for Palestinians to liberate themselves. How else is it to be done?

'When we left Beersheba we went first to my father's people in Dahiriya, as I told you, and then to Hebron, but there was nothing for my father there, and then his rich brother came to the rescue and got him the teaching post in Salt, and more or less adopted me and sent me to school in Ramallah. But before the term started I stayed with my family in Salt, and every day I used to go out and sit on a hillside and look down on to an Iraqi army encampment. I used to think they were the soldiers who were going to liberate Palestine. I went every day for weeks, wondering when I should see them march off in the direction of Jericho, heading for Latrun and across the border and into Occupied Territory. I even thought they might march through Jerusalem and down the road to Hebron, heading for Beersheba. It was a long time before I discovered that it wasn't an army camped out there below Salt, but only a base depot for depositing and picking up supplies. The soldiers there weren't going to march anywhere. Any day they would get into their lorries and drive back through Amman and Zerqa to Baghdad.'

Walid smiled, looking out of the window of the station-waggon at the desolate wasteland of arid land and bare hills of the last lap of the road to Hebron.

'It was a lovely dream whilst it lasted, that dream of an army preparing to march westward into Occupied Territory—I don't know how I would have lived through the empty, boring days of idleness whilst I was waiting to go to school if I hadn't had that dream to occupy me. I know now that Palestine isn't going to be liberated like that. We have to build up a resistance movement inside occupied Palestine itself. When the time comes. I told you I wanted to teach, like my father. I want to teach because a teacher can have great influence. Perhaps by the time I'm ready, in a few years' time, they'll want a teacher at the little school in Dahiriya. . . .'

Yusuf regarded with distaste the narrow, garbage-littered street into which he was directed to turn when they reached the ancient Moslem town of Hebron, and with profound mistrust the old and dilapidated house, with an open-fronted shop selling a conglomeration of cheap coloured glass, brassware, bead neck-laces, trashy jewellery, at which he deposited the young master and his friend. It was from just such a street in the *souks* of Lydda that Yusuf himself came, and where, if he had had the choice, he would have been content to live out his life, but he had the strong sense of propriety of his calling; what was all right for him was neither right nor proper for the young master, the son of Butros bey. He would return, he declared, firmly, the day after tomorrow. *Insh'allah.*

But scandalized as he was by the low social standing of the relatives of the young master's friend he was very happy to accept the invitation of the owner of the shop to come in and make him-self at home, regard the house as his own, and drink a glass of tea before making the long journey back to Jericho.

Walid took his friend up some dark stairs to where his aunt, his mother's sister, and various boy and girl cousins, waited to greet them. Walid was devoted to his aunt because she was like his mother, whom he greatly loved. She was a dark-eyed, middle-aged woman, her greying hair curling out on her forehead from under a white head-dress, her still slim figure totally concealed under a long straight dress of grey wool. She had a sweet smile and a gentle manner which overcame Anton's shyness with strangers. Walid was obviously very happy to be there with them all. He kissed his aunt's hand, affectionately patted the cheeks of his girl cousins, played with the small children, and was relaxed as Anton had never yet seen him. At school he was inclined to be arrogant, conscious of his intellectual superiority; at the Mansours he was always conscientiously not being impressed by the fine house and the social standing of Butros Bey. Alone with Anton he was consciously the more dynamic of the two and inclined to be, in a good-natured fashion, domineering. With his Hebron relatives he became immediately one of the family, all arrogance, affectation, and self-consciousness dispensed with.

Anton envied him his ability to be so relaxed and at ease with a crowd of people, and his ready flow of affection for relatives. He had never been able to feel or behave like that with his Dahoud cousins; only alone sometimes with Soraya had he felt really at ease. In Ramallah he had not thought about it; now it suddenly came to him that he was not Arab enough to enjoy this intensive family life, this strong family feeling, and he felt suddenly a little bleak and out of it.

The uncle was a thin, energetic man with a small neat moustache and a warm and ready smile. Such was his charm that he was able to persuade a high percentage of his customers that he made a special price for him or her alone; on those occasions when the price was still too much his manner was one of sad, gentle reproach, and more often than not the customer capitulated, then or later. His eldest son, Fuad, worked with him in the shop.

Fuad was a good-looking, gentle-mannered youth quite as proficient in the art of persuasion as his father. When Walid and his friend arrived he was released from the shop to go with them round the town.

He was interested in Anton, about whom he had already heard from his cousin, and now, meeting him, was amazed to learn that although he was nearly thirteen and had an English mother he had not yet been to England.

'Don't you long to go?' he demanded.

'Not particularly,' Anton told him. 'Sometimes I think I would like to know my English grandfather, because he was my father's friend when he lived and worked in Palestine years ago. Also my mother talks about him and is sure we would like each other. I suppose I will go to England eventually, because my father wants me to finish my education there, just as he did.'

'Doesn't your mother ever want to go back to her own country?' Fuad inquired.

Anton said, smiling, 'She always says Palestine is her country.'

'There's no such country any more.' The young voice was bitter.

Walid put in, quickly, 'There could be again—if Palestinians worked for it!'

'Our grandchildren might see it—or our great-grandchildren!'

'It could happen in our time!' Walid declared.

'If we live to be a hundred perhaps!'

They turned into a narrow passageway with flights of steps flanking the massive walls of the mosque.

Fuad turned to Anton.

'What do you say?' he asked him, challengingly.

'I think Walid might be right,' Anton told him. 'If there could be a resistance movement started in Occupied Territory later on——'

'It's a nice idea—but a dream!'

Walid said, with sudden passion, 'I suppose the whole idea of Israel began as somebody's dream! I read once in a book that the Chinese have a saying: What is so real as a dream in the heart of man? A million Palestinians dreaming of one day going home could be a beginning. They could make it happen if they dreamed hard enough! We young Palestinians could make it happen— people like you and me and Anton——'

'I'm an unbeliever,' Fuad said, smiling as he smiled at difficult customers who argued about the price. 'Leave me out!'

Fuad did not accompany Walid and Anton to Dahiriya next day; his father needed him in the shop, and Walid was glad; as Fuad was not sympathetic to the great dream the loan of his bicycle was more useful than his presence for the excursion.

Walid explained to his friend, 'Fuad feels as strongly about Palestine as the rest of us, but being a refugee makes a difference—you feel it in your blood then, as well. With Fuad it's all in the mind.'

Another bicycle was produced and the two rode out of Hebron and along the white dusty road to the border—the road to Beersheba. The road seemed to wind endlessly through the grey wasteland of rocks and boulders and strange volcanic-looking bare hills. There were occasional patches of cultivation and the biblical figures of men and women ploughing with camels and mules, scratching the stony ground into reddish furrows.

Walid told Anton as they cycled along over the rough road, 'When we lived in Beersheba I used to come with my family by bus along this road to visit my uncle in Hebron. Sometimes with one of my brothers I would come by bicycle. We would break the journey at Dahiriya. Now you can only go about nine kilometres along the road beyond Dahiriya before you come to the Demarcation Line. Once you could go all the way to Cairo! No one goes along the old Beersheba road now. There's nothing to go for. Whether you're living in Beersheba or on this side you can only go as far as the Demarcation Line.'

When they had been going for about an hour the country opened out and a small village rising in tiers of square flat-roofed houses on the side of a hill standing back from the road came into view.

'Dahiriya!' Walid exclaimed, with satisfaction. He added, 'Don't expect much of it or of my grandfather's place—it's a rough place and a poor life there. But we shall be welcome—a thousand times welcome!'

There were a few scattered buildings, including a boys' school, and the military post behind iron palings and rolls of barbed wire, and they turned off the road and followed a track up to the village. They wheeled their bicycles up narrow alleyways of dried mud, between ancient decaying walls topped by tamarisks and an occasional fig tree; gaunt dogs prowled among the garbage and bright-eyed, barefoot children crowded to wooden doorways in the walls, laughing excitedly at the sight of strangers; women sitting on the ground in the courtyards of houses suddenly revealed by the opening of the doors in the walls drew their white head-scarves across their faces.

Suddenly a boy in a shabby striped robe ran out and greeted Walid, seizing him and kissing him on both cheeks. When he could extricate himself Walid turned to Anton, laughing.

'My cousin Saïd,' he explained, and introduced Anton as a school-friend.

Saïd explained that his father and grandfather were out in the fields, but his mother and the children and his grandmother were up at the house. When they had been there and rested and refreshed themselves he would take them to his father and the others.

Wheeling the bicycles, and occasionally carrying them up flights of broken steps, they went on up through the labyrinth of alley-ways and stopped finally, near the top of the hill, at a wall in which the wooden door stood open. They stepped into a sunny courtyard of a whitewashed house where a number of young children ran about and two women, one fat and old, the other slim and young, sat on the ground facing the sun. The young woman wore a flow-ing white head-veil and was beautiful; she was mixing flour and water in a shallow pan on the ground, beside a smoking fire of sticks. She rose to her feet at the sight of the visitors and Walid introduced her as his aunt, and the old woman, wrapped in a black abbah, as his grandmother. There was a babble of welcome, ex-clamation, question, explanation, and when the general confusion had subsided the young woman disappeared into the house and stools were brought for the visitors and placed against the sunny wall of the house. Walid was asked for news of the outer world—Hebron, Ramallah, Jerusalem, Salt—and inquiries made about his family, and about the relatives in Hebron, and about his friend. Walid explained that Anton was a refugee from Lydda and there were exclamations of sympathy, and eager, sympathetic questions. Anton felt himself drawn into the warmth of the circle and ceased to feel alien and shy. His world and theirs were remote from each other, but they were all Palestinians.

Munir's wife came out of the house carrying a brass tray with glasses of tea. She wore a long dark dress with a strip of red em-broidery down each side and across the front, and she seemed to

Anton to glide rather than walk. There was such sweetness in her face that she reminded him of an icon of the Virgin.

When the tea was drunk and a sufficient number of questions asked and answers given they all rose and Saïd led them back through the labyrinth and down to the open country flowing away to the hills of the near distance—and Occupied Territory.

There was a rough track across ploughed land in which a number of people, both men and women, were working with mules and camels. At the base of a line of hills there were the black tents of bedouin—'They, also, are refugees,' Walid said, observing Anton's interest.

They walked a little distance over the rough ground to a path of red earth where an old man and a handsome man of about thirty-five were hoeing long stony furrows. They straightened up as the three boys approached, then broke into exclamations of surprise and welcome.

All over again it was explained who Anton was, and Munir's interest was immediately quickened. He did not have to be asked to take them to the point on the hillside from which, across the wide valley, his lands, now being cultivated by Israelis, were visible.

They followed a rough track for a few yards up to the brow of the hill and a wide panorama of undulating valley, with the long line of the hills rising like a wall at the far side. Very beautiful it looked in the mild sunshine of the April noon. They stood a few moments in silence, gazing at it, moved by the beauty of the scene and burning with the monstrous injustice it represented. The old man murmured, 'Our beautiful land!' and released the tension.

Munir touched Anton's arm and said, 'Do you see those olive trees over there to the left? A little way up the hillside? Those are mine. Below them are the market-gardens. I suppose no one ever thinks of the produce as stolen goods.'

Anton, deeply moved, said, with an effort, 'One day you will cultivate those lands again yourself.'

'Insh'allah,' the old man murmured.

Munir said, tensely, 'Whether I do or not, one day I am going back!'

They turned away and walked in silence back to the main track.

Below them now the old Beersheba road could be seen clearly, winding away between the bare hills closing in on it on both sides.

Walid halted Anton to point it out to him.

'You can't see Beersheba from here,' he said. 'It's away over there, behind those hills. The Israeli guards are on top of the hills at each side of the road——'

'We often see them as we work out here in the fields,' Munir put in. 'They look down on us as we work. We know they are there, watching us, and they know that we know.'

'At this side the check-post is manned by Jordanian National Guards—they have a clear view down the road. With their permission you can go as far as the white demarcation stones. If you go beyond there are Israeli bullets waiting for you from both sides of the road. Beersheba is only about fifteen kilometres by the road —imagine it, only about as far as we came from Hebron to here! But the road is no good except as a marker. Far out in the valley you'd lose sight of it for a time, behind the hills, but when you were round the hills you'd be parallel with it again——'

Saïd laughed.

'Walid has it all worked out. You would think he was planning to infiltrate!'

'I am, but not yet. Not for years yet. I have to spend many more holidays here yet, studying every rock and camel-track, until I could find my way on a moonless night. I have to come and live and work here, so that the National Guards and the Bedu all get used to the sight of me and I can come and go without exciting curiosity.'

Munir regarded his nephew with an affectionate, amused smile as they trudged back over the ploughed land in the direction of the village.

'You seem to have it all planned!' he observed, drily.

Walid returned his smile.

'Not yet,' he said, 'but I will have, by the time I'm ready to go. . . .'

Back at the house they rested again in the courtyard, this time on flat cushions and thin mattresses, refreshing themselves with small glasses of tea whilst the two women, with neighbour women who had come in to help, worked in a small yard at the side of the house preparing numerous dishes on open fires and a charcoal-burning brick stove. During the long wait Munir asked Anton questions about the trek from Lydda, and conditions in Ramallah when the refugees flooded in, and how it was now in Jericho, and in turn told something about Beersheba. Anton felt young and inadequate and wished that his father were there to do justice to the conversation, but Munir was impressed by the boy, and urged him, 'Persuade your father not to send you to a university in England—stay here and work with Walid and be one of us!'

Anton replied that he would like to, but that it wouldn't rest with him. He added, 'I can always come back.'

'*Insh'allah*. But you can never be sure. Once you have gone from a place it's not always so easy to get back.'

The talk became general, and in it Walid held his own, and Anton was full of admiration. It seemed most marvellous to have so brilliant a friend. He longed for the years to pass so that he could be more even with Walid, intellectually. When he was sixteen and Walid eighteen, he thought, there would not be such a gap between them.

After about an hour Munir's wife summoned them to the meal. They went first to a corner of the yard and Saïd poured water over their hands from a brass coffee-pot with a long spout like the beak of a bird. They dried their hands on a clean white cloth and then went into the house.

It seemed at first very dark inside, then as the eyes became accustomed to the dimness a very low round table in the middle of the earth floor became visible, laden with dishes, and in the centre a huge mound of rice and almonds into which pieces of fried chicken had been inserted. Whilst the males were washing their hands the women had brought the cushions and mattresses in and ranged them round the low table. Munir and his son and nephew and his nephew's friend seated themselves round the table, and because Anton was the guest of honour Munir dipped into the mound of rice and extracted from it a choice piece of the chicken which he handed to him.

Anton, who had never eaten in this fashion before, found it interesting but difficult; the chicken was easy enough to manage, but the rice, even with the strips of flat pancake-like bread with which each mouthful was picked up, he found not easy to negotiate. The women did not eat with them but hovered continually in attendance. Only towards the end did Munir's womenfolk join them, but disappeared to make coffee very soon after. There was a return to the yard for hand-washing, and then a brief relaxation on the mattresses again over the sips of bitter black Arabic coffee before Walid announced that he and Anton must start the journey back to Hebron.

The whole family came down to the main road to see them off, and they left with numerous injunctions to return soon, and many cries of *Ma'as-salama*, with its blessing in the goodbye.

'They are good people,' Walid said, warmly, as they pedalled back between the bare hills. 'I always feel so sad when leaving them. But one day I will go and live among them and take my parents with me.' He laughed, happily. 'We will be all together then, on the Beersheba road! I hope you'll come and stay with us—and that we'll get through to Beersheba together!'

'*Insh'allah*,' Anton said, fervently.

9

THE visit to Dahiriya made a deep impression on Anton and he thought about it continuously on his return—the things Walid and his uncle had said, and the old Beersheba road, where now nobody might go, winding away into the hills watched over by the Israeli guards. His response to Walid's impassioned talk about infiltration, and the creation of a resistance movement inside the Jewish state, was at that time not much more than schoolboy romanticism, but there was also in him the beginning of the germination of the seed of ideas Walid had dropped into his mind.

But back at school the familiar extroverted life reasserted itself and the Palestinian preoccupation retreated. Even Walid, when not studying for his exams, was more disposed to talk volley-ball and football than the liberation of Palestine.

The fearful summer heat engulfed Jericho again, and Anton stayed up in Ramallah. Marian was enervated by the heat to exhaustion point, and Butros continually urged her to go up into the hills; if she did not care to stay in Ramallah with Muna and Khalil she could stay with Nasri's parents outside Jerusalem. If she did not care to go alone he would go with her for a few weeks.

She gave him a sad affectionate smile when he talked like that, and her answer was always the same: it was less effort to remain where they were. Butros, she knew, had no desire to move; he could tolerate the heat more easily than the talk he must sustain if, as he thought of it, he went out into the world. The Jericho house, Dar el-Salam, was still for him the House of Peace. Marian, also, in spite of the prostration the heat laid upon her, preferred it to coping with the crowded family life shared with her in-laws. Sometimes she would go into Jericho with Yusuf or his wife to do the marketing and collect the mail at the post-office. Her father sent her the weekly edition of *The Times* by airmail; her mother sent her by sea-mail a woman's magazine, full of unsuitable recipes and even more unsuitable fashions and improbable love-romances. It was sent, her mother had once explained to her, to keep her in touch—presumably with English middle-class domestic life. Occasionally, when he remembered it, her father sent her a *Times Literary Supplement* to keep her in touch with culture. In the heat of the day she would sit on the porch, beside the fan, listlessly turning the pages of these publications, too full of inertia even to read the headlines.

In the evenings the heat would be a few degrees less, but it would not be cool. She and Butros would dine alone on the porch, caged in by the fine wire mesh designed to keep out the insects; there would be an incessant ticking of cicadas outside in the hot, thick darkness, and the occasional unearthly running-cry of a jackal, causing Marian to shiver even in the heat. When the meal was over and the servants had withdrawn they would lie back in the low rattan chairs listening to the radio; sometimes there would be a good programme of Western music from Beirut; mostly they merely listened to the news and an endless trickle of Oriental love-songs. They went early to bed, not to sleep, for the nights were too suffocating, but to lie on top of the bed, with the windmill-fan trundling overhead, talking desultorily, or lapsing into lonely silences. Then Marian would speculate about Butros's first wife, resenting her yet curious about her; and Butros would brood morosely on what Marian's life might have been had she not, quite deliberately, allowed herself to become involved with him. She might have returned to England with her parents and married an Englishman nearer her own age—and would not now be lying on a bed with an elderly and sick man in this smothering Jericho bottom-of-the-basin heat. . . . When that thought came to him he would grope for her hand in the darkness, for reassurance of its answering pressure.

On one of those nights he said once, brokenly, 'My poor Marian, why did you ever marry me? What have you got out of it?'

'You,' she answered him, 'and Anton.'

'An old man for a husband, and an only child. Not even a proper home any more, and Jericho all the year round!'

She said, loyally, 'I always loved Dar el-Salam, and Jericho.'

'You never had to endure it in August before!'

'It was pretty hot in Lydda in the summer!'

'Not like it is here—there wasn't the below-sea-level pressure.'

'One gets used to it, I find.'

He laughed, softly.

'Does one? Loyalty was always your strong point, my dear. Since we've been here haven't you longed for England's green and pleasant land? Own up, now!'

'Why do you say such things? I haven't longed for England! I've longed for Lydda, and Darat el Kheir. But we might have died in the wilderness like so many, and we're here and together, and I'm thankful! You're making me cry, and it's too hot to cry!'

She wept easily at that time, drained of all nervous energy. Life seemed to have ground down almost to a standstill, and she had a feeling of waiting for something to happen to get it going again. Something outside of herself.

As the first anniversary of the exodus from Lydda approached Butros became filled with a restless desire to go to the border and look across the coastal plain to the sea; it might even be possible to go to some point from which it would be possible to see Lydda. A military permit would be necessary, but for him that would present no difficulties.

Marian was distressed when he told her of his intention to apply for permission.

'How could you bear to see Lydda again from a distance and be unable to go to it?' she protested.

He smiled his rueful smile.

'In a way, I suppose, that a man in prison experiences some satisfaction in seeing his wife when she visits him, even though he may not embrace her. There is the longing to see the beloved again. It is torment, but also it is better than nothing.'

'It would be very upsetting,' Marian insisted, and then, despairingly, 'Haven't we suffered enough—you especially?'

He told her, gently, '*You* should not come. I will take Anton with me, and Yusuf shall drive.'

'I couldn't stay here and let you and Anton go off alone—if you insist on doing it we must do it together, just as we did the trek together. But I'm sure the whole thing is a mistake.'

'Not for me, my dear. For me it's something I must do.' He smiled his deprecating smile. 'You know—like going to church at Christmas and Easter!'

The trip was arranged for a Saturday morning, so that Anton could come. They started out soon after sunrise, driving up through the valley to Ramallah. Yusuf, disliking the rough dirt road through the wilderness, had suggested that it was now safe to go via Jerusalem, but Butros strongly objected—not from fear of snipers, but because he had a deep aversion to seeing Jerusalem divided, to see familiar landmarks and know them to be now in Occupied Territory. Marian was glad to be spared what would have been for her, also, an ordeal, but with her it was what Butros wanted which counted.

Bumping and bouncing over the valley road she recalled the journey of a year ago, but the laceration had yet to come. There were the encampments of bedouin refugees, their low black tents pitched at the base of the arid hills, their goats, and a few camels, grazing the grey scrub. How did they live, she wondered, in that waterless land?

They reached Ramallah at about eight o'clock, and the cool air, with the smell of pines on it, came in through the open windows of the station-waggon. They breathed it in gratefully and looked at each other and smiled. It was as though they had forgotten the simple pleasure of being able to breathe freely.

Ramallah was no longer wretched with the tragic squalor of a year ago; the refugees had gone from the streets and the olive groves, having gone down to Jericho for the winter and stayed there, camped out in the wilderness and on the hillsides. The Street of Dreams, in which the Dahoud house stood no longer arched the dark branches of its twisted pines over human misery.

Farid, Majdeh, Nadia, Anton, Walid, and the Dahoud girls were breakfasting on the wide first-floor verandah when the Mansour car drew up at the gate at the bottom of the garden. Yusuf sounded the horn and they all started up, expecting the arrival, and Anton raced down the steps and came running through the garden. Walid was there because Anton had begged his father to allow him to accompany them to Budrus, the border village opposite Lydda, and when the permission had been granted Walid had eagerly accepted. He was extremely glad the Mansours were making this trip; the more border-conscious Anton became the better.

There was an hour's delay, taking coffee and exchanging news: Nasri had been given a commission in the Arab Legion; Nadia's baby was due at the end of the month and Nasri expected to be home on leave for the event—Nadia, heavy in body but serene in mind, smiled happily. Muna and Khalil were away on a visit to his parents at Jenin in the north. Farid declined the invitation to join the Budrus expedition; he was starting up in business, running a garage with another Palestinian refugee, and had many things to attend to; he and Majdeh, with Nadia, would be moving into a flat in the centre of the town, near the garage, after the child was born.

Everyone insisted that Butros looked unwell and Marian worn out—even Anton thought they both looked tired, and that his father had aged in the few weeks since he had last seen him—and that they were fools to stay down in Jericho in the summer when they had a home to come to in Ramallah and were a thousand times welcome.

Butros and Marian smiled, at their relatives and at each other, and counter-insisted that they liked it there. . . .

'It is after all *dar el-Salam*,' Butros reminded them, almost apologetically.

They got away at last, heading for Ni'leen, Anton explaining to his friend that it was along this road that his Uncle Khalil's car, with Ahmad driving, had resued them—'Imagine, if we had had to walk all the way to Ramallah after all the walking we did the day before from Lydda!'

'But thousands did,' his father reminded him, sombrely. 'We were the lucky ones!'

'*You* might have died,' Anton persisted. 'With your bad heart.'

'Perhaps,' Butros said, simply. 'Perhaps. Thousands did.'

Outside Ramallah the road wound away through hilly bouldery

land, the earth red and stony, terraced with olive groves, until the landscape opened out into the broad-screen panorama of the high hills flanking the deep valley on the seaward side. They came to the tiny village of Ni'leen, and Anton cried to his father that they should stop here—he wanted to show Walid. . . .

Butros ordered Yusuf to stop and the station-waggon halted immediately opposite the stone drinking fountain, where now only a solitary woman stood filling an earthenware pitcher. The village seemed deserted in the bright sunshine.

Anton babbled excitedly to Walid of how it had been a year ago, when thousands of people had been milling round the fountain, of how long it had taken to get near it, of his blind friend, Amin, of his panic when he had been unable to find his parents—'And then my nose started to bleed again—pouring, like it did when the Jewish planes came over and dropped bombs on Lydda and I dived under the bed, and when they came over with machine-guns, so low you could see the men in them . . .'

He rattled it all off very quickly, almost lightly, laughing, but watching him Marian recognized the latent hysteria, and wondered whether it had after all been wise to bring him on this pilgrimage, to relive the terrors and horrors of a year ago.

She and Butros looked at the fountain and remembered and said nothing. After a moment Butros, sitting beside the driver, said, curtly, 'Yalla!'

They came soon to outcrops of prickly pear, then long hedges of it, flanking narrow lanes, and outlying flat-topped houses, and a check-post. They halted and Butros gave his name and a National Guard climbed in at the back of the station-waggon and they drove on into the small village of Budrus.[1] Butros sat leaning forward, his hands clasped on the knob of his cane, and his lips tightened at the sight of the coastal plain below, flowing away to the pale glimmer of the sea—the coast of Palestine, forbidden to Palestinians.

1. Four years later, on October 14, 1953, this small village was totally destroyed by Israeli bombardment, at the same time as the attack on the nearby border village of Qibya, where, at night, Israeli regular troops dynamited forty-two houses with the people inside them and fired on those attempting to escape. It was a massacre comparable with that of Dar Yassein.

Thin but bright-eyed barefoot children came running from all directions, cavorting in the dust, running beside the station-waggon. Yusuf drove as far as he could over the rough track, then stopped and looked inquiringly at his master.

'Wait,' Butros told him, and got out, followed by Marian, the boys, and the National Guard.

The Guard led the way over some rough boulder-strewn ground, rising slightly to a spur of the hill, beyond the last house of the village.

Then they stood looking down into the plain. In the near-distance there was the blue heat-hazed huddle they knew to be Lydda, the undulating line of the hills blue in the background. The Guard handed to Butros the pair of field-glasses he had until then kept slung round his neck.

Butros took them from him with a curt '*Shukran!*' and adjusted them to his sight; then stood motionless, gazing. Familiar buildings, a minaret, the water-tower. . . .

After a minute or two he turned and offered the glasses, mutely, to Marian, but she shook her head.

'Please—may I?' Anton was all impatient eagerness.

His father handed them to him and he focussed, then exclaimed, excitedly.

'It's so clear,' he cried. 'You can see everything!'

Butros said, painfully, 'But not our house.'

'Houses, though. Even some palm trees. Walid—look! Lydda! Our house is down there—with all our things in it! Imagine!'

Walid took the glasses from Anton, and Marian turned away, laying a hand on her husband's arm.

'It's too much,' she said, in a low voice. 'Even . . .' she managed a tremulous smile, 'even without the palm trees!'

Butros pressed her hand.

'Forgive me. I shouldn't have let you come. It was selfish of me.'

They stumbled back over the rough ground to the station-waggon, leaving Anton eagerly pointing out and explaining. Neither spoke; there was nothing to say; pain and bitterness went too deep, draining words of significance.

IO

AFTER that visit to the border Butros's heart condition deteriorated and very little exertion would induce the old fearful pain. He resisted Marian's plea to be allowed to telephone to Khalil to come with a doctor from Ramallah, or send someone down from Jerusalem. He had no faith in doctors; he had his pills and what they couldn't do for him no doctor could. To Marian's suggestion that now there were newer things than digitalis he replied that he didn't want any progressive young Beirut-trained doctor coming sticking needles into him and telling him to stay in bed and keep off whisky. Above all he didn't want any of his relatives trying to take charge of him and move him into any bright and shiny American hospital. All he wanted was some immediate relief from pain, and this he had; when his worn-out old crock of a heart finally came to a stop then it would be time enough to take him up to Jerusalem for burial. Until then he would stay down here in Jericho, in Dar el-Salam, the House of Peace.

All through the burning heat of July and August he sat on the ground-floor verandah looking across to the orange grove, whose dark green foliage gave an illusion of coolness. He liked watching the trickles of water moving along the irrigation ditches in the early morning and the evening, the precious life-giving water. He never went upstairs again after the visit to the border; he had a heart attack shortly after they got home, his worst yet; he slept downstairs that night, and for the rest of his time. This meant that he never saw again the refugee camp massed on the bare hillside visible between the cypress trees of his garden. But he did not have to see the camp to remember the thousands of men and women, young and old, and the children, who waited there in their miserable tents, dependent on charity for their mere existence, to return to their homes and lands.

From the radio and a sporadic reading of the newspapers he learned of the setting up of the United Nations Economic Survey Commission for the Middle East, which was to 'investigate the economic conditions of the Middle East and the problem of the refugees and submit recommendations for the solution of that problem'. He had as little faith in it as he had in doctors. The Commission, he was quite sure, would recommend the setting up of works projects in the host countries for the integration of the refugees into those countries—regardless of the fact that all the Palestinians wanted only one thing, which was to go home, and that this was their inalienable right. Count Bernadotte's recommendation that they should be allowed to do so, and any who did not wish should be fully compensated, had been accepted by the United Nations Assembly a year ago, and in that same month Bernadotte had been assassinated by the Stern Gang in Jersualem. No doubt the recommendation would be reaffirmed this year, and the new one along with it, he thought sardonically.

And in fact in December the United Nations Relief and Works Agency for Palestine refugees was set up, but this Butros Al-Mansour did not know, for by then he had been dead three months.

The end came very suddenly early in October, shortly after Anton's thirteenth birthday. It was just one more attack but this time one from which he did not recover. It was shortly after sunrise, when the air was breathable. Marian had hoped that with the cooler weather he would be better, but it had been a hot September, prolonging the summer exhaustion, and by the beginning of October there was little difference. If he could have held on another two months, she thought afterwards, sadly, but his heart had been unable to stagger along beyond that cool dawn.

She had stepped out on to the verandah of the room in which they slept to breathe the morning air, as always when she first got up. The house was astir and a smell of coffee came from the kitchen. There was a sudden choking cry from behind and she turned back into the room to see Butros sitting on the edge of the bed. He looked at her but could not speak and before she had reached the bedside table and his pills he had pitched forward heavily into her arms.

Anton, wearing only sandals and shorts, came in through the French window with a basket of oranges for the breakfast table.

She looked at him aghast over her shoulder.

'Anton!' she cried. 'Oh, Anton!'

He rushed to her and saw his father's face and knew.

In the night, holding her hand and talking into the hot darkness as they lay side by side he had said to her, 'When I'm gone don't stay on here. Go to England, to your parents. Anton is due to go soon anyhow. Khalil will take this place over probably—let him if he wants to. There will be enough money to send Anton to school. . . .'

She had asked him, distressed, 'Do we have to discuss all this now?'

'I don't know. But it could easily be later than we think. It's not morbid to discuss death rationally, my dearest. It's morbid to shrink from it. My time will come suddenly when it does and there will be no chance to discuss anything.'

He pressed her hand.

'You mustn't be unhappy when I'm gone. You will have Anton, and a new phase will begin for you—there's been no life for you here, and life finished for me when we left Lydda.'

'Try to rest,' she urged.

'Yes. I think I could sleep now.' He sighed, relaxing into sleep. 'Bless you, my darling,' he murmured.

That was the last thing he said to her. He was still dozing when she got out of bed in the morning, and when she turned back into the room he looked at her for the last time before the darkness closed over in the relentness finality of death.

PART 2

Exile

I

Robert Melby was at London Airport to meet his daughter and grandson. Eleven years ago they had been together on an airport in what was then Palestine. The fair land of Palestine. His heart contracted, remembering. He and Elspeth had been going home; at least that was what they called it, what everyone called it, though it had seemed to them both that what they were doing was leaving home. Jaffa was home, not London; Jaffa, Palestine. Elspeth had waved frantically from the window of the plane, her face streaming with tears, though Marian and the child were no longer visible. She had sobbed unrestrainedly as the plane taxied into the runway, demanding, piteously, 'When shall we ever see them again?'

Well, this chilly November evening eleven years later, in 1949, was when. And she was not there for the first sight of them. Because it was Annual Day for the Housewives Guild—or something of the kind; he was never quite sure of the names of the numerous associations, committees, societies, fellowships, which made up her life. She had to be there because she was in the chair, in charge of a stall, was one of the speakers—he was not sure of her roles in the endless succession of functions. Marian would understand about her not going to the airport, she said, and she would be home in time to welcome them at the cottage. 'So long as *you* are there,' she had added, and smiled the small resigned smile she had brought to bear, it seemed to him, on every aspect of their marriage for nearly half a century.

There was a time when he had pitied her the sterility of this resignation. Pitied her with an anguish of desire to have her feel something—anything; if not joy or sorrow at least anger or contempt.

That had been in the Palestine days. The days when there had been, as he thought of it, fire in his belly, in his passion for his wife, and his rage against all that was going on all round him in the 'sub-war'—the assassinations on both sides, the brutalities of the police, the hangings and shootings and imprisonments; the atrocities committed in the name of law-and-order. The long struggle was over now, and only the bitterness remained. His friend Butros Mansour was dead; of heart trouble, it was said; some long fancy name they gave to it, there being no such thing in medicine as a broken heart. Yet many Palestinians beside Butros Mansour must have died of just that.

For a long time now he had not pitied Elspeth; you do not pity a stone because it can neither sing nor weep; everything to its own nature, fulfilling itself in its own way. Since 1948 he had not even pitied Palestine, for in the confrontation of that epic tragedy pity is too mean a word. Despair neither rages nor weeps; it is its own black bitter fire, from which there is no respite whilst life lasts.

It burned in Marian, too, and now she too was alone. She had the boy, but a woman needed more than a son in her life. Thirteen years ago he would have said he needed more than a daughter. Now he no longer needed anyone to warm his bed; only his heart. And this she would do, his dear one, flesh of his flesh; she and her half-Arab son, Butros Mansour's son. Anton Melby Mansour. It was a good name. The boy had been proud of his father; perhaps he would discover that his English grandfather was at least a man of integrity—and proud to have been his father's friend. That Anton felt himself more of a Mansour than a Melby, as Marian had written, was to the good. Let the boy feel himself Arab—proudly Arab. Palestinian. The champion of a wronged people—his father's people.

Suddenly he saw them through the open doors of the Customs hall, standing beside a baggage-laden counter, Marian hatless, as always, her figure neat and slim as ever, and beside her a slim boy as tall as herself—a handsome olive-skinned boy; an *Arab* boy, his heart exulted. Marian looked up and saw him and waved; she said something to the boy, who looked in the direction his mother indicated, then, after a moment, shyly smiled and waved. Then the movement of people, breaking and reforming in waves, engulfed them, and it seemed a long time before at last they emerged into the main hall.

Tall and thin, and straight and gaunt as ever, almost a caricature of the traditional figure of the English sun-dried satrap, Marian thought affectionately, approaching her father across the gap of the years, but grown old, his hair completely grey.

'You haven't changed a bit!' she cried, in the confusion of greeting and embrace, shock and happiness.

He smiled and was not deceived. She, too, had changed, he realized, in spite of her still slim figure; there was grey in her thick dark hair and her face was lined; she was no longer a young woman in her early thirties, but a woman in her middle forties; eleven years is a long time in a woman's life, especially when she has suffered.

He smiled at Anton and addressed him in Arabic.

'I see that you are my friend Butros Mansour's son.'

The boy smiled confusedly and answered in English.

'We may speak in English,' he said, shyly.

'I know. But I hope we may sometimes speak in Arabic. I like the sound of it, and it's many years since I heard it spoken.'

Marian asked, 'Where is Mamma?'

'Committee-bound. Or a guild, or something. Anyhow, something she couldn't get out of. She said you would understand, and she'll be back by the time we get home. I ordered a car. . . . What sort of flight was it? Was it very hot when you left?'

'It was pretty warm in Jericho. The flight was merely dull.'

'How did Anton like it?'

They both looked at the boy.

He answered, laconically, 'It was all right.'

'He didn't want to come,' Marian explained, smiling to mask her frown, and not succeeding.

'I don't blame him.'

Melby laid a hand on the boy's shoulder.

'Don't mind it too much. Your exile's only for a few years. Mine's for life!'

'He doesn't see why he had to come at all,' Marian complained.

'I keep telling him he would have been coming to England soon now in any case.'

Anton offered no comment and they left the building and waited outside on the pavement for the car. There was a cold wind with rain on it, and Anton shivered, as when he had stepped out of the plane. It had been cold in Ramallah in the winter, but not like that; this was a kind of damp cold that seemed to creep in under your skin. It had been hot in Jericho that morning, and even up in Amman it had been very warm at mid-day.

They got into the car and Anton gazed out of the window at the vast straggling ugliness of the airport, and later at the factories floodlit and neon-lighted along the by-pass, and the miles of small suburban villas standing back behind little strips of gardens. His face was dark. Arab dark, Melby thought, sympathetically.

His spirits lifted slightly at the first glimpse of the Thames as they crossed a bridge; it seemed very wide after the Jordan. His spirits lifted still more when the first woods and dark open spaces of Wimbledon Common loomed up in the headlights of the car; here was loneliness and emptiness and breathing space again—something he understood.

Presently his grandfather said, 'It's a pity it's dark—otherwise just over there, at the edge of the Common, you'd see the school you'll be going to.'

Anton looked out apprehensively into the darkness, in the direction indicated.

'It's a good school,' Melby assured him. 'You'll like it.'

Anton wondered.

'Is it where my father wanted me to go?'

'Yes. Years ago he asked me to put your name down for it. He wanted you to go to an English public school, and the thought of your going to the one I went to pleased him.'

'I liked the idea too,' Marian put in quickly.

'It's a day school, too,' Melby added. 'You'll be able to live at home with us. Here we are—the house with the blue door——'

Anton was surprised at the smallness of his grandparents' house; it was hardly bigger than the adobe cottages in which the labourers had lived on his father's estate at Lydda. A lantern hung in the porch over the door, and there was a trellis with some kind of vine. He could make out rose-trees in a tiny front garden.

His mother cried out with pleasure as she stepped out of the car. 'It's a dear little house! No wonder you and Mamma are so fond of it! And looking straight out over the Common—you could be in the heart of the country! There's Mamma. . . .'

A small neat grey-haired woman came briskly down the path. There was a repetition of the embracing and kissing and exclaiming Anton had found so confusing at the airport. His grandmother kissed him and hugged him vigorously, crying to him that he was so tall, 'and you were only a toddler when I last saw you!'

She gazed at him with a raptness that embarrassed him. She reminded him of a bird. She had a bird's keen eyes, a bird's quick movements, and there was something pecking about her. She linked an arm through his and they went into the house, and he had the uncomfortable feeling that she was taking possession of him.

It did in fact mean a very great deal to Elspeth Melby to have her grandson under her roof. She was deeply convinced that if only Marian had been a boy her own life would have been different. Her first child had been a boy, but he had died in early infancy, and the child it was hoped would replace him turned out to be a girl—and her father's daughter. Robert Melby being a man of integrity there was nothing wrong with that; it was even admirable, but it left her, the mother, diminished and lonely.

There had been so many disappointments. She tried to be a good Christian and accept that it was all the will of God—and it was tiresome of Robert to point out, whenever she said this, that others besides Christians believed in God and accepted the divine will, the Moslems, for example—and to believe that whatever is is best; but there were weak moments, many of them, increasing with the years, when the sense of disappointment was oppressive.

It had seemed such a fine, romantic, adventurous thing to marry Robert Melby and go out with him to the Holy Land and help to run a school for blind Arab boys. She had liked their house in Jaffa, but not Jaffa itself; the high-light of Palestinian life for her had been access to Jerusalem. She had never been able to look at an ancient olive tree on a Judaean hillside without speculating as to the possibility of Our Lord's gaze having rested on the same tree—but Robert always said in his matter-of-fact way that that was most unlikely, that olive trees didn't live that long. . . .

He was so fundamentally kind, so really good, she would think sadly, and yet he could be so wounding.

Robert himself was really the first disappointment. He was a clergyman's son and had missionaries in the family as other people have twins, but he was a stubbornly unorthodox Christian, and distressingly sceptic about the authenticity of some of the holy places, even dismissing some of them as 'nonsense'. She had always been wishing they could be transferred to Jerusalem or Bethlehem; but Robert liked Jaffa for the chief thing she had against it—that it was predominantly Moslem. Or, as he always put it, Arab. If they hadn't been stationed there she was convinced he would never have become so deeply involved in Arab nationalism, and consequently not been recalled to London. Certainly if they had not been sent to Jaffa their daughter would not have met Butros Mansour.

Not that she had anything against Mansour, she would insist. He was a charming man, and a Christian. But the fact did remain—did it not?—that the Melbys were Anglicans and the Mansours Eastern Orthodox, which was almost as bad as being Roman Catholic. Mansour was anyhow old enough to be Marian's father, and it was embarrassing to have a son-in-law almost your own age. And they had been married by the Orthodox Church, and Anton brought up in that denomination. It was, to say the least of it, disappointing.

As disappointing as having to live in England again and endure the English winters. Not to mention the Battle of Britain. As disappointing as Robert's refusal to accompany her to church on Sundays or take any interest in her social work.

She never complained or criticized; by long habitude she was disciplined to acceptance. Robert was a good man, and she had no right to wish him any different. Marian had grown up to be intelligent, and a good daughter. If she was closer to her father than her mother, well, that was a law of nature and had to be accepted.

That the son who might have been close to her was not allowed to grow up was God's will and as such not to be questioned. She had tried not to be bitter, but to make a useful life for herself and to count her blessings, and she had more or less succeeded.

Her reaction to the news of the sudden death of Butros was a conflict of pity for Marian and a wild hope that now she would come to England with the boy and she would be allowed to know her grandson. Robert both cabled and wrote strongly urging return to England—'Jericho can hold nothing for you now,' he had insisted. When Marian had written back that she agreed and that she and Anton would come as soon as the sale of the property to Khalil had been effected, and all the loose ends tidied up, it had seemed to Elspeth such a blessing that her spirit had been hardly able to contain it. She had no illusions about the possibility of any great closeness between herself and Marian; they would meet as strangers, almost; but the boy, her grandson, the substitute at last for the son who had died—surely they in time would be close? Children, even modern children, were very often drawn to their grandparents. It was a well-known fact.

Elspeth had a life-long devotion to the well-known facts—in the face of all the disappointing evidence to the contrary.

She yearned towards her grandson with an intensity that was almost a physical ache. To be sure he was half Arab, but only half, and he had a look of his mother about him. There was nothing wrong with being half Arab, of course, but the Arab part of him, she felt, would be alien to her; though no doubt after a short time in England the English part would be uppermost. Particularly once he had become part of an English public school. He had his mother's blue eyes—though, to be sure, Arabs often had blue eyes —but despite this, and a general, fugitive look of Marian, he did not, Elspeth had to acknowledge, really look English, with his olive skin, full lips, strong nose—the strong Mansour nose.

Yet it was love at first sight with her, for he was undeniably striking in appearance—a handsome boy, a grandson to be proud of. If only, as time went on, he could come to feel even a little affection for her it would compensate for so much....

2

AFTER so long away it was not easy, Marian found, to adapt to English life or English weather. She shivered a good deal in the damp gusty autumn days, though both her parents assured her that it was really quite mild. 'Of course it's not *Jericho*!' her mother said, reproachfully, 'but it's no colder than Ramallah or Jerusalem at this time of the year.'

It seemed useless to remind her that that was a dry, mountainy cold, invigorating, whereas this was a damp cold which crept insidiously in the bones. Her mother was always advocating going out for a 'good sharp walk' or a 'good blow' across the Common as a means of restoring circulation and overcoming what she called the 'chillies'. Of course, her mother conceded, she was in a low state just now, due to the shock of Butros's death, and that would account for her being so shivery. 'But you'll get over it,' she assured her. 'We all get over everything in time, mercifully.'

Her tone was gentle and she did sincerely feel for her daughter, but words were not easy for her, and she had long ago lost whatever capacity she had ever had for demonstrating sympathy and affection; she persuaded herself, with a bitter satisfaction, that Robert had killed all that in her years ago.

Marian acknowledged that her mother meant well and that it was not her fault that she was incapable of really understanding; she had never known an impassioned love, and she had never known the intolerable deprivation of death. The loss of a baby which died when it was a few weeks old could be heartbreaking, but not to be compared with the loss of an adult person, very close and dear, after a period of years. It had been so short, the time she and Butros had had together, fourteen years only; but for the

Palestine tragedy there might have been at least another ten. It was simply not true that in time you got over everything; Butros had not got over the loss of his home, the loss of his country, the loss of his dignity as a human being. He had not got over the defeat, the humiliation, the intolerable loss of country and national identity. He had had to learn to think of himself no longer as a Palestinian but as a Jordanian—and he had failed. In the end it had killed him. He had died, as Khalil in his quiet cool way had said, of a broken heart.

With a terrible bitter passion Farid, weeping beside his brother's dead body, had said violently, 'The Jews killed him—as surely as if they had shot him!'

There was a sense, Marian thought, in her own tearless agony, then and later, and recurrently, in which he had been killed by the Israeli woman soldier who had spat at him.

She had known, of course, that the old walled Orthodox cemetery outside the Old City, near David's Gate, was now inaccessible in No Man's Land, and that when the time came Butros would not lie with his fathers on Mount Zion. Butros would be the first to agree that it didn't matter where you were buried, but he would also have agreed that it should be possible for the bereaved to choose, and the reasons for being buried in one place and not in another could matter intensely when principles and injustice were involved. She had wanted it to be Bethlehem, since it could not be Jerusalem. The service was held in the Greek Orthodox chapel in the Church of the Nativity, and Anton had had his friend Amin on one side of him and his new friend Walid on the other; Khalil was there with a group of Moslem friends and relatives, and Nasri had been given leave to attend.

Once Khalil, standing very straight and correct, had looked across to Marian and caught her eye and given her a small half rueful smile, as though to say, This is all very tedious but it has to be gone through. She returned his smile and was grateful to him; his cool detachment helped, which Majdeh's noisy weeping did not. Muna, so swathed in deep black as to be almost veiled, was a self-consciously tragic-heroic figure, too proud to weep, but genuinely under intense strain. She was bitter that the service and burial had to take place in Bethlehem; Butros had a right to be laid with their parents in the old cemetery on the lower slopes of Mount Zion.

Back in England Marian remembered Khalil, of them all, with the most gratitude and affection—Khalil who had always been difficult for Butros and whom he had never tried to understand, but who, by those very characteristics of quietness and detachment which had made him alien to Butros, had been for Marian, half drowning in the swirling currents of emotion, her own and other people's, a rock to cling to. She had been able to leave all the business in connection with the house and land to him, and he had begged her to believe that Dar el-Salam would always remain her home and Anton's and that their rooms would be left untouched for them to return to at any time. And he hoped they would return from time to time, if only to escape the English winters.

Marian told him, sadly, 'You are kind, Khalil, but I must try to find something useful to do in London, and Anton must go to school. Also Jericho was part of my life with Butros, and it came to an end.'

He said simply, then, 'Yes, I understand. Only remember Dar el-Salam is always there. I regard myself only as its caretaker.'

But it was no good, she thought, striding over Wimbledon Common in the gusty October weather, sometimes with her father and Anton, or with one or the other of them, sometimes alone, trying to acclimatize both body and spirit. She had to find something to do and launch both herself and Anton in a new life and forget about the orange groves and guardian cypresses and the hot bright sunshine of Jericho, the tremendous sunsets over the Judaean hills, and the shadows moving over the Mountains of Moab; just as it had been necessary to forget Lydda. She had to learn to live without Butros, who had been husband and father, lover and friend, to her for fourteen years. Butros in whose benign shadow she had lived, to which she turned so eagerly as a young woman and so gratefully in middle age. She had to learn to live with the deep inner loneliness, which not even her father, of the same calibre as Butros himself, could reach. Only it was so very bitter that Butros with his failing heart should have, miraculously, survived the terrible trek from Lydda only to die less than fifteen months later in the peaceful haven of Jericho. And bitter for Anton, who had been so proud of his father, loved him so dearly, and who had already suffered so much—too much, too soon; Anton who thought of himself as Arab, and for whom England, whatever its beauty and interest, whatever it had to offer, must remain exile.

3

FOR Anton the whole of the first year was a confusion of new experiences and sights. Frequently he felt overwhelmed by it all. In his mind he talked continuously to Walid, but though his mind wrote innumerable, and graphic, letters to his friend the thought of trying to get even a part of it down on paper defeated him by its magnitude. So he sent only coloured picture-postcards—of the Tower of London, Trafalgar Square (with pigeons), Piccadilly Circus, Wimbledon Common (with windmill), Wimbledon Common (with birch woods), the parish church ('where we go on Sundays'), and later on coloured postcard reproductions of pictures in the National Gallery ('which is free').

Walid studied all these postcards with interest and tucked them into school-books and was glad to get them; but he himself did not write, though in his mind, too, long conversations took place.

Anton would not be going to school until the January term, and in the three months until then Marian did her best to show him London—which seemed to him quite unbelievably vast, as though a number of cities had all flowed into each other. Viewed from the top of a bus it seemd to go on for ever, he thought, like the desert, only it was as crowded and noisy as the desert was empty and silent. He had no experience of cities, and the biggest town he had known was Lydda, with some fifteen thousand inhabitants; Ramallah at that time was little more than a large village, and Jericho little more than a main street. Jerusalem was something different and apart. The alleyways of streets of the Old City, to which he had been taken occasionally before partition, were packed with people and donkeys and merchandise, but the streets of London were solid masses of traffic—cars, taxis, and the enormous high red buses—and the pavements seemed like nothing so much as an overturned anthill, the same dark moving mass. Everyone, it seemed to him, men and women alike, wore dark clothes. And the buildings were dark, and the skies. There seemed to be very few American cars, and the English ones seemed very small.

He was interested in Tower Bridge and had the good fortune to see it open up for a tall ship to pass under. He thought that he must tell Walid about this, and how wide the River Thames was, and how dirty, but interesting because ships from all parts of the world came to it. The Tower of London was interesting, too, and he bought a selection of postcards to send one by one to Walid. St. Paul's Cathedral impressed him; it reminded him of the Dome of the Rock—at least, from a distance. One day they went to town by a different line and from the train window he saw, to his astonishment, a mosque. When he exclaimed upon it, bewildered, his mother said yes, it was a mosque all right, and down the line, in the other direction there was another. There was also in London a Greek Orthodox cathedral to which one day she would take him. Truly London was the most marvellous place; and yet he was homesick, most desperately homesick, for the familiar scenes, the cypresses black against the Mount of Temptation as you drove towards Jericho from the Dead Sea, the quilted folds of the Mountains of Moab, the great tawny haunches of the Judaean hills, the little twisted pine trees of Ramallah, and the smell of *falafel* frying on the braziers at the street-corner booths in the evening, the smell of it blending with the smell of the pines, the evening smell of Ramallah.

He was homesick, too, for Jericho, the old house with the cool tiled floors, and his father sitting on the verandah, his hands clasped on the silver knob of his cane—the one possession he had brought from Lydda. He was not homesick for Lydda; it was written-off in his mind, and associated now only with terror. He knew now, in his blood and bones, they would never go back. (But his grandfather said that never was a long time. . . .)

He liked the London parks, and was amazed at the size of the great trees, and by the greenness of the grass. But he preferred

Wimbledon Common and its silver birch woods full of bracken, golden just then, with narrow paths threading through, because all this was wild and you could get away from people, and it was a kind of green and gold wilderness. There were also, he discovered, ponds where wild duck settled, and seagulls came in from the river, not far away. It seemed to him most marvellous that all this was, as his grandfather assured him, only nine miles from the centre of London.

During the first few weeks before he started working with a tutor, preliminary to starting at the new school in January, he walked every morning across the common with his grandfather to a big old house which was a home for blind people, some of whom were also deaf. His grandfather explained to him that he tried to help these people by being friendly with them, talking to them, and taking them for walks, and that he talked to the deaf-blind people by spelling out words to them on their hands. He talked to Anton about the school he had run in Jaffa for blind boys of all faiths—Moslems, Christians, Jews. He told him also about the struggle of the Palestinians at that time, before the Second World War, for independence, and the promises the British made to them during the First World War, when they were fighting the Turks. It was a story of betrayal all along the line, he said, sadly. Anton knew something about it all from his father, but not as factually, and he understood very well that the tragic happenings in which he and his family—and hundreds of thousands of others—were rooted in all this.

He enjoyed walking and talking with his grandfather. He reminded him very strongly of his father and he felt drawn to him because of it. What he felt for his grandmother was something very much less; he got along with her and didn't mind her. Every Sunday morning they went to church together. He liked the church with its tall spire and its coloured glass windows; inside it was very much lighter than the little Orthodox church in Jericho, with its deep shadows and the small stars of its candles, and he preferred the religious mysteriousness of the candlelit gloom; also in the Anglican church he found all the standing and sitting and kneeling confusing. At first, too, he found it disturbing that men and women sat together, but going up to the altar for Holy Communion the pieces of a recognizable pattern seemed to fall into place and he felt reassured; it was not after all so very different; anyhow not the most important part, and one day he would go to the kind of service he was used to, at the Orthodox cathedral, Agia Sophia. Not, he thought, that God wouldn't be just as pleased with one form of service as another, when it was offered up sincerely, but attending a service in an Orthodox church was a way of keeping in touch with the old life, which he thought of as his true life, and to which he would one day return—for it was unthinkable that he should live out his life in England, where he felt, although it was his mother's country, he would never belong, never be able to think of as home. The strong Palestinian blood ran in his veins, and the strong Palestinian sunshine. And there was something he and Walid had to do together in a few years' time.

But of this he said no word to anyone, not even to his grandfather; the dream of the Beersheba road had to remain locked, an inviolable secret, in his heart until his exile came at last to an end and he returned to what had now to be thought of as Jordan.

Finally, at the beginning of November, he wrote to Walid, writing in English, as they had agreed: 'Dear Walid: I hope you have had the postcards I have sent. I couldn't write a letter before this as I have felt so confused with the newness and strangeness of the life here. I have been taken to see the headmaster of King's College School here, where I am to go. He was friendly and seemed to think me O.K., but I have to sit for an entrance examination this month, and if I pass it I have to go before a board of examiners so that they can see for themselves that I am all right. The rule is for everyone, not just for outsiders like me. My grandfather says he is sure I will pass. He was at this school himself in 1905. Now that I have seen it I don't think it's going to be much different from the Friends School. I expect I will manage, but first I have to do three months' hard work with a private teacher, what the English call a crammer—because he crams you full of learning in a short time, so that when I start at the school I will be what the headmaster called 'in line with the English syllabus'. I am not quite sure what it means, except that I have to study very hard and won't have much time for anything else, so I may not write again for a few months, but you will know I am thinking of you and all we did together and what we talked about and plan.

'I hope you are getting along all right. I wish I was back and that we were going around together. But that will come—*Insh'allah.* Remember me to Fuad.

Your friend
Anton Mansour.'

Walid was very happy to receive this letter, and he read it many times, during class, strolling alone during breaks, in his room at nights in his uncle's house. At the weekend he made a special trip by bus to Hebron to show it to his uncle and Fuad. But he did not answer it, because he was not in the habit of answering letters, and he knew that his friend would not expect him to write. One day they would be together again and carry out their plan—his Uncle Munir's plan. This was the time of waiting; and preparation.

Another month went by before Anton wrote again, and then it was on the inside of a Christmas card.

'This is to let you know I passed my entrance exam for K.C.S. It was very easy. I go six mornings a week now to a tutor—the crammer I told you about in my letter. He is very nice, and knows a lot about Palestine, my grandfather being an old friend of the family. I would like to hear from you, even if you only sent a postcard saying *marhaba.*'

Walid sent the postcard, a garish coloured picture of the Dome of the Rock. He wrote in English: 'I thank you for your postcards of London, also letter and Christmas card. I am working hard for examinations. I saw Soraya Saba the other day and she asked about you and wished to be remembered. I also saw your cousin Nasri, very smart in officer's uniform. Please write again soon. W.H. (Your friend who waits.)'

It was, however, some time before Anton wrote again, so overwhelming were the new experiences and impressions, so numerous the adjustments to be made. His greatest difficulty was in adjusting to the dampness in the English winter climate. He shivered and caught cold, and crouched continually over the very small coal fire in the cottage sitting-room, scorching his face without ever warming his body.

He was fortunate in liking his tutor, a pleasant and intelligent young man called Gerald Johns, who had been struck down by polio in his last year at Oxford and was now confined to a wheelchair. He lived with his widowed mother in the ground-floor flat of a large seedy house that had once been grand. Anton walked to it across the Common and liked going there, because he liked Mr. Johns, and Mr. Johns's room, which was full of books, from floor to ceiling, and very warm from a big black stove which glowed red through a small door with a mica window.

Gerald had developed an interest in Middle East affairs, and had great sympathy with the Palestinians; he had planned to tour the Arab countries when he came down from Oxford. He had accepted the calamity which had overtaken him with philosophical fortitude, resolving that since physical adventures were debarred him he would enjoy intellectual ones. Tutoring young Anton Mansour was something of an adventure; he found him not at all brilliant, but receptive and eager. He encouraged him to talk about his father, feeling that he needed to. Eventually Anton talked about the trek. The young man, listening, would be filled with horror, anger, pity. By what right did one people do this to another? Because they themselves had suffered did that give them the right? In any case these Palestinians were not the cause of their suffering.

Anton told him, 'In Ramallah I have a friend who came with his family from Beersheba. He believes that Palestinians can win back their country if they organize. But my father never believed it. He wouldn't even talk about it.'

His tutor said, 'History has seen great empires and whole civilizations pass away. In our own time we've seen the passing of the British Empire. It used to be said that it was the empire on which the sun never set—though the Indian nationalists used to say that was because God couldn't trust the British in the dark! Anyhow, it passed—its sun set. And Hitler's Third Reich, which was to last a thousand years. So why shouldn't young people like you and your friend live to see the passing of Israel—the liberation of Palestine? In the end injustice destroys itself—all evil does. History demonstrates the fact.'

In his mind Anton reported all this to Walid, but it never got on to paper. In his mind he talked to Walid all the time, and in this way stayed close to him, in spite of all that was strange and new impinging from outside in this crowded new life.

Christmas was a thoroughly confusing business with a huge clutter of cards which his grandmother strung on lines across the room, and a Christmas tree decorated with tinsel and small coloured electric lights and crowned with a silver cardboard star-of-Bethlehem, and numerous people coming in for glasses of sherry and to say Happy-Christmas and leave small parcels wrapped in fancy paper.

Several times, also, Anton accompanied his mother and grandparents to parties in other people's houses and flats, and at these parties there were a great many people and a great deal more than sherry to drink, and Anton sipping a soft drink of some kind, grown warm and sticky in his clutching hand, would reply politely to endlessly repeated questions—Yes, it was the first time he was in England; yes, he liked it very much, thank you; yes, he was going to King's College School next term; yes, he came from Palestine; yes, he spoke Arabic; yes, he did find it rather cold here; yes, it was his first English Christmas. . . .

At one such party a stout woman, red-faced and strung with beads, came up to him saying she had heard he was a refugee and she wanted, she said, to shake him by the hand, because she always felt so sorry for Jews and always stood up for them.

She beamed down at him, compassionately, full of ginny goodwill.

'My great-grandmother was a Jew,' she told him, kindly.

Anton said, confusedly, 'I am sorry—*yani*—I mean I am not a Jew. I am a Christian.'

Goodwill ebbed from her like an outgoing tide.

'You're not a refugee?'

'Oh yes, we're refugees—I mean my family. Refugees from Palestine. My father was a Palestinian—an Arab.'

'An *Arab*?'

She stared at him as though he had declared himself a leper, then accosted a man who stood near her talking to a girl.

'Did you hear that? The boy says he's an *Arab*!'

The man looked from her to Anton.

'So he is. Half-Arab, anyhow. He's Bob Melby's grandson. Marian Melby married a Palestinian.'

He gave Anton a friendly smile then turned away to resume his interrupted conversation with the girl. Anton seized the opportunity to escape whilst the woman was still gazing indignantly at her informant's back.

When he reported the incident to his grandfather afterwards Melby smiled in the way which always reminded Anton of his father.

'It'll probably happen to you many times yet,' he told him. 'The great British public has been hearing for years about Jewish refugees —from long before the war. Very little has been heard about the refugees from the Jews. . . .'

During the Easter holidays Anton wrote Walid a long letter:

'I didn't want to write again till I was settled in at K.C.S. The photograph I send with this doesn't mean I have joined the British Army but that I am a recruit in the Army Section of the School Cadet Force. We wear khaki battledress, like the Army, and black berets. I am very keen on this; it's useful to know how to shoot and to know about the different types of machine-guns. We have a rifle range here at the school, and we go out on to the Common for cross-country runs and manœuvres. I enjoy all this very much and wish we were doing it together. In the summer we will go camping.

'I miss going to Mr. Johns, the tutor I told you about, but I go and see him at weekends, and although he is no longer teaching me he helps me quite a lot in other ways, such as making up my mind what I want to do when I finish at King's. He thinks I should do some kind of social work, and that now that the United Nations Relief and Works Agency has been formed to take care of the refugees I might be able to get work with them later on. I have discussed it with my grandfather, also with the Headmaster at King's, and it's been decided I shall study to take a diploma in Social Science at London School of Economics, which is a college of London University, but I will have to have a job of some kind first, for a year, because students have to have had some experience of working conditions before being accepted. That's all far ahead, but now that my career is planned I have to have special classes in Economics, as I will have to pass in this subject when I come to take my G.C.E. examination.

'I wish my father could know about all this. I was so undecided about what to do when I was at school in Ramallah, and my parents couldn't help me—my father was too ill, and my mother too worried about him. But now it does all begin to be clear as to what would be useful, and what would be possible for me, not being brilliant like you but only fairly intelligent, and good at what the English call "swotting", which means working very hard at something in a very concentrated way.

'The first few days here were not as difficult as I feared they were going to be. It's not really very different from the Friends' School, and the boys don't seem to find me all that foreign. There were the usual questions: What's your name? Where are you from? When I said Jericho they thought I was kidding. They've no idea where it is, but they all seem to know about the walls falling down, and apparently they have a saying about oh, go to Jericho, like saying go to Hell. Some of them thought if I came from Palestine I must be a Jew. I explained that my father was a Palestinian Christian and that my mother was an English Christian. One boy said that made me a half-caste. I said it made me Anglo-Arab. I had an idea they were trying to get me rattled and I was determined they shouldn't.

'Afterwards one of the boys came to me when I was alone and asked me if I really came from Jericho. When I said yes he wanted to know if it was true it was below sea-level and asked me about it. He told me he'd got to this school by scholarship, his family being poor. He said most of the boys' fathers are doctors and lawyers and business directors and so on. He wanted to know what my father did. I told him he was dead, and about our house in Lydda, and everything, and how we were fortunate to own a house and land in Jericho and not to have lost everything like thousands of others. He was very interested in all this and said I must visit at his house sometime as his Dad would be interested. He said it was a pity I hadn't told the others my father was an Arab prince or a sheik because then they would have been impressed. He said he hadn't joined the Cadets because he didn't believe in militarism, nor did his Dad. I said I thought it handy to know how to shoot. He said "That's because you've got Arab blood!" I think he meant to excuse me for something I couldn't help. I said I guessed that was it. I think he's what the Americans call a good guy, but a bit too serious.

'That's as far as I've got with making friends, but it all seems all right; there's no bullying, and the masters are all right.

'The trees are all bright green now, and there are a lot of blossoming trees in the gardens everywhere, but it's so cold still. I think of the almond trees in bloom in Jordan.

'Since Christmas my mother has a job with a Middle East trade publication in London and now has an apartment in town and only comes out here on Sundays, or I go and spend a weekend with her and we visit the parks and museums. Sometimes I wish you and I could be exploring London together, but mostly I wish I was back in Jordan with you. There is one bright spot, though— my mother has said that when I finish at K.C.S. and before I start work at the job, whatever it is, I can have a holiday in Jordan. Only another three years. Roll on the day!

Your faithful A.M.'

4

IT WAS generally considered—by his grandparents, his mother, his school-masters—that Anton had adjusted splendidly to English life. Only Gerald Johns, who knew more than most people about adjustment, was not so sure. Externally Anton was extrovert and uncomplicated; he played all the school games, enjoyed the Cadet training and was admirably tough in all its more rigorous aspects; he was good-natured and good-tempered and always managed to grin amiably at the endless jokes about sheiks and harems—the words invariably mispronounced. He got along with everyone, joined in the general fooling and ragging, was well enough liked, but made no special friend. He joined a model yacht club which met on Saturday afternoons to sail its boats on a pond on the Common, and a model aeroplane club which met on Sunday mornings farther across the Common. He went occasionally to the home of Philip Edwards, the boy who had asked him about Jericho and was initiated into the rites of high-tea; when he was not too burdened with home-work he went to the house of another boy, Michael Lindley, to watch the television, there being none in his grandparents' house. Sometimes Lindley would assure him there was a smashing film at one of the local cinemas and he would go with him to see it; the smashing films were always war pictures, or 'epics', or thrillers, and usually disappointed; Anton was not much interested in any of them, good or bad; he went because he was asked and it was easier to say O.K. than anything else.

The things he liked doing were walking on the Common with his grandfather, walking alone in the woods and thinking about Walid and all that life which was more real to him than the present, visiting picture-galleries and museums with his mother, and talking with Gerald Johns.

He never thought of Johns as his special friend in the way that Walid had been—and in his mind still was—because Johns was quite old, about twenty-five, but he liked going to the shabby book-lined room in the ugly old house and being treated by Johns as an equal; it made him feel less immature, a feeling from which he frequently suffered, even with Walid. He could tell Johns things about Palestine, things he was interested to know, and it made a change from that endless process of being told things which was called education. Johns asked him questions and listened with respectful attention to his replies. Mrs. Johns, also, treated him as an adult, asking him what he had thought of the Guinness film he had told Gerald he was going to see, calling upon him to admire a piece of Georgian silver or an early Victorian paperweight she had bought for her antique shop. In this atmosphere he felt relaxed and at ease and could be himself—his fundamentally disturbed self. At school there was always the necessity to pretend, to be what was expected of him, to enter into the spirit of whatever was going on, in order not to be different—to overcome the handicap of having a name that was different, a face that was a little foreign, a father who was much more foreign than if he had been of any European nationality, of being what one of the boys had called a half-caste, of being altogether, one way and another, odd. At the Johns' it was not odd to be different; it was merely interesting.

But not even to Gerald Johns did he confide the dream of the Beersheba road. That was something between him and Walid, an unspoken pact. Just as the cross was the symbol of his Christian faith the road to Beersheba was the symbol of his ultimate aspiration, a road which had eventually to be trod, a spiritual way which had to be undertaken and to which all things led, and though he did not, as yet, think of it in those terms there was in him this fugitive, restless comprehension, an imperceptibly growing awareness.

It was this restlessness, this unease, just below the surface of the external cheerfulness and normality, which made the young man immobilized in the wheel-chair uncertain as to what extent the boy had adjusted. He, too, at school, had been regarded as such a nice, natural, normal boy, so good-natured, and—that dreadful word—jolly. . . . But it hadn't felt like that inside; nor had it at Oxford, where again he had been considered so splendidly extrovert. Then the disaster had happened, releasing him from the necessity of keeping up the pretence any longer.

Young Mansour had considerable charm; he had an engaging manner, very good manners, and an attractive smile. There was a choir-boy bloom of innocence on him—as spurious as the carefully applied dust on a faked antique. This boy had heard the screams of women being raped, had seen men and women drinking their own and each other's urine, human beings dehumanized by terror and suffering; this boy had known the fear of death and seen it, face to face, in all its pitifulness and horror. This fundamentally Arab boy disguised as an English public school boy with the cheerful, candid, open manner, so normal and uncomplicated. Johns didn't believe it, any more than he believed in the splendid adaptability and resignation—acceptance was a word they were very fond of—attributed to himself. He was quite sure that young Mansour was desperately homesick, and in spite of finding a father-substitute in his grandfather, desperately lonely; and profoundly disturbed. He had been twice uprooted and each time it had been associated with shock, the first time from Lydda, to the accompaniment of terror, humiliation, and unspeakable suffering; the second time from Jericho, associated with the shock of his father's sudden death. There had been the prolonged shock and horror of the trek to Ramallah, the mental, emotional and physical ordeal; and finally the shock of the impact of a new life in a new climate in another country. Only a moron could have come through all that unaffected by it, and Anton Mansour was intelligent, sensitive, aware. Below the charming, ready smile, the easy, amiable manner, there were tensions, and not very far below the surface. Of this Gerald Johns, observing the boy with sympathy and affection, was convinced.

Anton knew only that at the Johns' there was not the necessity to be on guard about being different; and that out of school hours, when he could be himself, he thought endlessly about the wide

Jordanian plains flowing away to meet the sky at immensely far horizons, and about the tawny Judaean wilderness with the strange shapes left when the sea went out, and Jericho at the foot of the Mount of Temptation, and the jasmine smell of Jericho and the pine smell of Ramallah, and the dusty white road snaking down from Hebron; and of Walid, endlessly of Walid, who had signed himself 'your friend who waits', and remembering all this he would feel restless, and in some indefinable way lonely.

This loneliness he admitted to no one, and was careful to conceal. It was effectively camouflaged by his numerous activities. At weekends, and during the holidays, he would announce that he was going off on his bicycle with Edwards to Box Hill, going up the river with 'some chaps', going to the pictures with Lindley, or popping along to his place to see something on the telly, going over to the Johns'. Or merely just going for a walk on the Common.

He had always something on, was never at a loose end. And yet it was all loose ends, because with the exception of Gerald Johns they none of them meant anything to him; like the masters at the school they were all right; they were part of his English life, like the chilly weather, and the Common, the Anglican church, and King's College School. You became absorbed into it all, and yet there was always the feeling of it all being temporary, like the life you lived on holiday—only it didn't feel like a holiday because it went on too long, and school came into it. There were the anniversaries, too; the anniversary of the Lydda trek, the anniversary of his father's death. And his private anniversaries: the anniversary of his Hebron-Dahiriya trip with Walid; the anniversary of the day he and his mother flew to London.

In the first summer he wrote to Walid: 'There have been a few warm days here lately, about 80°F, and people put on black glasses and suffer and say how hot it is. The boys at school call the days "scorchers". When I tell them that in Jericho it's so hot at this time of the year that even the flies die they think I'm joking.'

During the school holidays he spent a week with his mother in Britanny. Marian, with a week's leave from her office, had a sudden yearning for the sea—and to get out of England. She had had a holiday in Brittany with her parents, as a young girl, on leave from Palestine, and St. Malo of all the places they toured had remained most vividly in her memory, because it was a walled city, and it was to this her mind turned when she thought of a week by the sea with Anton. She knew that some three-quarters of St. Malo had been destroyed by incendiary bombs when it was liberated in 1944, but had been told that it had been restored, and that the twelfth-century ramparts had remained intact.

The night-crossing by steamer was very exciting to Anton, who had never been in a ship before, and his mind wrote endless letters to Walid about the experience.

It was a good way to travel, Marian thought, standing on the deck as they slipped down Southampton Water, with the gulls wheeling and crying in the wake of the ship, and the green fields and cliff-tops slipping past. Why hadn't she and Butros gone sometimes to Europe and done such things together? Why had they never gone farther afield than Beirut? But the answer, of course, she reflected, was that they had never wanted to. Butros always liked Beirut when he wanted a change, and she had always liked doing what he liked. Only if he had lived, she thought, with Anton at school in England, then we might have come, and we might have found many things to do, including this. If he had been allowed to live a little longer; if his heart hadn't been broken. . . .

She looked at Anton leaning on the rail beside her, his thick dark hair blowing in the wind, his face alight with eager interest. This was so much more Anton, Butros's son, than the boy who went around wearing the cap of an English public school. This was Anton who had gone off so eagerly with Walid to Hebron that Easter—in older worlds long ago, it seemed now. This was Anton released from the English bondage; Anton being himself. The Anton who would one day go back to the country of his birth, his father's country.

In the morning when they came up on deck, almost under the ancient walls, Anton exclaimed, delightedly, 'It's like Jerusalem!'

'In a way, but this is four hundred years older, and what's inside the walls is different.'

They stayed in a small hotel in a steep narrow street in which the holiday-makers swarmed up and down, and perhaps with the crowds, and the open-fronted fruit and vegetable shops, and the small cafés, it was faintly evocative of the Old City of Jerusalem, Marian conceded, but it was for the sea they had come, for Britanny, the old *Armorica*, was the Country of the Sea. And the sea was shining emerald, streaked with the white curling lines of breakers, and could never be looked at enough from the top of the ramparts at all hours of the day. They were agreed it was most wonderful, and something to remember always.

Long afterwards Marian was to remember that handful of days of wonder and beauty, and intense happiness and closeness, with Anton, her son.

At low tide they walked out to the islet on which the granite tomb of Chateaubriand faces out to sea; there was a smell of warm grass and the honey scent of gorse and the fugitive sweetness of wild flowers stirring in the sea wind, wild geranium and clover and yellow toadflax and ladies' slippers and wild lupin, with out-crops of seapinks among sudden boulders—small unimportant flowers, weed flowers, flowers in the grass.

They came to a hollow, a sunpocket out of the wind, with gorse crowding over, and sat down.

Anton sighed with contentment.

'I wish we need never go back to London!'

'I thought you liked it—the school, the lovely common, all your friends——'

'It's all right. It's just I feel I don't belong there.'

'You're half English!'

'I know, but I wasn't born there and I never lived there till now.'

'You'd belong even less here, not even speaking the language.'

He said quickly, 'No, that would make it easier! I wouldn't have to be sociable.'

He pulled the head off a dandelion and flicked it towards the sea.

'I don't always feel sociable,' he explained.

'I know what you mean. But you had to be educated.'

'I was doing all right in Ramallah.'

'I couldn't have stayed on in Jordan, Anton. And the night before he died your father——'

She broke off and groped for a handkerchief in her handbag, desperately fighting back the sudden tears.

He was instant contrition.

'Oh, now I've made you sad—just when we were so happy! Please don't be sad! I'm all right in London, really. It's only that I get a bit homesick. And miss Walid. And then being here, just the two of us, and feeling different——'

It was his turn to become choked and inarticulate.

Marian resolutely smiled.

'I know, but think—you'll be fifteen this year, and in three years' time you'll be back in Jordan—*Inh'allah*! It's not so long, is it?'

'Not really.'

He scrambled to his feet and held out a hand to pull her up beside him.

'Let's finish walking round the island then go back to the ramparts and have an ice-cream on the terrace of that café with the sun-umbrellas!'

Sun and wind and sea reasserted their enchantment; nostalgia retreated; there was only the present.

5

THE Breton memory was to remain isolated, for there were no more holidays together. Robert Melby opposed it: 'A boy of fifteen shouldn't be going around with his mother!' and Marian regretfully agreed. The pattern of their lives changed, too. By the second summer she was more absorbed in her work and Anton in the Cadet Force; when he went camping that July he had one stripe up and was intensely proud of it; it made him feel very much more than a year older than the boy who had gone to St. Malo with his mother. Lance-Corporal Mansour; corporal by the end of the year, and next year sergeant. He assumed authority and self-confidence with the uniform; he no longer had to pretend to be something in order not to be different; he *was* something. He indulged fantasies of making the army his career, but always at the back of his mind was the pull of his allegiance to Walid, the insistence deep down in himself of another and quite different road awaiting him.

Marian became involved on the editorial side of her Middle East paper and when Anton was camping on Salisbury Plain she was in Beirut collecting material. In the winter she flew down to Kuwait. Then scandalized her mother by writing that she would not be back until after Christmas and recommending that Anton be encouraged to go off to Switzerland on a winter sports holiday with his friend Lindley, whose family had invited him.

Anton did not need encouraging; it was what he desperately wanted to do, with his memories of his first English Christmas, and what had seemed to him the endless and boring succession of people and parties. He liked Lindley, a little older than himself, because he shared his own keenness for the Cadet Force, and for going swimming early on summer mornings, before school, in the

Queensmere, a small lake in a hollow, surrounded by woods, near the old windmill. Anton liked those mornings when Lindley would arrive on his bicycle at the cottage around six and they would cycle together across the Common the short distance to the lake; after a quick swim in the always icy cold water they would cycle back to the cottage for breakfast, their skins tingling and glowing, their appetites enormous.

Lindley was a tall, fair, good-natured boy, not particularly intelligent, always only narrowly scraping through examinations, with whom Anton found it easy to get along because no ideas were involved in the banter that mostly passed for conversation between them. Other than with Gerald Johns and his grandfather Anton did his best to avoid serious conversation, because sooner or later it led round to his nationality, and then the Jews came into it, and uninformed assertions were made and arguments started, and once, even, a fight.

It happened in the school grounds during morning break. Anton was strolling with Lindley and the serious Edwards, and a boy called Farrow who didn't care for Anton but who tacked on because he liked Lindley.

Farrow deliberately provoked a quarrel with Anton. It annoyed him that he could never get Lindley alone, that the A-rab, as he always referred to Anton, was always with him. It was the beginning of the autumn term, and joining the group he greeted Anton, 'I see your king got bumped-off during the hols! Oughtn't you to be wearing a black armband, or something?'

Anton replied, mildly, 'I wasn't so keen on King Abdullah.'

Farrow said, smiling unpleasantly, 'I forgot. It was one of your lot that shot him dead! I wonder why he would do a thing like that?'

Anton explained: 'Many Palestinians didn't like all that was left of their country becoming part of the Hashemite Kingdom. They felt the king had betrayed them.'

'Well, I never! A measly lot of Pallywhatnots who got licked by the Jews!'

'Pack it up, Farrow,' Edwards pleaded.

'You go and boil your head! I'm talking to our tame A-rab. That's correct, isn't it, Mansour! Your lot were licked?'

Anton's heart quickened, but he replied, levelly, 'The Arabs were outnumbered.'

Lindley said, nervously, 'I don't see the point of all this. Why don't we change the subject?'

'The point is, Mansour's anti-semitic,' Farrow insisted. 'That's correct, isn't it, Mansour?'

'It's a silly expression,' Anton said, keeping a grip on himself. 'Arabs are Semites too.'

Farrow grinned at the other two.

'Now he's trying to make out Jews and Arabs are all the same!'

'I wish you'd chuck it,' Lindley said.

'I'm waiting to hear Mansour give three cheers for Israel!'

Anton managed a desperate smile.

'Why should I?'

'To show you're not anti-semitic. It's the Jews' country, isn't it?'

Anton gave up trying to laugh it off.

'I'm sorry,' he said. 'Israel is Palestine, an Arab country.'

'Now you've got your answer—buzz off!' Edwards said, bravely, blinking behind his hornrims. He had gone a little pale and was feeling frightened.

'Buzz off yourself! Mansour's going to take that statement back and give three cheers for Israel, or put his fists up. What's it to be, Mansour?'

Anton did not answer. He took off his coat and handed it to Lindley, then squared up to Farrow.

'O.K.,' was all he said.

Farrow laughed.

'Aren't you scared of being outnumbered or something?'

Anton waited whilst Farrow removed his jacket, folded it neatly, and laid it on the ground. Then Farrow came at him like a bull charging.

A number of boys who had stood a little way off listening to the quarrel, sensing the fight to come, closed in, forming a circle. They were joined by others running from different parts of the grounds.

Farrow was bigger and heavier than Anton, but not as light on his feet. Anton who, when it began, had merely thought the whole thing silly, suddenly discovered when he was locked in a clinch with Farrow that he was violently angry; he fought strenuously to break free, then came at his opponent with a force that had fury behind it. It went on for some minutes and Farrow was getting the worst of it; partisans were yelling excitedly, 'Go it, Mansour!' and commiseratingly, 'Stick it, Farrow!' and they were locked in another clinch which neither was able to break and neither was prepared to relinquish, when a prefect appeared on the scene and commanded them to 'break it up!'

When they had separated and stood sheepishly apart, Anton with his nose pouring blood, Farrow looking hot and red, and secretly relieved by the intervention, the prefect said, casually, 'If you chaps want to fight go to gymnasium and ask gym instructor to let you put the gloves on!'

He then looked at Anton, who was desperately trying to stanch the flow of blood.

'Want first-aid for that, Mansour?'

'It's nothing,' Anton mumbled through his handkerchief. 'I get attacks of it.'

It was his first and last fight at school, and it seemed to him quite pointless; it left Farrow still believing him to be anti-semitic and unable to see the injustice done to the Palestinians by the creation of 'Israel', and himself unrepentent for stating the simple truth. Did Farrow really think he had punched a different idea into him? There might sometimes be good reasons for fighting someone; if someone went off with something of yours and refused to give it back you might be justified in hitting them—starting a fight; that was why the Arabs had fought the Jews in 1948; that made sense. But to be falsely accused, and provoked, and then required to stand up to a bashing—that made no kind of sense that he understood.

Lindley didn't agree. There were times when you had to scrap. He had once had a scrap with a chap who had called him a liar—he wasn't going to stand for that.

'Who won?' Anton asked.

'Well, no one, really. Old Smithy turned up, and you know what he is——' he mimicked, "Really, I thought you knew how to behave better than that! I'm surprised!"'

Anton laughed, and started the nose-bleeding off again. The

humiliating part was that he was quite sure that Farrow and his supporters believed that the blood was evidence of his defeat.

He told no one about the fight. It seemed to him better forgotten than kept alive by words. The beauty of his friendship with Lindley was that it didn't use up a lot of words. It didn't use up much in the way of ideas, either, but that didn't matter, because it wasn't, as he saw it, all that important a friendship.

He and Walid had not written to each other all that year, but that they were still close friends, and each other's special friend, Anton did not for a moment doubt.

Nor did Walid.

Anton sat for six G.C.E. subjects that summer and to his relief passed; he felt himself well on the way to his objective. He would be sixteen in October; only two more years. . . .

Marian was at home for Christmas that year, and the pattern of the first English Christmas was repeated, but Anton escaped from the round of parties into parties given by the families of his various friends; these at least had the virtue of consisting largely of young people. He met girls, but didn't feel at ease with them, and because he was shy and gauche with them they wrote him off as school-boy.

He went with his mother to Trafalgar Square on Christmas Eve to hear the carol-singing, and that he liked, and the tall Scandinavian Christmas tree, and the crib in the church of St. Martin-in-the-Fields, and when they all went to church—even his grandfather—on Christmas morning. But he was glad when it was all over and life reverted to the normal routine.

The first term of the New Year saw a certain deterioration in his friendship with Lindley, who during the Christmas holidays had become interested in girls; there was no one girl, but the species in general attracted and disturbed him. They still walked together with solemn little Edwards during break at school, but they met less and less out of school hours, since Anton felt incapable of sharing this new interest. This didn't matter to Anton because he had developed an interest of his own: he had discovered books.

Until then he had felt too unsettled to read other than what was required for his studies; there had been very little time for reading for pleasure, but also he had not felt capable of being interested; when he was not concentrating on the subjects required for passing examinations his thoughts were always in Jordan, with his father in Jericho, with Walid in Ramallah, and always the obsession of the Beersheba road.

But that Christmas Gerald Johns introduced him to the first volume of the memoirs of Chateaubriand, on the strength of his having been to St. Malo, where he was born, and seen his tomb on the Grand Bé. 'He was a desperately lonely boy,' Gerald told him, 'and full of imagination. You might be interested. His father made him sleep all alone at the top of a tower of the château. It was reputed to be haunted, and to reach it he had to walk along the battlements where owls screeched and the wind wailed. . . .'

He roused Anton's interest by stirring his imagination, and he read avidly. Young François-René's adolescent yearnings for female love did not strike a responsive chord in himself, but his fears and shyness and uncertainties did, and his sense of 'the burden and the weary weight of all this unintelligible world' pressing on him. He was resolved one day to return to Britanny and go to Comburg and tread the battlements the young Chevalier had trodden night after night, fighting his terror. His mother to whom he confided his interest in Chateaubriand promised they should go together—in the Easter holidays, in the summer holidays, but somehow it didn't work out, and it didn't matter. He went on to other books, other interests.

He discovered the real-life adventure story through *The Kon-Tiki Expedition*, which he read rapidly and with intense excitement, and came to travel books through Dr. Johnson's *Journey to the Hebrides*, and Arthur Young's *Travels in France*, both of which he found on Gerald John's shelves. His first action he found on his grandfather's shelves in the shape of a shabby old volume called *Saïd the Fisherman*, by Marmaduke Pickthall. Saïd was not a very likable man, but he had courage, and in the end, when he died a martyr for Islam, you wanted to cheer for him. There was another book by the same author, *Oriental Encounters*, with the sub-title, Palestine and Syria, 1894–5–6. This book excited him intensely; from the Introduction he gathered that the author had gone to Palestine and Syria when he was nineteen, and ridden about the plain of Sharon with a dragoman, meeting the *fellahin* and sitting in the coffee-shops of Ramleh, Lydda, Gaza. He wrote about the orange groves of Jaffa and the mountains south of Hebron; and he knew Jerusalem.

Anton found that his grandfather, whose name appeared on the fly-leaf of the battered old volume, had underlined something in the Introduction: 'I had a vision of the tortured peoples of the earth impelled by their own misery to desolate the happy peoples, a vision which grew clearer in the after years.' He developed a love for the Arabs which, he wrote, he was made to understand was hardly decent.

Anton asked his grandfather about Pickthall. Melby told him: 'He was the son of an English clergyman and he ended up a Moslem. He acquired Arabic and he translated the Koran. He saw that the Zionists could only survive in Palestine protected by British bayonets—it was in 1929 he wrote that. He had a great success with *Said the Fisherman*, but nobody reads him today, and not many remember him. He had his limitations, but he knew something about Arabs, and he loved them. He saw the injustice being done in Palestine, but he wanted nothing to do with post-war Palestine. Turkey was his great love, and there he committed himself.'

Melby smiled, ruefully.

'People like us who hold minority opinions have to learn to be thankful for small mercies—for any crumb of sympathy flung to us. He died in 1936—the Koran was his last work. He thought giving part of Syria to alien immigrants was unjust. He was spared living to see Palestine carved up.'

Anton discovered that his mother knew about Pickthall and had read his books; she admired those set in what was then called the Near East, but thought his English novels 'dreadful'. She thought *Said the Fisherman* the best of the Arab stories, 'But of course he knew nothing about educated Arabs, any more than T. E. Lawrence did,' she declared.

He had heard his father and his grandfather speak disparagingly of 'Lawrence of Arabia', as a man who had deceived the Arabs, leading their revolt against the Turks knowing that at the end of it all the British would not honour their pledges for Arab independence—that they would be so much 'dead paper' as he himself put it. His father had had a copy of *The Seven Pillars of Wisdom* at Lydda, but he had been too young for it then; his grandfather had a copy, but he had come belatedly to books and was only now ready for books of his own choosing. Now, suddenly, when he was sixteen, a House Prefect and settled in his English school life, and beginning to see his way clearly through what had at first seemed the dark forest of education, he was impatient to read in all directions; there seemed suddenly all the books in the world demanding to be read, and everything in the world demanding to be found out about, and the falling-off in his friendship with Lindley released him for it. It seemed to him now that he had wasted a lot of time with Lindley, going to the pictures and cycling aimlessly about the Common, with all the exciting—and important—books there were to read waiting unopened on the shelves. There was for him no time for girls. There wasn't even time for thinking about them.

Edwards had a wistful hope that now that Lindley and Mansour were not so 'thick' his own friendship with Mansour might become closer, especially as they were both now prefects. He, after all, had been Mansour's first friend, and they had much more in common than Mansour could ever have with someone like Lindley, who had never really been keen on anything except games and sports and the Cadet Force, and had now added girls to that non-cultural list. Anton admitted that he now had more time for reading and reported on his current literary enthusiasms. They were not enthusiasms Edwards shared—his own tastes ran to Aldous Huxley and T. S. Eliot among the moderns. He was quite shocked to find that Mansour was not much interested in poetry, a cultural omission he attempted to repair by giving his friend, on his seventeenth birthday, a copy of the *Oxford Book of English Verse*. In a neat hand he wrote in it, 'For Anton Mansour from his friend Philip Edwards in abiding affection'.

Anton was so touched by the gift, and so effusive in his thanks for it, that Edwards felt for a little while that their friendship was at last on a more intimate footing; but hope died as the term wore on. Mansour, it seemed, liked almost everyone a little and no one a great deal; he gave a little of himself to everyone and the whole of himself to no one—unless it was to that Moslem friend of his out in Jordan who wrote to him once in a blue moon but whose letters when they did come seemed to send Mansour into a dream for days on end, he thought, jealously. Full of adolescent longings complicated by something like a fear of girls—they got on his nerves, he would declare—he yearned for romantic friendship with one of his own sex, with whom he could feel safe and at ease. But Mansour, he was to discover, had no inclination to see more of him because he was seeing less of Lindley.

Anton was aware that Edwards was fonder of him than he was of Edwards, whom he continued to think as dull as when he first met him, but he attached no significance to it until Lindley told him one day, laughing, 'Poor old Edwards has quite a crush on you!'

'Crush?' Anton was startled.

'You know—has a special kind of feeling for you. Not just common or garden friendship.'

The colour flamed up into Anton's cheeks.

'Why on earth should he have?'

'Don't ask me. It's not my line!'

'It's not mine, either. How awful! What am I to do?'

Lindley grinned.

'Just be nice to the poor boy. Don't forget he suffers!'

'Oh shut up! It's not funny. It's bad luck on him. I feel sorry for him. I wish you hadn't told me.'

'I wouldn't worry! Edwards was always a drip, anyway!'

Anton did not, in fact, worry for long; his first reaction had been of dismay, followed by pity, but this in turn was followed by irritation. He had been thinking of giving Edwards a book-token for Christmas, as Edwards had given him the *Oxford Book* for his birthday, but then decided not to; and the next time they met he was more casual than ever. It was bad luck on Edwards, but people had no right to force themselves on you. Suddenly he remembered the day at the Friends' School in Ramallah when he had spoken to Walid for the first time under the twisted pine tree. He had asked him, at the end, if they could be friends. Had he forced himself on Walid? 'Why not?' Walid had said, and had flicked a fir-cone. There hadn't been anything emotional about it, though now in his English exile when he thought of Walid it seemed that all the emotions he was capable of rushed to the surface—his love for Palestine, his hatred of its usurpers, and all he had felt for his father, and for Amin, all the love and hate and loyalty he was capable of, somehow centred in Walid Hussein, who accepted a friendship as casually as he flicked a fir-cone, and who seldom wrote, but who was always there—waiting. . . .

Suddenly it came to him: Why shouldn't I do my year's work in Jordan? I couldn't go back just for a short holiday and then come back here. But if I had a whole year, and Walid and I made it to Beersheba together—then I would have achieved something, and whatever happened after that wouldn't matter—could look after itself——

His grandfather said: 'I don't see why not. Provided your mother agrees, of course. She might not feel like your being away for a whole year.'

Anton said quickly, 'She'll let me go if you tell her it's a good idea. If you tell her you're sure my father would have approved. You do think that, don't you?'

Melby looked at his grandson's eager face and said thoughtfully, 'Yes, I think so. He wanted you to stay Arab. He only wanted you educated in England. On the other hand he wouldn't have wanted you to have deserted your mother . . .'

'But I won't be deserting her. I'll be coming back, and then I'll have to be here for a year or two, taking the course. Anyhow she only sees me once a week when I'm here, and sometimes not that! I'm sure she won't mind.'

'We'll discuss it with her on Sunday. In the meantime had you thought what you might do in Jordan?'

'I wondered if I might help at the blind school in Bethlehem where my friend Amin is—I mean,' he went on with a rush, his face flushing with excitement, 'I thought as it's run by the organization that ran your Jaffa school you could probably get me in, and also I know a little about the blind, through being with Amin so much and then going with you to the place here. It would be something I could do—something useful——'

'It's an idea. In fact it's a very good one. I'll go and see them and have a chat with them. We'd better start the ball rolling, because these things take time.'

'Oh, thank you!' Anton said, fervently, and added, 'I'd work, you know that. I wouldn't let you down. I'd be really interested, and with Amin being there, and able to see Walid in my spare time—it would be wonderful!'

Melby regarded his grandson quizzically.

'What started all this in you? Was it an attack of homesickness?'

'Oh, it's complicated. There's a boy at school likes me more than I like him, and someone told me about it and it annoyed me. I thought about Walid, and how it wasn't sloppy like that, but—well—different. Then everything came back somehow—Lydda, Ramallah, Jericho, my father—everything. My real life. I thought I couldn't bear to go back just for a few weeks, and I suddenly got this idea——'

'I understand. Indeed I do understand! Your real life. Palestine was my real life too. I'll do what I can. We'll make it happen. *Insh'allah.*'

'*Insh'allah,*' Anton repeated, like the Amen to a prayer.

The conversation took place in the sitting room of the cottage on a cold November evening with fog creeping up over the Common and thinly penetrating the house despite closed windows and drawn curtains. Melby sat in a shabby armchair beside the fire; Anton sat on the fender—a position his grandmother always defined, impatiently, as 'almost on top of the fire'. But that evening Elspeth was out at a local committee and Anton could crouch as close as he pleased and, what he dared not do when his grandmother was there, feed the fire with lumps of coal to prevent it from getting low. His grandfather never raised any objection, and Anton even thought that secretly he approved. It was always cosy when Grandmamma was out and they were alone. Poor Grandmamma! She was another of those people, it came to him, who loved you more than you could love back, and whom you might love more if they loved you less. Presently, when his grandmother got back, more lights would be snapped on—'Why are you sitting in such gloom?'—the fire frowned at as being too high—'The heat in here is frantic!'—cushions crumpled in her absence pulled back into shape, the evening paper lying discarded in a chair whisked out of sight, and order, generally, restored. There would then be a bustle and clatter in the kitchen and tea would be made and brought in and the kettle refilled for the hot-water bottles. After a cup of tea and a biscuit Anton would be expected to do what Elspeth called 'retire'—no one ever did anything as vulgar as go to bed—first going into the kitchen and filling his hot-water bottle and then refilling the kettle and replacing it on the cooker—'on a very low gas,' as his grandmother always warned—for use later.

But it was then not much after eight o'clock and Grandmamma would not be back for about two hours and he and Grandpappa could talk or be silent as they felt inclined, relaxed and at peace. Grandmamma did not believe in silence, unless someone was reading or writing; persons doing neither were expected to converse, to keep the flow of words going, even when there was nothing to talk about, otherwise there was a general accusation of 'everyone being down in the dumps'. The radio was used sparingly, mainly for the news and the weather forecasts. When they were alone Grandpappa sometimes twiddled knobs and got light, easy music from Luxembourg or Brussels; he regretted the inability to get Radio Cairo, or Amman.

That evening they talked about the Jordan plan. The more they discussed it the more feasible did it seem to Melby and the higher Anton's spirits rose.

'Only one more year! Do you think I could have the Christmas after this in Bethlehem?'

'Perhaps. But your mother would probably be hurt! Not to mention your grandmother!'

'Mamma had Christmas in Kuwait when it suited her,' Anton pointed out.

'She didn't stay away for a year. Look, let's ring her now and try and get the general idea settled——'

Marian was at her flat and surprised to receive a telephone call from her father; her first thought was that something might be wrong, with her mother, or with Anton. Her father set her mind at rest by coming immediately to the point: 'What do you think of the idea of Anton doing his year's work in Jordan—possibly at the blind school in Bethlehem?'

She was first startled and then slightly irritated.

'Do we have to decide about it now? It's not till the year after next!'

'These things take time to arrange, and Anton and I are a bit excited by the idea.'

'Is it your idea?'

'Anton's. But it seems to me a good one.'

'That he should be away from home for a whole year?'

'He's not a child. Besides, on one of your trips to the Middle East you could fly up to Jerusalem and see him!'

'I wouldn't like to be in Jerusalem again, any more than you would! Why does he want to do this? We were agreed he should have a holiday in Jordan before he started a job here—it ought to be enough.'

'He's homesick, Marian.'

Melby smiled at Anton, who sat watching him, anxiously.

'His home's here now.'

Melby ceased to smile.

'You forget he's Butros Mansour's son. His home is in Palestine.'

'There's no such place any more!' Her voice was hard with bitterness.

'The West Bank is still there—Nablus and Ramallah, and Bethlehem and Jericho and Hebron. It's possible to be homesick for a part even when you can't have the whole.'

Marian said, impatiently, 'We can't discuss it over the phone. We'll talk about it Sunday.'

'Anton won't sleep unless he knows you agree to the idea in principle.'

'Let me speak to her!' Anton pleaded.

Melby added quickly, 'Anton wants to talk to you himself. Just a minute——'

He held out the receiver to Anton, who was already at his side.

Marian heard her son say, eagerly, 'Please say yes! *Please!*'

'Do you hate England so much?'

'I don't hate England—you know I don't! But I want to see Walid again, and Amin, and Uncle Farid and the others. If I get back at the end of next year I'll have been away four years.'

'People sometimes stay away from their own countries for twenty or thirty years—even whole life times!'

'I couldn't—I'd die! Darling Mamma, please say yes!'

Marian knew suddenly that she was defeated; that she had been defeated at the outset.

'Oh, all right—if it means so much to you. Now let me speak to Grandpappa again, please.'

'I love you I love you I love you!' Anton cried wildly into her unwilling ear. 'Here's Grandpappa . . .'

Marian said, 'You'll have gathered I've given in. But I don't like it. I'm sure it's a mistake.'

'I don't see how it could be, my dear.'

'Let's not talk about it any more now, shall we? Say good night to Anton for me. I'll be over Sunday for lunch—*Insh'allah.*'

'*Insh'allah.* Good night, my dear . . .'

Melby hung up and he and his grandson smiled at each other.

'It's going to be all right,' Melby said. 'At present she isn't keen, but we'll reassure her on Sunday.'

'It's wonderful!' Anton cried. 'I wish you were going, too, and Mamma—that we were all going back—going home——'

Marian did not move away from the telephone. When she had hung up she buried her face in her hands and, unaccountably, wept.

6

ELSPETH was deeply opposed to the Jordan plan, hurt that Anton should wish for it, and angry that Robert should be a party to it and Marian weak enough not to stand out against it. She was convinced that if Anton returned to Jordan for a year the past four years of Anglicization would have been lost and the process would have to be started all over again. But this, apparently, weighed with no one but herself, since neither the boy's mother nor his grandfather saw anything wrong with him feeling himself more Arab than English. It was perhaps understandable in Marian, who had after all married an Arab, but Robert should have known better; he should have realized that it was not in the boy's best interests. Apart from what it would mean to her, his grandmother, to have him removed from her for so long that in the real sense he could never come back to her; after a year in his own country, among his own people, he would be lost to her for good. It would mean, in effect, that for the second time she would have lost a son, she thought bitterly, but that, of course, would never occur to Robert.

To be sure, Anton had never come as close to her as she had hoped. Robert had an unfair advantage there, since he stood to Anton in the place of his father; also Robert encouraged him in his Arabism. For herself, she felt, Anton had a kind of casual affection; he would probably say he was fond of her; he was certainly very nice to her, giving her little presents at Easter, Christmas, and on her birthday. He was very polite to her, opening doors for her, jumping to his feet when she entered a room, insisting on carrying trays for her, and always very willing to run to the post for her, or to the shops. But he always shied away from any attempt on her part to establish a cosier, more intimate relationship; he had no wish to talk about himself, confide his dreams and aspirations, reveal the secret places of his heart; well, anyhow, not to her—who would have received such confidences with sympathy and understanding. He was, she supposed, an extrovert; his enthusiasm for the Cadet Force, and the fact that he was so good at games and keen on all outdoor activities seemed to suggest it. But being an extrovert he should surely take some interest in girls, now that he was in his eighteenth year. It seemed strange to her that he showed no such interest, and also a great pity, because if only he would fall in love with some nice girl it would be the one thing which could make him give up the Jordan idea. Perhaps at one of the Christmas parties of his school-friends this year he would meet a nice girl—the sister of one of them, perhaps.

But Christmas came and went and as the previous year he was evidently relieved when it was over, and went so far as to say, hopefully, that perhaps next Christmas he would be in Bethlehem. Then she hoped that in the spring, by which time he would be seventeen-and-a-half, something would happen, and she watched for some sign of change in him. But there was none; he worked, he read, he was promoted to School-prefect, he visited Gerald Johns, and in uncertain Coronation June went swimming in the Queensmere, sometimes with Lindley, sometimes alone. For some time now he had not gone to the parish church with her on Sunday mornings having established the habit of going to the Greek Orthodox Church in town instead, so to that extent he had grown away from her. But surely, soon now, there must be a girl. With his looks and charm he couldn't fail to attract girls—and surely he must eventually meet one to whom he could respond? It would be only natural that he should.

She thought a good deal about this hypothetical girl. She would be, preferably, the daughter of someone known to the Melbys. She would be—she did not hesitate to admit the word—a lady. Anton would meet her at a sherry party given by her family or his, or at the house of mutual friends, or at a church social, or at one of those summer garden parties organized for charity—she would be helping at the cake stall, perhaps, whilst he would be lending a hand getting the children's sporting events organized. Perhaps they would be introduced; perhaps they would meet informally—only to discover that their families would be acquainted. It would all be very correct, but entirely charming—first-love at its most lyrical. Without undue haste they would become engaged, and a year or two later they would be married at St. Mary's, a delightful occasion, a white wedding, with bridesmaids, church bells, and a well organized reception, nicely done, at an hotel as a grand finale. They would make a handsome young couple, and in due course there would be two or three lovely children, bringing fulfilment into her own life. Anton would settle down then, all thoughts of returning to Jordan finally set aside as so much boyish fantasy.

It was her most cherished dream, and she knew several girls who would most admirably fill this romantic role, but she recognized that this was long-term planning; the immediate thing was for Anton to fall in love with a nice girl this year, so that he would give up the Jordan plan and do his year's work in England instead.

Feeling unable to discuss the matter with her husband Elspeth finally mentioned it to her daughter.

'Don't you think it odd that Anton should be so uninterested in girls? You don't suppose he's emotionally arrested, do you?'

Marian said, shortly, 'Why should he be? He's only seventeen, and boys of seventeen, still at school, don't reckon to be emotionally mature!'

'He's nearly eighteen, and in some ways older than his years, and with Eastern blood I'd have thought he would have matured early rather than late.'

Irritated by the reference to Eastern blood Marian exclaimed impatiently, 'He's a perfectly normal average boy. When he's ready for a girl-friend no doubt he'll find one. In the meantime his studies are the most important thing and it's a good thing he hasn't any emotional complications to distract him from them!'

'If he became interested in a girl he wouldn't want to go to Jordan for a year!'

Marian said, bitterly, 'I don't see any girl deflecting him from that! Anyhow girls don't come into the picture yet, and it's just as well.'

Her tone indicated that the discussion was closed. She was both impatient and irritated. Anton was a schoolboy still, emotionally as well as in fact, and that boys matured more slowly than girls was also a fact. Anton was Butros Mansour's son, and obsessed with the idea of England as exile, and by the dream of return to Jordan—to Palestine. His lack of interest in girls was in all probability due to the fact that he was already in love—with his dream.

But as it happened, at the time that conversation took place Anton had been interested in a girl for some weeks past, and had been secretly meeting her.

He met her in circumstances which would have horrified his grandmother: that is to say on the Common, and without benefit of introduction or the sanction of mutual acquaintances. She was also very far removed from the type of girl his grandmother had in mind for him.

The encounter occurred late in the afternoon of a sultry day in August. Anton had felt suffocated and restless in the house and had put a book in his pocket and set out across the Common in search of fresh air. He walked in the familiar direction of Queensmere; there were some seats looking out across the wooded hollow that held the lake, with a view over the tree-tops to Richmond Park; he would sit there, he thought, or if all the seats were occupied go down through the woods to the lake itself. He wanted to be away from people, and he hoped that on such a grey heavy evening there wouldn't be many about.

There were in fact not many people on the Common at that time and the row of benches facing the view were all empty. He chose a central one and after sitting idly for a few minutes pulled the book out of his pocket. It bore the formidable title, *The Significance and Basic Postulates of Economic Theory*. He thought gloomily that it was a title as oppressive as the whole sunless day had been. Since the exciting news that his grandfather's Arab welfare organization were prepared to let him work at the end of the year in their school for the blind in Bethlehem he had found it difficult to concentrate on economics or anything else outside of that prospect. He had written immediately to Amin and Walid; the blind boy had replied by return, expressing his happiness in a neatly typed letter; Walid had belatedly sent a garish postcard of a mosque, unidentified, saying simply, 'Splendid news. I wait for you. W.H.'

He opened the book and settled himself on the bench and stared at the printed page, reading without absorbing.

Suddenly a female voice said, 'Excuse me!'

He looked up to see a dark-haired girl in a flowery dress standing beside the seat. He was confusedly aware of heavily made-up eyes, a bright red mouth, a film-star bosom hoisted high under the tight bodice of her dress.

'Excuse me,' she said again, 'but is that mac yours?'

She indicated a bundle on the seat—a plastic mackintosh packed up into a pink plastic envelope. He had not noticed it when he had sat down.

'No,' he said. 'No, it's not mine.'

'Then it's mine.'

There was relief in her voice, and she smiled, and suddenly he felt less confused; it was rather a sweet smile, and he was suddenly reminded of his Cousin Nadia.

'You see,' the girl continued, 'I went on down to the lake and suddenly realized I hadn't my mac with me any more. I thought I might have left it on this seat, as I was sitting here. When I saw it I thought it might be yours—there are a lot of these macs about, aren't there?'

'Yes. I've got one. Not pink, though.' He grinned. 'Mine's dark blue. But I didn't bring it.'

The girl sat down beside him, hooking her fingers, with pointed red-painted nails, through the carrying strap of the bundle.

'I wouldn't like to have lost it,' she said. 'I paid nearly four pounds for it and only had it new last weekend. Isn't it an awful summer?'

'Not up to much,' he agreed. 'But English summers never are, are they?'

'Not really.'

She looked at him.

'You're not English, are you?'

'My mother is.'

'I'd guess your father was Spanish.'

'You'd be wrong.'

He smiled, to take the edge off the snub.

She opened a white plastic handbag and took out a packet of cigarettes and a plastic-covered lighter.

'Sorry,' she said. 'It's none of my business. I just thought you looked Spanish. My family's Spanish. A way back.'

She lit her cigarette and was about to replace the packet in her handbag then withdrew it.

'Beg pardon. I should have asked you.'

'I don't smoke—thanks all the same.'

She replaced the packet of cigarettes and the lighter, then glanced at the book lying between them on the seat. She turned it over.

'Anything exciting?' Then she saw the title.

'Good God! What's the idea?'

'I'm studying economics.'

'For the hell of it, I suppose?'

'That's right. How did you guess?'

They smiled at each other, and it came to him that she was rather pretty—in a Spanish way.

He said, 'Are you really Spanish?'

'I told you—way back. I was born in London. So was my old man, and his. But *originally*——' she lingered over the word, savouring it—'we came from Barcelona. The name's Rosado. I'm Rosa Rosado.'

He laughed.

'It sounds like a wine! My grandfather drinks a pink Spanish wine called that!'

She fanned the smoke away from herself.

'I daresay. It's a common Spanish name.'

'I think it's nice—Rosa Rosado.'

'I suppose yours is John Smith?'

He laughed again.

'It's Mansour,' he said. 'Anton Mansour.'

'What kind of name is that?'

'Guess!'

'I can't. Unless it—it's not French by any chance?'

He said, almost aggressively, 'It's Arab!'

She said, as he had known she would, '*Arab?*'

'Arab.'

'Where are you from, then?'

'Palestine.'

She stubbed out her cigarette at the side of the seat.

'You said your mother was English, so you're only half Arab.'

'Does that make it better? Or worse?'

'I don't care what people are, so long as they're nice.'

He offered no comment, and after a moment she asked, 'You been over here long?'

'Four years. My family lost everything when the Jews came into Lydda in July, 1948—our house, orange groves, our capital—everything. It killed my father. We lived for a year in Jericho, where we had a house and some land, but my father's heart was broken and he died. My mother and I came to England—my father wanted me to go to school here anyhow.'

'I'm sorry about that—really I am.'

'Thank you. There's a lot I could tell you, but it's a long story and I don't feel like it just now. Let's talk about you—what are you doing here on the Common all by yourself?'

'All by myself? Why shouldn't a girl go for a walk by herself?'

'I don't know. No reason really, I suppose. It's just that where I come from girls don't go about by themselves. I don't suppose many English girls walk about on the Common by themselves, do they?'

'I wouldn't know. Some do and some don't. Depends whether you're the nervous type or not. I always come up here on early closing day for a bit of air—I'm in a shop all the week. My old man runs a dress-shop. It's a family concern—my father and brother look after the business-side, my brother does the buying. My mother works behind the scenes, on the alterations for customers. I serve in the shop. Just ladies' dresses. What do you do?'

'I'm not through school yet.'

'Fancy that! College, I suppose?'

'If you like. Public school. I hope to get to London University the year after next.'

'I left school when I was fifteen.'

'It depends what you want to do. I want to get a diploma in social science.'

'I suppose you're the interlekchal type. I just wanted to live.' She laughed and crossed her legs and her short tight dress rode up over her knees. 'You don't need education for that,' she added. 'It's an education in itself.'

'I'm not sure I know what it means. *Yani*, what do you mean, live? We all live—till we die!'

'Don't you believe it! Some people don't live—they walk around half dead. You've only got to look at them—you can see it in their faces!'

He was silent, confusedly pondering this assertion. She sat swinging a foot in a high-heeled sandal composed of pale blue plastic straps, watching his serious reflective face, and thinking him terribly attractive, but slow, slow. . . .

He said at last, 'What's living then?'

'Aren't you funny? Having a good time, of course—enjoying yourself. Oh, *you* know——'

'The trouble is I don't!' For a moment he looked troubled, then suddenly smiled and added recklessly, 'You'll have to teach me!'

She smiled at him, then, deliberately coquettish.

'You'd better put up an L plate!'

She had at last got the conversation on to the right level of flirtatious banter, like a game of table-tennis; she flicked the ball across the net and he flicked it back again—though sometimes he missed, because he was slow, and the ball rolled away, holding up play. But the to-and-fro lasted them for quite a time, and then Anton glanced at his watch and was surprised how late it had become and declared that he would have to go.

'We eat at seven,' he explained.

'Where do you live?'

He told her and she suggested they should walk across the Common in that direction and she would get a bus.

They got up and he picked up the plastic bundle.

'Don't let me forget to give it to you,' he said.

They made their way over the rough grass, with its patches of heather, to the path, she tippeting along beside him on her spiky heels, plump buttocks swinging under the tight skirt of her dress. He had often seen girls like her on the films; he had never thought he would be walking beside one. It was an odd feeling. He had never walked with a girl of any kind before, not even his girl cousins. He wondered what Lindley would say if he could see him, and how old she was; about his own age, he thought.

He asked, presently, conversation having totally lapsed since they left the seat, 'When is your birthday?'

'June—the month of roses! That's why they called me Rosa. When's yours?'

'October.' He added, to draw her, 'I'll be eighteen.'

'Then I'm four months older than you!'

'I thought you were younger!'

'Funny, because I thought you were older. I thought you were about twenty, which is why it seemed funny you were still at school. A man never minds being thought older, does he?'

She babbled on until they came to the bus stop on the main road at the side of the Common.

Whilst they waited it was for him to say, 'When may I see you again?' but he didn't say it, being too bemused by the whole encounter, and when the bus loomed up and he still hadn't said it she asked quickly, 'How about seeing each other again Friday evening, about half past eight, at the same place? If it rains we can go to the pictures.'

'Yes,' he said, confusedly. 'Yes, of course. I'd love to! I was wondering if I dared suggest it!'

Then she had skipped on to the bus, sideways because of the tightness of her skirt, pursed up her mouth in imitation of a kiss in his direction, and was gone.

For Anton, walking back across the Common in a dream, the basic postulates of economic theory had ceased to exist. Even Jordan had retreated into the background. He had, astonishingly, spent some time with a girl, and he was meeting her again the day after tomorrow. Some people walk around half dead, she had said. Perhaps that was what he had been doing till now, with all this swotting for exams? She would teach him to live. Rosa Rosado. Spanish *rosé*. Rosa.

When he reached the cottage he found his grandfather in the front garden finger-and-thumbing greenfly off the remaining roses.

'It's gone seven,' Melby reproached him.

'I'm sorry, Grandpappa. I didn't notice the time.'

Melby followed him up the path, then asked, 'What have you got there?'

Then Anton realized he was still carrying the girl's plastic bundle.

'I found it on a seat,' he said, confusedly. 'It's one of those plastic macs.'

'Pink!' his grandfather observed, with distaste. He added, 'You'd better run it down to the police station tomorrow.'

'I'll pop down with it after dinner,' Anton said.

In fact he took it to Lindley. He could hardly wait to tell him, anyhow.

'Keep this for me till Friday,' he said. 'I was out with a girl this evening and went off with it by mistake. I can't take it home.'

Lindley stared at him.

'Did you say what I thought you said?'

Anton grinned.

'It had to happen sometime.'

'Where'd you find her?'

'I didn't. She found me, sitting on a seat on the Common reading economics.'

'Aren't you the outside limit!'

'I daresay. I can't stop now. I've got to get back. I'll be around about eight on Friday—I'm meeting her at eight-thirty.'

He rushed off, leaving the astonished Lindley holding the pink plastic proof of his adventure.

7

HALF an hour after hopping on to the bus the girl who called herself Rosa Rosado was sitting in a pub animatedly recounting her adventure to her great friend, Alice Meyer.

Miss Meyer had a film-star bust well hoisted and fine dark eyes heavily made up; she was twenty-five, a year older than her friend Rosa Rosenberg, for whom she felt a mixture of admiration and disapproval. Rosa was undeniably attractive and very good-natured; you couldn't help liking her, but she was dreadfully irresponsible, both where the opposite sex was concerned and *politically*—Alice's own political consciousness was such that she tended to italicize the word both in her mind and in speech. She was an ardent Zionist.

She worked in the records department of a music shop and fancied herself cultural. She hoped to marry Rosa's brother, Len, who had similar cultural and political interests, and whom she had met when he came in to buy records. A big part of his attraction for her was that he dreamed of emigrating to Tel Aviv—the very heart of Hebrew culture. She could think of nothing more wonderful than to go 'home' to Israel with the man she loved. Len's parents—lamentably in his eyes and hers—did not share this Zionist dream; they were born and bred in London and anywhere else would be foreign for them; they had no use for the great in-gathering; you belonged where you were born and bred; nationality was one thing, religion another. So far as they were concerned they were Londoners, of the Jewish faith.

Rosa had no very strong views one way or another; London was all right for her too. It was all part of what Alice and Len thought of as her light-mindedness; both hoped that she would eventually fall in love with a nice serious young Zionist and become more serious herself. In the meantime there she was sipping gin-and-lime and rattling on about picking up some college boy—if you ever heard of anything so preposterous—on the Common.

'I felt depressed after you had to call off our trip to town,' she was saying. 'I always hate being at a loose end on half-day, as you know. And I get restless in this thundery weather. I thought I'd take a bus to the Common and perhaps meet some nice boy also all alone on his half-day and go to the pictures. I left my mac on a seat and when I went back for it there was this Spanish-looking lad sitting there all alone studying a book with a title a yard long. I thought he was about twenty, but he said he would be eighteen in October.'

'Cradle-snatching,' commented Miss Meyer, delicately sipping her gin.

Rosa laughed.

'I told him I was eighteen last June, and he said he thought I was younger! I told him my name was Rosa Rosado and that we had Spanish blood a way back.'

'Are you crazy, or what?'

'If I told him my name was Rosenberg it might have put him off and I didn't want to risk it. But you'll never guess what *he* is!'

'An Arab probably,' Miss Meyer said, bitterly.

Rosa gazed at her in wonder.

'How ever did you guess?'

'I didn't, but with you making out to be Spanish I thought it only wanted that as a finishing touch. But is he really an Arab?'

'Uh-huh! Palestinian. He said they had to get out in 1948 and his family lost everything and that it killed his father. I felt sorry for him.'

'Felt sorry for him? It was they who started the war against us, wasn't it? Better not tell that to Len!'

'I don't care. He's ever so attractive. I'm seeing him again Friday.'

'Wait till he finds out you're Jewish!'

'I might not tell him!'

'He'll find out in the end.'

'So what? Jews and Arabs don't have to hate each other, do they? He's a Christian, anyhow.'

'He's still an Arab!'

'Only half—his mother's English.'

'You bet he's as Arab as they make them, when it comes to it. Don't be a fool, Rosa! Don't see him again. Sooner or later he'll find out, and then he'll hate you. What's the good of it, anyhow? He's far too young, and even if he weren't you could never marry!'

'Who's talking about marriage? I'd just like him for a boy-friend for a bit—he's going away to Jordan at the end of the year anyhow. He's awfully nice—and ever so innocent. I don't believe he's ever kissed a girl. He said I'd have to teach him how to live.' She laughed, happily. 'I bet he's a fast learner—he's got that look about him. You know—sexy!'

'One of these days you'll get yourself into trouble,' Alice warned.

'Why should I? I've had plenty of boys—some of them very experienced. But I know when to stop.'

'The experienced ones are safer. You might not find this one so easy to manage. Anyway, it's crazy. There are plenty of nice Jewish boys around. What about that boy we met at the Palais last Saturday—the one you danced a lot with? What was his name?'

'David Marks? I don't want him. He's too conceited—thinks every girl falls for him. It's why I wouldn't make a date with him. This boy's different—shy. I'll—educate him!'

'That's what you think! He might teach *you* a thing or two!'

Rosa's eyes sparkled. Her smile was childish and sweet.

'That would be lovely!'

She sighed, then said, wistfully, 'He's *nice*! You don't understand. Promise you won't tell Len. Promise!'

'Don't worry. I won't tell. All the same—it's not right, say what you like! You'll regret it.'

'Regret it! Why should I regret it? I intend having a good time with him, and no one's going to stop me! Let's go. The big picture starts at eight....'

The next encounter, so longed for, was for Rosa what she thought of as a dead loss.

She arrived at the spot facing the view ten minutes late to find

Anton sitting there with a bicycle propped up at the end of the seat. When she exclaimed about it, asking what was the idea, he explained that he had run into difficulties over getting away. He had announced after dinner that he proposed to go over to his old tutor for a little while to clear up some points of economic theory, and his grandfather had immediately said that he would walk over with him, as he would like to stretch his legs.

'I told him I was going by bike as I wanted to call on Lindley first—the friend I went to Switzerland with. That was true, as I left your mac there and wanted to go and fetch it. But I hadn't intended taking the bike—I was going to pop down by bus.'

She took the plastic bundle from him.

'I don't see why you had to take it there.'

He explained, adding, 'The alternative was saying I'd met you and would be meeting you again and that would have meant a lot of questions. I didn't feel like it.'

Rosa was irritated and vaguely resentful.

'Can't you go out without having to say where you're going?'

'Not very easily. They naturally like to know.'

'I don't have to say where I'm going. I just say I'm going out.'

He said, apologetically, 'Perhaps if I lived with my mother I could do that. My grandparents are old-fashioned, I suppose.'

'I'll say they are!' She added, 'It's going to rain.'

She began extricating the mackintosh from its envelope and he helped her into it.

'But for your bringing the bike we could have gone to see a film,' she complained.

'I couldn't stop out that late anyhow, I'm afraid.'

'There wasn't much point in coming, then, was there?'

'We could go for a little walk——'

She gave him a scornful look but led the way in the direction of the woods. The air was heavy, with a spit of rain on it. It was hard-going for Rosa over the tufty grass; she was wearing her high-heeled sandals, not having expected to walk farther than down the short road from the windmill to the bus stop; she had planned a cosy evening at the pictures, with heavy petting in the back row.

They reached the sandy track of a horse-ride through the woods,

166

and there the sand and small stones got into her sandals. Anton followed, wheeling his bicycle, seeing no point in this plunge into the woods, uncomfortable for them both, when they could have stayed comfortably where they were on the seat; the more so as he had very little time. He wondered why she wore shoes it was almost impossible to walk in. He looked desperately about for a seat, but there was only the tumbled green sea of bracken at each side of the track and the silver birches rising from it like the masts of ships; there were occasional narrow grassy paths threading deeper into the woods, but not a seat in sight.

Suddenly Rosa said, 'Let's go down there,' and indicated a path slightly wider than others he had noticed.

They left the sandy track and followed the path, which seemed to lead nowhere in particular and was crossed by similar paths. The woods themselves were thinner than he had expected and there was a good deal of bramble.

Rosa looked about her.

'We could sit down,' she suggested.

'There are no seats.'

'What's wrong with sitting on the ground?'

She halted beside a small oak tree; there was a shabby, bare space in front of it littered with dead leaves, acorns, twigs, a cigarette carton, a decaying newspaper.

'We can sit here,' she added, kicked aside the newspaper, and sat down.

Anton leaned the bicycle against the tree then seated himself rather gingerly beside her. That she should wish to sit on the ground seemed to him strange, since it was neither comfortable nor clean; also it seemed to him not the sort of thing a respectable girl would wish to do. There were ants, too.

Rosa emptied the sand and stones out of her sandals.

'My feet were killing me,' she told him.

'It's those shoes,' he said. 'I don't know how you can walk in them.'

She said, tartly, 'I can walk in them—I didn't know we were going hiking!'

He offered no comment, not knowing what to say; she seemed

very annoyed, still, and it was all his fault; he had so looked forward to meeting her again, and it was all messed up. He felt helpless and, with no experience to draw on, lost.

She looked at him and was suddenly filled with contrition. She moved closer to him and leaned her head against his shoulder.

'Well, anyhow, we've got the place to ourselves.'

He should have put an arm round her, bent his head and kissed her; instead of which he remained sitting bolt upright and made no move of any kind.

She waited a moment, then said, 'You don't know what to do with a girl, do you?'

He was embarrassed by her directness and laughed awkwardly.

'It's all so new to me,' he said, then, recklessly, 'I'd like to kiss you!'

She turned her face up to him.

'Then why don't you?'

He put an arm round her, clumsily, and kissed her cheek. He was about to move away when she took his face between her hands and planted a kiss firmly on his lips, darting her tongue between, to his great astonishment. She tilted her head back and smiled at him.

'You're very sweet,' she told him, 'but such a big baby!'

'I'm sorry,' he said, nettled, and she moved away impatiently and groped in her bag for cigarettes.

'Haven't you ever kissed a girl before?' she demanded.

'No, never.'

'Or even wanted to?'

'Not really. Not till I met you. I haven't thought about it. I can't explain.'

Because there was too much to explain—his whole life up to that point, she couldn't begin to understand; how could she?

'Since we left Palestine everything's been so confusing,' he added, helplessly.

'I suppose so. You had bad experiences——'

'Terrible experiences. I still have nightmares about it——'

'But that's all over and done with. Now you can relax. Now you've got yourself a girl-friend!'

168

She waved away a smoke-screen of cigarette smoke and smiled at him.

He returned her smile.

'Yes. It's wonderful. I can't realize it. I haven't been able to think of anything but you——'

'We must find a way to be together properly. What about Sunday?'

He shook his head and said gloomily, 'Weekends are no good. My mother comes out and I have to be around. If she doesn't come out Saturday evenings I meet her in town after church Sunday morning and we come out together.'

'Fancy going to church! Are you religious?'

'I don't know if I am or not. I like going to church, and I believe. Don't you?'

'Me? Oh, I'm not orthodox!'

'I know—you're Roman Catholic—being Spanish.'

She had been caught off her guard and now recovered herself.

'I'm not anything really——'

She stubbed her cigarette out against the trunk of the tree.

'We ought to move—it's beginning to rain quite hard——'

'Yes. I have to get back anyhow.'

He scrambled to his feet and pulled her up, and then close to him. She had been quite sure he would kiss her again then, but he didn't, and in the moment in which she waited he turned away from her to wheel his bicycle from the tree.

At the bus stop she gave him her telephone number and they parted without another meeting having been arranged. He would have to work, he said; he couldn't say offhand when he would be able to be free; he was swotting for an exam. . . .

It was agreed he would ring her when he could suggest something. A dead loss, she thought, as she settled herself in the bus; she was not even sure whether she wanted him to ring her. He was attractive and nice and all that, but so slow. That was a slip-up, too, over religion. She hadn't given that aspect of it a thought when she had invented her Spanish ancestry.

Perhaps he was just a mixed-up kid as a result of his Palestine experiences. Perhaps he was best left alone. Perhaps Alice was right about the whole thing being a mistake. One thing was certain, though; the evening had been a wash-out; a dead loss. It was too early to go home and too late to go to the pictures. And she had laddered a new pair of nylon stockings on a bramble in that beastly wood. . . .

8

FOR Anton, however, the evening had by no means been a loss, in spite of the awkward start, but a wonderful and exciting experience. When the bus had borne her away, that astonishing creature, Rosa Rosado, he propped his bicycle against a seat under a lime tree at the edge of the Common, facing the main road, and sat for a few minutes trying to collect his thoughts.

When his grandfather had said he would walk across the Common with him to the Johns' he had felt mean making that excuse about the bicycle; he and the old man had always been such good friends, and then suddenly he was not merely rejecting him but deceiving him; and more than that—lying to him. Just as he had lied about finding the mac on the seat. If he hadn't done that in the first place he would have had no need to lie and deceive this evening; he could have been open and frank. He could have said, 'I am going to meet the girl whose mac I went off with the evening before last.' But then his grandmother would have known, and his mother have been told, and questions would have been asked, and the only answers he could truthfully give have caused alarm, dismay, disapproval. Since neither in Mansour nor in Melby circles were acquaintanceships formed with girls of whose family and background nothing was known, and who had been casually met. There were, in fact, no such casual meetings. You met girls at the houses of school-friends, or at the houses of friends of the family, and were properly introduced. This girl Rosa, he realized, was not the sort of girl he would meet in Mansour or Melby circles. She was, he knew well, what his grandmother would call common. He was not sure about his mother. It occurred to him suddenly, disconcertingly, that really he knew more about his grandmother than about his mother; he had some idea of her reactions to things, and of her attitudes of mind. Of his mother, it seemed to him, he knew very little.

I couldn't tell them, he thought; I couldn't tell any of them. They wouldn't begin to understand. Only Lindley could understand, because he liked girls, any girls, and he didn't care about proper introductions and all that. But Lindley didn't tell his family. Lindley also lied and deceived.

Rosa. She was so pretty with her thick dark hair and her big dark eyes, and that smile which reminded him of Nadia. He had been shy and clumsy, but next time he wouldn't find it all so strange and would do better. Next week he would telephone her and make a date, and they would go to the pictures, as she wanted; in the warm darkness of the cinema he wouldn't feel so shy. They would sit in the back row and hold hands—and kiss; he had seen couples doing that. Lindley boasted of taking girls to the pictures and never seeing the film at all. . . .

He would have to be going. Roll on next week.

He got back to find his grandfather sitting by the open window engaged in his nightly practice of what he called 'finishing off *The Times*'. There was a scent of petunias from the flower-box on the window-sill.

For the sake of something to say when he entered the room Anton observed, 'The rain didn't come to anything after all.'

Melby took off his reading-glasses and regarded his grandson.

'That's so. There's thunder about. We might get a storm in the night.' He folded his paper, then asked, 'Did you clear up whatever it was you wanted to clear up with Mr. Johns?'

'Yes, thanks. Where's Grandmamma?'

'Making the tea.'

'It's too hot for tea. There's no air. It's like being in Jericho. I need a glass of cold water. Then I think I'll be off to bed, if you don't mind—I've got a bit of a headache. It must be the thunder.'

'Probably,' Melby said, and took his pipe out of his jacket pocket and began filling it.

Anton escaped to the kitchen, feeling guilty in relation to his grandfather, and wanting to be alone.

A few minutes later Elspeth came in with the teapot; the cups were already set out on a side table.

'Anton's gone up,' she said. 'He doesn't seem to be feeling well. I hope he's not sickening for anything.'

'Perhaps he's in love.'

Elspeth looked startled.

'Why do you say that?'

Melby prodded the tobacco in the bowl of his pipe with a stump of pencil.

'It occurred to me. It's probably about time he had a girl.'

'I've thought it for some time now, but he doesn't seem interested.'

'How can we know? He wouldn't tell us.'

'Why shouldn't he? He's no reason to think we'd object!'

'He might pick a girl he knows we wouldn't approve of.'

'What a thing to say! Where would he meet such a girl? He only meets girls of our own class.'

'The world is wider than you think, my dear!'

He got up and moved over to the tea table.

She said, firmly, filling his cup, 'When Anton has a girl we shall know all about it.'

She closed the subject by crossing to the small radio set on a bookshelf and switching on the ten o'clock news.

An hour later, alone in his room, Melby lay staring at the heavy airless darkness thinking of the two figures he had seen emerging from the woods on his walk that evening; the dark-haired girl in the pink plastic mac, and his grandson. The girl had been laughing up into his face and Anton gazing raptly down. They had been so engrossed in each other that he had been able to retreat quickly into a clump of pines without being seen. After that he had made his way to the north side of the Common and kept to the road and gone into the first pub he had come to and ordered a large whisky.

He had felt stunned. Then, when the first shock had subsided, hurt. Deeply hurt.

Why had Anton done this to him? Why had he lied to him in the first place about finding that horrible pink mackintosh on a seat? And then pretending to take it to the police station; possibly he had taken it to his friend Lindley, and then fetched it from there this evening—he had said he was going there. That at least might have been true. But why all the other lies and deceptions?

That had been his first hurt, resentful reaction; but now laying wakeful in the darkness he thought: He couldn't tell me because she's a pickup; because in his heart he knows she's an unsuitable young person; because he knows he would have to say how he met her, and that it will none of it do.

Only what is he doing with this unsuitable young person? He's a good-looking boy and there are plenty of girls in his own sphere; he meets them all the time. Why does he have to sneak off to the woods with this little tippet?

What would Marian say? And is Marian to be told? But impossible to tell Marian and keep it a secret from Elspeth. Marian might even encourage the affair, whatever she might think of the girl, in the hope of it putting him off the idea of the year in Jordan. He wouldn't put it past her. She might think there was no harm in it and that it would run its course and finish naturally without outside intervention. She might be right, too. Nowadays young people did what they liked, anyhow, without reference to their elders; the old standards of social conduct didn't obtain any more, the class distinctions being no longer so sharply defined—in the West. In the East, Near and Far, the situation could not have arisen. Butros had probably not envisaged this particular risk when he had been so keen on having his son finish his education in England.

Only it wasn't a question of whether Butros Mansour's son was to be allowed to run round for a bit with this unsuitable young person; the question was what had gone wrong that this boy, brought up along the lines of a scrupulous rectitude, and of a natural integrity, inherited from both parents, should be involved in such a situation, and should lie and deceive in order to protect it?

Where had he, who stood in the relation of a father to this boy, failed him?

Because of course, he thought, I have failed him somewhere along the line, that he finds himself incapable of confiding in me. Whereas, no doubt, he has told young Lindley the whole exciting story. Is it that age is age and youth is youth and never the twain shall meet? Did I, like an old fool, just delude myself that there was closeness, communion, communication, between us? Is it just *because* I stand in the relation of a father to him that he can't be open with me?

And then—what to do about it? Keep silent and let the thing run its course? Or confront the boy with it, demand: Why did you lie? Why did you deceive? And who *is* this vulgar young person? And what are your intentions? No, no, that would be ridiculous. This was 1953, God help us all. Impossible to drive the boy into a corner like that; it might only drive him into closer association with the girl—possibly even into her bed. Not to mention driving an iron curtain down between us for good and all. Better to let it ride. Watch and wait, as the evangelists say. Masterly inaction. Not to worry, as they so extraordinarily said nowadays. Not to be hurt . . . but that wasn't so easy; it was a matter of vulnerability.

'Go ahead, boy, and get it over with! But don't lie to me any more!' He could say that to him. But he knew he wouldn't; because Anton, too, was vulnerable, and he loved him.

9

WHEN Alice Meyer promised Rosa to keep her secret she was sincere, but there are secrets which burn holes in the pockets of their keepers, and for Alice this was one. She was also in a cosy and confiding mood that Saturday evening sitting with Len Rosenberg on the terrace of a riverside hotel at Richmond drinking her second large gin—the second one that does you good, she always called it. Driving out to Richmond at weekends, in the good weather, was a thing she and Len liked to do. They parked the car in the fore-court of the hotel, had a few drinks on the terrace above the river, then went inside for a meal, taking their time over it, and as far as Len was concerned no expense spared—one of the things Alice liked about Len—and then driving up Richmond Hill and along the terrace to the park. When the problem of where to park the car had been successfully solved they took a short stroll, as far as the first reasonably shady tree not already sheltering another couple, then sat down on a raincoat Len was always careful to bring in the back of the car, and waited for it to get dusky enough to permit of the passionate interlude which was a major part of the night's programme. Alice prided herself on knowing when to stop, though it was a little risky and sometimes frightening, but not only did mutual passion demand it, it was also, she was con-vinced, by stopping short this side of consummation, a compelling force towards marriage. Sooner or later Len was bound to cry, 'We can't go on like this!' and then somehow, she was sure, in an access of frustrated desire they would find themselves engaged. Any Saturday night it could happen now. It was because that Saturday evening in particular she felt so sure of it, with Len hardly able to keep his hands off her even before they got to the park, that she relaxed into the cosily confiding mood in which the secret would no longer keep.

'I've been longing to tell you,' she told him, halfway through the second gin, 'but you'll never guess who Rosa's latest boy-friend is!'

Len's curiosity was hardly roused; Rosa had a succession of boy-friends.

'Haven't a clue,' he agreed carelessly. 'Why should I care anyway? She's never serious with any of them. A bit of snogging at the pictures or in the back of some bloke's car——' He laughed. 'I know my little sister!'

'Serious or not you'll sit up over this one!'

He looked startled.

'Don't tell me it's a married man, this time!'

She burst out laughing.

'This one's still at school! He's eighteen—not that!'

'Cradle-snatching! But it's none of our business. Drink up and let's go and eat!' She was aware of the excitement in his voice as he added, gaily, 'It's going to get dark early this evening!'

She turned her glass and regarded it thoughtfully.

'You don't understand what I am trying to tell you.'

'Well, what are you trying to tell me? Rosa's new boy-friend is still at school. So what?'

'He's a refugee—from Palestine.'

She looked up then with something like triumph in her eyes to be confronted by the consternation in his.

He stared at her for a moment, then said, 'Say that again!'

'Rosa's boy-friend is a Palestinian refugee. I can't say it any plainer.'

'How do you know? I mean did she tell you herself?'

'How else would I know?'

'She must be crazy!'

'That's what I told her!'

'What did she say?'

'Oh, something about Jews and Arabs didn't have to hate each other, and feeling sorry for him.'

'Sorry for him?'

'His family lost everything when they had to get out.'

He said violently, 'They didn't have to get out! You know damn well! They went because their leaders told them to—those that didn't just run away.'

His anger filled her with dismay; she had gone too far, but there was no getting out of it now; poor old Rosa's secret was out. Well, she shouldn't have told her. There shouldn't have been any secret. It served her right.

She said, quickly, conciliatory, 'Well, you know what I mean. It's nothing to worry about, anyhow. It won't last. I just had to tell you, that's all.'

She drained her glass, then smiled brightly.

'Shall we go?'

But now it was his turn to make no move. His dark, good-looking face had become pale with anger.

'Of course it's something to worry about! What about all the anti-Zionist propaganda he's going to dish out to her? It seems he's already told her a sob-story about how his family were turned out!'

'Well, there's nothing we can do about it. Do let's go and eat—I'm starving.'

She got up and he also got to his feet, knocking over a glass with the angry violence of his movements.

'Nothing we can do about it? I'll see about that!'

She felt frightened. Rosa will never forgive me. Why did she have to tell me, damn her! I wish I hadn't mentioned it. It was the two double gins did it . . .

Len was determined to have it out with Rosa that night. He talked of nothing else all through dinner, and afterwards declared that he was too upset to drive up into the park. He wanted to get home before Rosa; he wanted to be waiting for her when she came in, the little bitch.

'I don't think she sees him Saturdays,' Alice told him.

'She won't have stopped in. I've never known Rosa stop in on a Saturday night since she left school!'

Alice could find no way of placating him. He seemed quite

unaware when she laid her hand on his thigh under the table, and not even to notice when she leaned forward so that he had the full benefit of her low-cut dress. He wasn't in the mood—and it was the first time she had known him not in the mood. And he had been so much in the mood before I started all this, she thought, miserably. People shouldn't tell one secrets; it wasn't fair. People weren't meant to keep secrets; it was unnatural.

Still trying to repair the damage she pleaded, 'Supposing he does propaganda with her—you can soon correct that!'

'Don't be a bloody fool! How can I? What makes you think she's going to take notice of what a brother says when she's in love with this street-Arab?'

She was suddenly angry.

'I won't be talked to like that! I'm fed up with you, going on all night about poor Rosa! You ought to be ashamed. I'll never tell you anything again.'

'You're on her side, is that it?'

'Of course I'm not. I care as much about Zionism and Israel and all that as you do!'

'That's news, anyhow!'

'Oh, shut up! You make me tired. I'm going!'

He let her go. She was tippeting away down the courtyard, packed with cars, when he came after her.

'Oh, for God's sake!' he said, grabbing her arm. 'I'll take you home . . .'

After tears and kisses in the car the quarrel was at least patched up; it could not be properly made up because that would have taken more time than Len was prepared to give to it, in his pre-occupation with his sister and his impatience to get back and have it out with her. The full reconciliation, with probably more tears, forgiveness, and intensified passion, would have to wait till next time. But there was at least reconciliation enough to enable her to plead with him, 'Don't be too hard on Rosa! It's nothing, really! I mean—a schoolboy!'

'Don't let's go over it all again. It's got to stop, and I intend to stop it.'

'I don't see how you can. I mean—what can you do, really?'

'Frighten her,' he said. 'Frighten her so that she doesn't dare!'

'She'll hate you for ever! She'll never forgive you . . .'

'I can't help that. Love—hate—who the hell cares? There are more important things.'

Rosa was in fact so frightened that after the first instinctive defiance she crumpled up and promised never to see Anton again, except for the last time, to say goodbye. Her brother remained adamant. Not even for that.

'Tell me where you were meeting him Monday and *I'll* go along and explain. I'll explain all right!'

She had arranged to meet Anton at the seat above the lake at eight-thirty. The previous Wednesday, her half-day, they had met at the bus stop and gone to the cinema. This session had been so successful that they had met again by the seat on the Friday and had a similarly successful session in the woods; both felt they could hardly live through the weekend to get to Monday; their obsession was mutual and complete.

Then Len forced that terrible promise from her, but she knew that if it was the last thing she did she would go to meet Anton that Monday evening.

She got there early, because she had to get out of the house whilst Len was out. She had nearly an hour to wait for Anton and was terrified that Alice—the treacherous Alice—would have told Len that they met on the Common and that he would come haring up there. She hid in a clump of trees whilst waiting and was in an acute state of nerves by the time Anton arrived, a few minutes early.

He was surprised when she emerged suddenly from the trees, but alarmed when he saw the expression on her face as she came up with him.

'What's the matter?' he demanded. 'Anything wrong?'

'Yes, everything. Let's get down into the woods. I'll explain there . . .'

From the horse-ride she plunged off immediately into a narrow track, without heed for her stockings on the brambles.

'There's some bracken—we can hide in there——'

He followed her into the bracken, protesting, half laughing, 'What's all this about? Who are we hiding from?'

'My brother.'

She plunged in through a density of bracken some four feet high, surrounding a silver birch tree, and flaying at it in all directions made a place to sit. She dropped down and he came down beside her.

'What is it?' he said again. 'Why do we have to hide from your brother?'

He put an arm round her and pulled her close to him, kissing her wildly.

'I've so longed to be with you again,' he told her. 'Sweet, lovely Rosa!'

She clung to him, tightly.

'Darling Anton! Oh darling! I'm so unhappy!' She began to cry, helplessly.

'What is it?' he beseeched. 'What's wrong?'

'My brother has made me promise to give you up. He said if I tried to see you again he would have me watched, and he would find out where you lived and what school you were at, and he would beat you up . . .'

'Beat me up? Why? I don't understand. I'm not so easily beaten up anyway—I can put up quite a good fight, if I have to. But what's it all about?'

Rosa got her tears under control then asked in a low voice, 'Do you truly love me, Anton?'

'Of course I do. You know I do. Have you forgotten last time?'

'Could anything change it? I mean—supposing you found out I wasn't what I'd made out I was—that my name wasn't really Rosado and that I hadn't any Spanish blood—that I'd made all that up——'

He picked up one of her hands and kissed the palm.

'You're a funny girl. Did you really make all that up?'

She nodded. 'Uh-huh.'

He laughed.

'If you're not Rosa Rosado—then who are you?'

'You'll hate me when I tell you.'

'I might hate the name but it wouldn't make me hate you. Come on—out with it. What is it? One of those funny names——'

She said, desperately, 'It's Rosenberg. My name is Rosa Rosenberg. My brother Len is a keen Zionist. That's what it's all about! Someone told him about us.'

He dropped her hand and stared at her, unable to believe.

'You're Jewish?'

She nodded again, her eyes holding his, despairingly. He continued to stare at her, aghast, and she said, almost inaudibly, 'We can't help how we're born.'

Then as he continued in his silence, 'If it doesn't matter to me that you're Arab why should it matter to you that I'm Jewish?'

He buried his face in his hands, pressing back the scenes crowding behind his eyes, his head humming with the sound of the small black planes coming over, coming in low. He felt very cold suddenly and shivered; evil recollected in anguish. He forced himself to look at her, sitting there in the bracken beside him, her dark hair—the lovely thick dark hair like Nadia's—framing her pale face, her big dark eyes swimming with tears; he saw it all and it no longer meant anything. He groped for the words and said, painfully, 'In the ordinary way it wouldn't matter. I mean if the Jews hadn't taken our country—done to us what they did do. Now that I know—it couldn't work any more. It's not your fault. It's just bad luck on us both. I wouldn't see you as Rosa Rosado any more. I can't explain. It wouldn't work that's all.'

Unable to look at her he sat looking down miserably at the soles of his shoes, the crushed bracken, a small beetle picking its way through the wilderness of stalks and pieces of twig . . . the wilderness.

Rosa looked at him and her heart hardened. When she spoke the words seemed spat at him; like machine-gun bullets; like the words the Israeli woman soldier spat at his father.

'Anti-semitism,' she said, with cold bitterness. 'That's all it is. Anti-semitism.'

He looked at her, then, despairingly.

'No. How can it be? We're all Semites, Arabs and Jews.'

'All the same—you hate Jews!'

'I never used to. There were always Jews in Palestine. We all lived together, went to the same schools—Moslems, Jews, Christians.'

She scrambled to her feet, brushing the leaves and pieces of twig from her gay cotton skirt. She had the skirt new at the weekend and had looked forward to wearing it.

Anton got up and stood looking down at her. She was the girl he had seen emerging from the clump of trees less than an hour ago, his heart quickening at the sight of her, the girl he had been kissing so hungrily only a few minutes ago; his mind acknowledged these facts but it seemed all unreal. His mind knew also that she was bitterly hurt and unhappy, that his conduct was unreasonable and cruel, but he could not feel pity; nothing but a despairing dismay.

As they moved out of the bracken she said in a flat voice, 'I never really thought it would be goodbye. I thought we'd find a way of being together in spite of Len. I thought you wouldn't mind. That you really loved me.'

'I'm sorry,' he said, perfunctorily, feeling himself accused.

When they came out on to the sandy track she said, 'Don't come to the bus with me—there's no need. It's better we shouldn't be together in the open—in case Len's prowling about. He threatened to half kill you when he caught you!'

'I'm not afraid of your brother.'

They stood looking at each other, numb with hopelessness.

'It's goodbye, then,' she said at last, unsteadily.

'Yes.' He wished she would go; or that he could find a way to.

'All right, then.' Her voice was suddenly hard. 'Goodbye!'

She turned abruptly and began picking her way across the sand of the horse-ride. At the other side she walked very quickly across the grass and did not look back.

Anton did not watch her go. He walked slowly along the edge of the track, his eyes on the ground. He felt humiliated and deeply ashamed. It was no more his fault than what had happened to Nadia had been hers, but what your mind knew and what you felt inside yourself were different things. He wondered if he would ever have the courage to tell Walid.

With the thought of Walid he knew an upsurge of longing for Jordan . . . for Palestine. For the last few weeks it had receded into the background; he had been unable to think about anything but Rosa, and guilt was added to the sense of shame. He thought that if Walid knew he would despise him—not for having made a fool of himself over a girl, but for his weakness in being so overwhelmed by the infatuation as to deviate from his singleness of purpose: the steadfast following of the straight and narrow way that led to the road to Beersheba.

As he approached the cottage he saw his grandfather sitting by the open window with *The Times*, and knew with a sudden upsurge of relief that he would confess to him.

10

MELBY said, at the stammering end of the recital, 'It's not news to me that you had a girl. I saw you together one evening on the Common. I recognized the pink mackintosh.'

'You saw us? Where?' He felt something like panic.

'Leaving the woods, near the windmill. What upset me was that you had thought it necessary to lie to me.'

'I felt awful about it. I never meant to. I don't know why I did, really——'

'Now you're trying to deceive yourself. You deceived me because in your heart you knew this girl wasn't suitable. If it had been Lindley's sister, or someone like that, you wouldn't have felt it necessary to keep it a secret.'

Anton said, miserably, 'England's supposed to be so democratic, but there's all this class thing——'

'It isn't really a matter of class. Your friend Edwards is of humble family, but he's not—vulgar. I'm only surprised you could have been attracted in the first place. Such a lapse of taste—I don't mean because she's Jewish. Most of us are born to one religion or another.'

'That was the worst part for me. It made it all seem—ugly!'

'Was she all for Israel?'

'I don't know. We never discussed it. She just told me this evening that her brother was a Zionist. He told her if she went on seeing me he'd have her watched and find out where I lived and what school I went to and when he caught up with me he reckoned he was going to half kill me. She was frightened of him. I told her I wasn't. But that I couldn't see her any more because I didn't feel the same about her—now I knew.'

'She was upset?'

'At first. She was crying at first, then she got angry and said it was anti-semitism.'

'Poor girl!'

'Why do you say that? After all the Jews did to us!'

'That girl didn't do anything to you. If she shared her brother's views she would never have taken up with you. Not all Jews are Zionists. A big majority—but not all.'

'You said she was what you call unsuitable, but now you're defending her!'

'I thought that before I knew she was Jewish. I find her pathetic, trying to pass herself off as Spanish, and wanting to go on seeing you in spite of her ferocious Zionist brother! Courage and loyalty are always admirable. I feel sorry for her and think you were too harsh.'

Anton said, despairingly, 'What she told me came as the most awful shock to me. I suddenly saw everything again—the wilderness and the dead children, and the planes I was so afraid of. And I remembered what I'd found out they'd done to Nadia, and a servant girl we had—all the terrible things the Jews did to us, and how it killed my father—how they killed him, and I'd been kissing one of them——'

Melby was aware of the mounting hysteria in the boy's voice, then, 'You don't understand,' Anton cried, wildly, and rushed from the room.

When Elspeth returned from a Women's Institute social an hour later she found the room in darkness and Robert's chair occupied only by *The Times*. She switched on lamps, drew the curtains, and was straightening up the room when she heard a step overhead and a moment later Robert entered the room.

Inevitably she said, 'Fancy sitting in the dark!'

'I was upstairs with Anton. He came in a bit overwrought from his walk. We've been having a talk.'

'Overwrought—what about?'

'Just things getting on top of him. He's more homesick for Jordan than we realized. I hope Marian will agree to let him go back before Christmas.'

'I thought he'd been a bit odd these last few weeks. I even wondered if he'd got a girl. Wishful thinking, I know! What exactly is up with him—did you find out?'

'I think he has worries and difficulties he doesn't tell us about. For one thing he had no close friend at school since he and Lindley drifted apart.'

'There's that nice serious young Edwards.'

'I gather he finds him a bit of a bore—too solemn. One of his worries is that he feels he had been neglecting Walid Hussein.'

'I understood they didn't reckon to write to each other much.'

'They don't, but Anton has some sort of a thing about what he calls keeping faith with Walid, and he feels that lately he hasn't. It's all churned up in him again, too, about the trek, and his father's death. It's good that next term is his last at King's. I feel strongly he must go back and have that year in Jordan—be with Hussein again, feel himself Arab again . . .'

'I'd hoped that after nearly four years here he was getting over that!'

'No one ever gets over what's in their blood.'

'To me it all seems a great pity. Anyhow, has he settled down after the great heart-to-heart?'

'Yes. I gave him one of your sleeping pills.'

She stared at him.

'A sleeping pill? A boy of that age?'

'I wanted him to sleep without nightmare. When I went up to him he'd had an attack of nose-bleeding.'

'All over the sheets? I put a clean one on this morning!'

'No. He wasn't in bed when it happened.'

'I suppose he's what used to be called highly strung?'

'You could call it that,' Melby said, drily.

All his life, he thought, he would remember that sound of stifled sobbing in the dark.

II

MARIAN, with nothing specific to go on, the picture blurred by her mother's vagueness and her father's evasions, decided that all that was wrong with Anton was that he had been overworking and needed relaxation and a change. She would have him spend the rest of the holidays in town with her at her flat. They would be able to do a few things together, she said, and whilst she was at the office he could amuse himself visiting picture galleries, museums, the Tower; he could go by water-bus to Greenwich, visit the Nelson museum, go over the *Cutty Sark*; he need never be at a loose end—and if he had anything on his mind he might eventually find himself able to tell her.

Anton welcomed the plan; he did badly need a change both of scene and atmosphere. His grandmother, with her continual probing, got on his nerves—and all the more because she came very near to the heart of the matter. Elspeth was convinced that behind whatever had transpired to cause Robert to describe Anton's condition as overwrought, the night he took one of her sleeping pills for him, there was a girl. She also suspected that Robert knew about the girl and she resented it, bitterly, that he refused to discuss the matter with her, and that Anton seemed visibly to shrink, when she invited his confidences. Anton did in fact experience a sensation of physically shrinking away from her when she attempted to come closer to him emotionally; his body seemed to contract with distaste. Everything in him shouted: Leave me alone! But that was the one thing she was incapable of, because her love demanded that he come close to her, confide in her, be emotionally possessed by her.

It was a relief when his mother suggested he finish the holidays with her. He never felt that she made emotional demands upon him; he could not even feel that he knew very much about her, yet there existed something strong and deep between them, beyond the normal mother-and-son bond—something to do with having made the terrible trek together, experienced the same terror, witnessed the same horrors, suffered the same hell of exhaustion and thirst, shared agony and anguish—and the searing moment of truth in which Butros had died.

In the first few days in the London flat he wrote to Walid and told him about Rosa: 'My grandfather thinks I was unjust to her, and of course I was, but I couldn't help myself; it was a great shock to me and brought back everything the Jews had done to us. I haven't told anyone about it except my grandfather, and now you. There was a friend at school I told in the beginning, but not how it ended; I just said it fizzled out. While it was on I couldn't seem to think of anything else; I couldn't work or read or concentrate properly, or even think about Jordan. Now that it's over I am ashamed that it could have got such a hold on me, even to deceiving my grandfather, whom I love as a father. Until all this happened I never thought about it, but now I wonder whether you have a girl, and if so whether you are still able to work and read and think properly, and be yourself. I think I want that more than anything—to be myself.

'The other day my mother and I stood on London Bridge looking down into what is called the Pool, where ships from all parts of the world tie up along the wharves to discharge or take on cargoes. There was a Swedish ship unloading timber, and there was a beautiful white ship, very modern, streamlined, with low-raking funnels. We wondered where it was from—and then we saw that it was an Israeli ship, and we didn't look any more but walked on over the bridge. It was probably bringing citrus fruits; there are a great many Jaffa oranges in the shops—perhaps some are from the Mansour estates.

'Sometimes my mother tries to explain to the shop people. We were going to buy some flowers for the flat, but the ones my mother wanted were long-stemmed things called gladioli and were very expensive. She asked where did they come from that they should be so expensive, and the woman in the shop said from "Israel". My mother said, "That's another reason for not buying them, then!" and explained that "Israel" is Jewish-occupied Palestine, and that she who was the widow of a Palestinian was only one of a million or more people who had lost their homes and lands and money there, without a single penny of compensation having been paid in all these years, or a single refugee being allowed to go back.

'The flower-shop woman was very surprised at what my mother told her and said she had no idea, and agreed that it was very terrible. She even used the word "shocking". But next time we passed the shop she was still showing gladioli in the window, and the fruit side of the window was stacked with Jaffa oranges. I think most of the people here don't know what "Israel" is and how it came about, but even when they do they don't care. The Jews are real to them; they are meeting them all the time—they are everywhere and they can't escape them even if they wanted to, but Arabs are strange far-away people who wear Biblical clothes and live in deserts and go about on camels. T. E. Lawrence and all that. Or else they're dark shifty greasy people, traders, from the Levant, though they are not very sure where or what the Levant is. So it's not easy for them to get up any sympathy for or interest in Arabs; they know Jews as writers, painters, musicians, stage and film producers; they know Indians and Japanese, but not Arabs. It's odd when you think that Jerusalem and Beirut and Cairo and Damascus are only a few flying-hours away from London. Now that air-travel has made the world so small—still the Arabs are the unknown people who live somewhere out there in the desert, backward and forgotten.

'Soon now I'll be back, Walid; they're going to let me go to Ramallah for Christmas, and I will go to Bethlehem to see Amin— if you are in Ramallah then we can go together. I can't tell you how much I long to be back. . . .'

To this Walid replied surprisingly quickly and what was for him at length:

'It's good news that you will be back in December. Let me know what plane you're coming on and try to arrange to arrive on or after the 22nd, as since October 8th, the beginning of the semester, I have been at the American University of Beirut, and the Christmas vacation begins then, for one week. I'll be spending most of the time in Hebron with my relations—perhaps we could have a few days together there—though we'll hardly get beyond there this time.

'You ask about girls, but I am not interested. I am much too busy with my studies, and have too much else on my mind. I am sorry you made a bad start. Better luck next time, but better postpone the next time until after your "sabbatical year"—to avoid complications in connection with anything we might decide to do.

'I have grown a moustache since I've been at the A.U.B. I enclose a photograph so that you can see what I look like and will be able to recognize me on the airport!

Ma' as-salama.
W. H.'

12

His last term at school dragged; all his real life seemed lived out of school hours. His interest in the home for the blind and the deaf-blind at which his grandfather visited revived and he took to accompanying Melby there every Saturday morning, eager to accustom himself to being with the blind, and to practise speaking manually with the deaf-blind. He visited at the Johns' a good deal, returning books and borrowing them; Gerald introduced him to the novels of Joseph Conrad, which he began reading as seafaring and adventure stories and then for their obsessional quality which seized upon his imagination; he did not understand all he read, but knew the excitement of new things imperfectly understood, glimpses of something beyond his grasp, intimations of wider worlds, infinitely complicated. The women in the stories seemed always shadowy, and this he liked, and that the men were always heroic, searching, and lonely. The description of the aging sea-captain in *The End of the Tether* reminded him of his father, both in physical appearance and in his courage, honourableness and dignity, and that he too was destroyed by disaster brought about by the forces of evil, so that in the end 'he had nothing of his own—even his own past of honour, truth, of just pride, was gone. All his spotless life had fallen into the abyss.'

Anton was profoundly moved by this story, and innerly wept; when he had finished it he had been unable to read anything else for some days. After that he lost himself in *Heart of Darkness*, the philosophic implications of which he only imperfectly understood, but there was for him the 'terrific suggestiveness of words heard in dreams, of phrases spoken in nightmares'.

It was the waiting time, during which the dream world was

more real than the material world—from which he was always escaping back into the reality of dream.

Outwardly he was unchanged, his smile as ready, his good nature as unfailing; as a prefect he was more tactful than authoritarian, and therefore popular; in the Cadet Force he put on authority with his uniform. He took a polite interest in the photographs Lindley showed him of his girl-friends and made appropriate smiling comments. He conscientiously read, or anyhow looked at, the books and periodicals Edwards was always bringing him and urging upon him—he had become an ardent reader of the *New Statesman*—and always went back to Conrad. Because he would soon be going away he resumed going to the parish church with his grandmother on Sunday mornings—it was the one thing he could do for her, and a relief to him that there was this one thing.

He wished there was something he could do for his mother but short of giving up the Jordan plan, which had become intensified in importance to him since the Rosa interlude, he knew there was nothing. She had agreed to the plan but told him she hoped he would change his mind before the time came. He in turn had told her he knew he wouldn't.

'Why are you so against it?' he had demanded, implicitly pleading.

Unable to say to him 'Because you're all I have of Butros, and if you go back to Jordan for a year you're lost to me for a year and perhaps for always,' she said simply, 'I shall be lonely without you.'

'I shall be writing to you regularly,' he had urged, and added, 'You could come out for a little while, perhaps—when you get your holidays from the office——'

'I could never go back to Jordan. Not possibly.'

He said, helplessly, 'You make me feel bad about going——'

'I'm sorry, darling. You must do what you want—it sounds contradictory but I even want you to do what you want. It's just that I wish you didn't want to do this particular thing. It's selfish and unreasonable of me, but there it is. You have to be yourself, but I have to be myself, and being ourselves cuts us off from each other.'

'Not really,' he said, and again pleaded with her, 'Really not!'

She smiled, in an effort to ease them out of the emotional morass.

'I hope you're right. We'll see, won't we?'

They had left it there at the time and the discussion had never been renewed. He continued to feel guilty about her knowing he was hurting her, but with another part of himself ruthless. There was something he had to do, and this was it.

As his eighteenth birthday approached his mother and grand-mother joined forces to urge a party upon him—he would after all not be there for Christmas, nor for his nineteenth birthday; it would also be the last party whilst he was still at school, and the date falling on a Saturday was very convenient. There seemed, in short, every reason for giving such a party and inviting all his friends.

He protested, laughing to cover his dismay, 'I haven't any friends—except Gerald. Really I don't want a party—really and truly I don't!'

Elspeth said, disappointed, 'I thought we would hire a small hall or banqueting room locally, such as they use for wedding receptions, and have the catering done, and make it a really good teenage party! It would be a farewell party for you as well as a birthday party. You could ask all your school-friends, and their sisters—we could even have some of the parents.'

Anton looked appealingly at his mother.

'Really I'd rather not,' he pleaded.

Marian sighed.

'You're an odd boy. Most boys of your age have swarms of teenage friends. You're popular at school, and for years you've been going to Christmas parties at the houses of other boys—if we have a birthday party for you it would be a way of repaying——'

It was his grandfather who saved him.

'Why not let the boy choose what he'd like to do on his birth-day? After all it's *his* birthday!'

Marian looked from her father to her son with equal displeasure and demanded of Anton, 'Well, what would you *like* to do?'

Released from tension Anton grinned.

'That's easy—have dinner at home as usual, just the four of us, with a bottle of fizzy wine!'

'Fizzy wine?' Melby was puzzled. 'You don't mean champagne, do you?'

'It doesn't have to be champagne,' his grandson assured him, lightly. 'We had some Italian wine at Lindley's last Christmas—Asti something. It was smashing.'

'We'll make it champagne,' his grandfather said.

Stubbornly determined that Anton should have more of a party than the family circle for his eighteenth birthday Marian, without mentioning the fact to anyone, invited a couple called Wyncott-Brown to come in after dinner. Desmond Wyncott-Brown was the advertising manager of the Middle East publication for which she worked; he was in his early thirties, good-looking, informed on Middle East affairs, and, she considered, a very pleasant young man; his wife, Suzie—she insisted on the z—was not, she acknowledged, highly intelligent, but beautiful and decorative. Marian had several times been their guest in their narrow and elegant house in Knightsbridge, and she had once taken them out to her parents' cottage, but Anton had been away camping at the time. Now seemed the opportunity to invite them to meet him, and they would brighten up the occasion with their glossy decorativeness, she thought.

Towards the end of the meal she announced, casually, that she had invited them for coffee. Her mother was delighted, her father raised his eyebrows and remarked drily that it was a good thing he had laid in some Courvoisier, and Anton was annoyed.

'I thought it was agreed we should be just ourselves?'

Marian said, serenely, 'You turned down a dinner party, and we didn't have a dinner party, but there's no reason why we shouldn't have a couple of friends in after dinner—you didn't want any of yours, so we're having a couple of mine!' She added, to balance the asperity of this speech, 'They're nice—you'll like them. They're not old fogeys—she's not yet thirty, and *very* glamorous!'

Anton continued to look sulky, demanding, 'Who are they, anyhow?'

Marian filled in the background and assured him, 'They're all right—they know the Middle East. He does, anyhow.'

Melby recharged his grandson's glass.

'Not to worry,' he said, cheerfully. 'The thing is just to look at her and listen to him. She's a good eyefull!'

Elspeth regarded him with astonishment.

'Really, Robert! I think the wine must have gone to your head!'

'Probably,' he said, carelessly, and Marian was reminded of Butros.

He went over to the radio and twiddled knobs, producing roars and shrieks, and in the middle of the commotion the after-dinner guests arrived.

Marian annoyed Anton still further by introducing him as 'My grown-up son!'

Confusedly he shook hands with a bright-haired woman in a tight black dress. He was aware of peculiar jewellery like chunks of bronze and of an almost suffocating perfume which he recognized as expensive, being like one his father used to buy for his mother in Beiruit. She gave him a radiant smile and wished him many happy returns of the day, then turned to Marian to exclaim, 'Isn't he the image of you?'

Anton smiled as always when embarrassed and shook hands with the husband, who wore a very well-cut dark suit, a bow tie, and a complacent smile. His good looks were a trifle florid and in a few years he would be fat. Anton disliked him on sight.

Elspeth bustled off to make coffee, chairs were drawn up, Melby invited Mrs. Wyncott-Brown to have some champagne— there was still some left, he declared, as only he and Anton had really been doing it justice.

'Champagne!' Mrs. Wyncott-Brown exclaimed, ecstatically, adding, playfully, 'You *are* doing yourselves well!'

'Well, we're only eighteen once,' Melby said, filling her glass.

'Also, of course,' Marian reminded her, 'Anton's going away for a year to Jordan at the end of term.'

'Yes, of course.' Suzie gave Anton a sweet, encouraging smile.

He looked away from her to her husband.

Desmond made easy confident conversation:

'Going back to the lowest spot on earth, I hear?'

Anton told him, 'I'll be going to Jericho sometime, I expect, but actually I'm going to stay with my uncle in Ramallah before going to work in Bethlehem—I'll only be passing through Jericho on the way up.'

'Why don't you fly to Beirut and get the morning plane to Jerusalem? Simpler.'

Desmond Wyncott-Brown always knew the simpler thing, the better thing, the more sensible thing, and loved to tell it.

'It would mean spending a night in Beirut,' Marian pointed out.

'So what? We've got plenty of contacts in Beirut, haven't we?'

Anton said, nettled, 'I'd sooner go to Amman. It's nice to drive through Jericho in the early morning. I have a friend who'll meet me and we'll go and have beans for breakfast in Amman before going out.'

'Beans?'

'Beans,' Anton confirmed, happily, his smile very bright, because he felt he disliked Mr. Wyncott-Brown more than anyone he had ever met.

'Eaten by the hand,' Melby amplified, 'with the aid of that flat thin peasant bread. Very popular with Palestinians.'

'First thing in the morning—I couldn't!' Suzie cried. She smiled at Anton over her champagne glass, then inquired of Marian, 'How did you get on with the food out there? I mean living down there in Jericho—how could you cope? It always sounds so terribly cut off——'

Desmond put in, 'Suzie's a girl likes her village stores handy— little places like Harrods'——'

Elspeth came in with the coffee and Melby brought out Courvoisier and brandy globes.

Elspeth poured and Anton handed.

Marian explained, 'There's a market and shops in Jericho. I could get most things there. The thing I missed most was fish. Sometimes someone would bring us some packed in ice, all the way from Aqaba—all across the desert.'

'Aqaba?' Suzie looked blank.

'On the Red Sea,' Melby told her, and explained, 'The Israelis have all the Mediterranean coast. Jordan has no sea—only the Dead Sea.'

'What about the Sea of Galilee?'

'That's in what is now called Israel.'

'Occupied Palestine,' Anton said, firmly, offering sugar and cream.

'Whether one likes it or not Israel is a *fait accompli*,' Desmond stated.

'It's still Occupied Territory,' Marian murmured.

'It's not a useful expression. It's like the Irish nationalists who like to refer to Ulster as British Occupied Territory. It's just silly. Unrealistic.'

He sat with his legs crossed, swinging one foot as he talked, and his smile was as complacent as his neat little bow tie.

Marian thought, despairingly: Desmond is being tiresome.

Anton hated him. He wondered if his grandfather did. But Melby merely thought him a bore—and poured the Courvoisier less liberally than he otherwise would have done. A pity to waste good liquor on a bore. Or good conversation either.

Anton, excited by champagne and anger, said, boldly, 'I call it unrealistic not to call things by their proper names! You can call a stables a cow-shed but it doesn't make it one! I was born in Palestine, not in Israel! And one of these days it'll be Palestine again!'

'*Insh'allah!*' Melby murmured.

'You might live to see it, but I doubt it,' Desmond said.

The supercilious smile infuriated Anton and he became reckless.

'My generation of Palestinians will see it because we shall work for it,' he declared, wildly. 'Palestine will be liberated by Palestinians.'

Desmond was now genuinely amused. This boy of Marian's was the authentic chip of the old paternal Palestinian block.

'By the Palestine Army of Liberation?' His tone was mocking.

'By a fifth column inside Israel,' Anton said. Even as he said it he was filled with horror to hear himself saying it all out loud, but something inside himself drove him on and he couldn't stop.

'Massive infiltration, is that it?'

'Not massive—gradual. It will take years.'

Desmond turned the brandy globe in his hands, warming it.

'I'm afraid it will. More years than you can live!'

Anton was, furiously, aware of his amusement.

'Youth must be allowed its dreams,' Melby said. 'Didn't you have wild dreams at eighteen?'

Desmond said drily, 'When I was eighteen it was nineteen-thirty-nine and no time for dreaming!'

Anton suddenly yawned, then laughed.

'I'm sorry,' he said. 'It must be the fizzy wine. If I may be excused I'd better be off——'

He shook hands with the Wyncott-Browns, who said they had been very pleased to meet him—Suzie clasped his hand in both of hers and said they must meet again when he got back from the Holy Land—and escaped.

In the coolness of his room he felt suddenly dizzy. He tore off his clothes and pitched into bed without cleaning his teeth. Fizzy wine was a mistake, he thought, it made you say more than you meant, and it gave you a headache. It made you—pass—out. . . .

He wakened late and with a headache, and came downstairs to find that his grandmother had already left for church and his grandfather, his mother told him, had gone out for a walk.

'It's nearly eleven,' she pointed out.

'I'm sorry. I have a headache. I don't think champagne suits me.'

She said, severely, 'You certainly talked a lot of nonsense—if that's anything to do with it!'

'He annoyed me.'

'He?'

'Mr. Wyncott-Brown. I don't know how you can like him. I think he's horrible!'

'Well, I do like him. I like them both, and I don't think I have to discuss them with you. Go and get your breakfast.'

She picked up the wad of Sunday papers lying on the table and stood staring at the headlines, her back turned to him. He hesitated a moment, then accepted his dismissal and went off to the kitchen, feeling miserable.

He found his breakfast laid on the corner of the table with the things he liked—some yoghourt, dish of black olives, cheese, apples. He helped himself to an olive and went over to the stove to make himself a cup of Turkish coffee. Whilst he was waiting for it to come to the boil he stood sniffing the jar of ground cardomom seeds, which, next to the scent of orange blossom, he thought the most beautiful smell in the world.

The coffee came to the boil in the little bronze pot, he put in a pinch of the seeds, and carried it over to the table. He poured the thick sweet brew into a tiny cup and was peeling himself an apple when his mother came into the kitchen.

She sat down at the table opposite him.

'I want to talk to you whilst we're alone,' she said.

He looked at her, steadily.

'About what I said last night?'

'About this talk of infiltration into Occupied Territory. Is that what you want to go back for? Some schoolboy romanticism about liberating Palestine? Is that what you're up to—you and Walid?'

Anton averted his eyes.

'You know why I want to go back. I get homesick, and I've no real friends here.'

'It was agreed you should go for a holiday when you finished at King's and before you started your year's work. Why do you want to do the year there—cutting yourself off from your family?'

'Uncle Farid and Uncle Khalil are my family too,' he mumbled, defensively.

'They're not as close to you as your mother and your grand-parents.'

He swallowed the coffee, so lovingly made, without pleasure. It had grown cold; she had spoilt it for him anyway.

She went on:

'I couldn't sleep for worrying about you last night. The wine loosened your tongue—you've never talked like that before. All that talk of infiltration and building up a fifth column inside Israel—it's crazy, Anton! Don't you see that it's crazy?'

He stared down at his plate, pushing olive stones around with a forefinger, vowing not to touch fizzy wine again, or any wine at all, if it came to that; perhaps it was better to be like a good Moslem and never touch alcohol at all. Walid's father didn't, and Walid didn't intend to.

He came out of his reverie to hear his mother demanding, sharply, 'Did you hear what I said? I want you to swear you won't get into mischief if I let you go to Jordan for a year.'

'I'm not a child,' he mumbled.

'In some respects you are a child. What you were saying last night was pure childishness. I was ashamed of you. Fortunately everyone just thought the wine had gone to your head.'

'It had.'

'Then you weren't serious about that fifth column idea?'

'I think it's a very good idea. I didn't invent it.'

'It might be a good idea if it were feasible, but it's not. Your father would have said the same. Would you like him to have heard you talking like that?'

Anton said, 'I'm not sure I remember all I said—those two got on my nerves.'

'It doesn't seem to occur to you that you might have got on theirs. You certainly got on mine! You've got to promise me not to do anything foolish if I let you go to Jordan—nothing you know I'd disapprove of. You've got to swear to me!'

He looked at her, then, anger rising in him.

'Why should I swear? Can't you trust me?'

'After last night no, unfortunately.'

'That was the wine——'

'*In vino veritas!*'

He made a movement of impatience.

'What is this—an inquisition?'

She got up.

'All right—if you want to worry me——'

'That's blackmail! You've no right——'

She said heavily, 'I have the right, because I'm your mother, and you're my son—all I've got. You can call it blackmail. I call it asking you to behave decently. Either you swear to me not to do anything foolish or you don't go!'

She went out, leaving him sitting at the table. He was still pushing olive stones morosely round his plate when Melby came in a few minutes later.

'What about some coffee?' he said, cheerfully.

Anton got up and went over to the gas-cooker.

His grandfather said, fumbling for his pipe, 'Your mother has been telling me of your little argument. She's worried about you. Can't you set her mind at rest?'

'I suppose so. But why must she blackmail me into swearing?'

'Because she's worried. I, also, would like an assurance you won't do anything foolish.'

You, too, Anton thought, watching the coffee rising in the copper pot, sniffing the fragrance of the cardomom seeds, even you. He wanted to say: What is foolish? Who's to decide?

He brought the coffee to the table.

'You have my assurance,' he said, miserably.

'Thank you. You must give it to your mother, also.'

'I'll try.'

'Try?'

'I can't if she blackmails me.'

He carried his coffee cup and plate over to the sink and rinsed them under the tap. Drying his hands he said, 'I've a bit of a headache. I'd like to go out for an hour, if I'm not wanted for anything.'

'Your mother might need help getting lunch.'

'I'll ask her.'

He went into the sitting room. His mother was sitting on the window-seat reading what she called the Sunday culture.

He said, 'Do you want any help—with the potatoes, or anything?'

She said coldly, without looking up, 'No, thank you.'

'In that case I'd like to go for a walk—my head aches.'

'Be back by one,' was all she said, turning the page of a paper and not looking at him.

He hesitated by the door.

'Please don't go on being cross,' he said.

She still did not look at him.

'Oh, go *away*,' she said. But he had the feeling she would smile if she allowed herself. Encouraged by the slight thaw he said, as a parting shot, 'I hope to—all the way to Jordan!'

No more was said after that until the evening they were on London Airport, three days before Christmas. Then Marian beseeched her son for the last time.

'Promise me you and Walid won't do anything foolish! Promise me, darling!'

He took the hand she laid pleadingly on his arm and raised it to his lips.

'I wish you wouldn't worry about me—just because I got a bit tight on my eighteenth birthday and talked some airy-fairy nonsense!'

'So long as it *was* only nonsense!'

'What do you think? What contribution do you suppose Walid and I could make towards liberating Palestine?'

At that point his grandfather returned from the bookstall with the evening paper and some magazines.

Anton asked him, 'Don't you wish you were coming?'

'Not really,' Melby said. 'Not during the Occupation. But salute the old tree in front of the church when you're in Bethlehem for me, and give Jerusalem my love . . .'

His grandmother was not there—it was one of her committee evenings, as on the evening of his arrival just over four years ago. She had said that she would anyhow prefer to say goodbye at the house—goodbyes were best said in private, she declared. So she had embraced him and wept over him, said how much she would miss him, and all over again how sad that he should be going just before Christmas, begged him to write to her frequently, said that she would pray for him, and for his safe return. If it had to be that kind of farewell, he thought, it was certainly better conducted in private.

On London Airport nobody wept. When the time came for passengers to pass through barriers forbidden to those who saw them off his mother kissed him, held him to her for a moment, and said only, 'Take care of yourself, darling!' His grandfather shook hands with him and said, 'Safe journey—and safe return,' to which Anton had replied, simply, '*Insh'allah*', and that was all.

Then he marched off with the other passengers, and when he was in the plane he could not distinguish them from among all the other people crowded on the roof to watch the plane take-off, and they could not distinguish him.

As they descended into the building, on the way back to the car Melby had hired to bring them out to the airport, Marian said, 'Bethlehem—isn't it odd, he's going back to Butros!'

'I thought that too—that it had to be Bethlehem. It makes a pattern——'

In the car she said, 'I feel so sad—so indescribably sad. He's doing what he wants to do and I ought to be glad for him, yet I feel so sad I could die of it!'

'Perhaps you should have flown out with him for a few weeks——'

'I couldn't go back—any more than you could. But he had to go. In my heart I do feel that. It was a kind of compulsion. I resisted the idea, but in my heart I knew it. He had to go.'

Melby said slowly, 'Yes. I think he did.'

PART 3

The Return

I

FLYING into Amman over the bare desert hills, into the sunrise which had not yet reached the West, Anton felt an exhilaration entirely new to him. For the first time in his life he wanted to sing and shout for joy. He laughed up into the face of the air-hostess as she approached to see that his safety-belt was fastened.

'Amman!' he cried, exultantly.

She smiled and nodded.

'Your home town?'

He said yes because that was what it felt like—home. He had come home; there had been exodus and exile and now there was return.

In a few moments he would be seeing Walid, embracing him, speaking to him, after all this time, four years; they had been schoolboys when they had parted, and now he was a young man with a moustache. Anton could not imagine it. He extracted from his wallet the photograph Walid had sent him and looked at it. He became aware that his heart was beating very fast. He told himself: We shan't know each other, but could not make himself believe it. Your mind could say one thing and something inside yourself another, and what you felt was truer than anything the mind could say.

Then with a few light bounces the plane touched down and was skimming along the runway and Anton was peering eagerly through the window by which he sat trying to make out Walid among the figures waiting by the airport buildings. It seemed an age before the cabin door was opened and passengers came out into the cool freshness of the Jordanian dawn. Anton could not see his friend, but because he was sure Walid could see him he waved, joyfully.

Crossing the space between the plane and the airport buildings he became aware of women in long flowing dresses and head-veils, men in white robes and head-dresses; of roses in bloom in a small garden, and the pink gleam of oleanders. The air was cool and clear as a mountain stream. Officials came out to the plane and the sound of Arabic fell on his grateful ears. He went on into the building with other people and waited by a counter for his passport to be restored to him, and then, suddenly, to his astonishment, saw his Uncle Khalil approaching from a door at the far side, beyond the baggage counters, and behind him a handsome young man with a dark moustache, and a dark-haired girl in a summery dress.

Khalil bore down on him and seized him and kissed him on both cheeks crying welcome-back in Arabic and English, and then the young man was hugging him and crying to him in Arabic, a thousand welcomes, and praise be to Allah for this morning of good which had restored the beloved ... The warm flowery Arabic phrases fell sweetly into Anton's heart and mind, and all that was English fell away from him and he wept unashamedly from pure joy, and it seemed to him they were all laughing and crying together.

He didn't know whether he would have recognized Walid or not; the little black moustache made him look different, but it was Walid embracing him, and Walid's voice crying welcome to him, and it was Walid's laugh.

When the first confusion abated he became aware of the girl. She came forward shyly, asking him in Arabic, 'You remember me?'

He hesitated and Walid cried, 'Of course you remember Soraya!'

She laughed then and he was aware of her irregular teeth, but it no longer mattered, because somehow in four years she had become beautiful.

He smiled at her and said, 'You were at my Cousin Nasri's welcome-home party. You were going to study medicine——'

She told him, 'I'm at the medical faculty of the A.U.B.'

There was the interruption of Anton's name being called for the return of his passport, and Khalil rescuing his baggage, and then, 'Let's all go and have breakfast!' Khalil said.

In the car Khalil inquired of Anton about his mother, and the possibilities of her coming out, and when these formalities were disposed of, 'Where would you like to have breakfast—in Amman or in Jericho? And what sort of breakfast?'

Walid put in quickly, 'I'll die of hunger if I have to wait till we reach Jericho—Anton probably had something on the plane.'

'I'd like it in Amman, too,' Anton said. 'I'd like to have beans!'

He turned to Soraya:

'What would you like?'

She said promptly, 'Turkish coffee and beans!'

'There's a new restaurant in Amman we can go to,' Khalil told them, adding, 'You'll hardly know Amman, Anton, it's grown since you last saw it. You have to look now to find the old buildings!'

Anton did in fact find the town he had remembered very much changed, with its many modern buildings, but it was all part of the general dreamlike unreality of being back, with Walid the same and yet different—become so strangely adult, and Soraya grown from a gawky, self-conscious schoolgirl into a lovely young woman, and his Uncle Khalil, of whom he had always been a little afraid, thinking him haughty and aloof, grown so warm and human and easy—but perhaps he hadn't really changed, Anton thought, perhaps it was only that he himself had grown-up. He wondered if the old house in Jericho would seem different now that he was four years older.

The restaurant in the main street to which Khalil took them was new and modern, with mosaic-tiled walls and strip-lighting and loud-speakered music. Its sliding glass doors were folded back so that it was opened on to the street and took in the blare of radios from open-fronted shops on either side. The day was already warming up and there were a few flies. Anton flicked them away happily. He was back home, and flies belonged, like the blare of radio and the greasy mess of beans on his plate and the sound of Arabic all about him. He felt intensely happy. Khalil thought he had never seen a human being so completely lost in a trance of happiness, but because he wanted to hear him say it he smiled at him and asked, when they were leaving the restaurant, 'How does it feel to be back?'

Anton's answering smile was radiant.

'It feels wonderful,' he said. 'It's like a dream, and I never want to wake!'

'We're all down at Dar el-Salam for Christmas,' his uncle told him, adding, 'I hope that won't be too sad for you?'

'Oh no,' Anton cried. 'If you knew how often I've longed to go back there! What is sad is being away from it!'

Khalil drove down to Jericho by the Jordan Valley route, with its great hills and wide vistas, and Anton felt his heart swelling with love; it seemed to him that though he had never ceased to think of it all he had forgotten the immensity of its beauty.

His ears crackled from the long descent and by the time they had crossed the Allenby Bridge into what had been Palestine he was a little deaf, and he noticed that Soraya, also, was pressing her fingertips to her ears. She caught his glance and smiled ruefully.

'I always get deaf going down to Jericho,' she told him, 'whether it's coming down this way or from Jerusalem.'

'But it's worth it when you get there,' he suggested, and her fervent assent made him happy. He wanted her to love Jericho; he wanted that they should agree; he wanted her to like him, and her smile was so warm and friendly he felt that she did, and it was all part of the great enveloping happiness.

'We should send your mother a telegram from Jericho,' he heard his uncle saying from the front seat, and glanced at his watch and saw that it was half-past eight and thought how it was still only half-past six in England and his mother would be asleep in her flat in town, and his grandparents in the little house at the side of the Common, and it all seemed remote and unreal.

'This afternoon you must go and see Mr. Shapley,' his uncle continued, 'but he knows you're not starting work there till after Christmas.' He added, 'You will like Arnold Shapley. When he was a young man he knew your grandfather very well, also your father, in the old Jaffa days. Your blind friend is teaching there now—I understood you would be sharing a cottage with him.'

'Is it the school for the blind that's run as a community centre—on the side of a hill off the Hebron road, a little way out from Bethlehem?' Walid asked.

'Yes. It's more than a school. The boys learn trades, and to adapt themselves to community life. Anton will find it an interesting experience, I think.'

'Convenient for visiting Hebron, too,' Walid commented.

'In work of that kind there's not much free time,' Khalil pointed out.

'We shall have to make the most of what there is,' Walid said, and looked meaningly at Anton. But Anton was gazing raptly at Soraya. Walid stared fixedly ahead, at the road snaking down into Jericho; he was frowning, and did not speak again until they were nearly there.

At the sight of the Mount of Temptation in the near distance, with the familiar tall cypresses in the foreground, Anton cried out in pure happiness.

'Oh, there it all is! Just as I'd remembered it all this time!'

He turned to Walid, eagerly. 'Let's go up it this afternoon, shall we? For old time's sake! Remember last time?'

'This afternoon you're calling on Mr. Shapley,' his uncle reminded him.

'Tomorrow, then! Walid must stay the night and we'll go tomorrow morning—get an early start. We can take our lunch and picnic at the top.' He turned eagerly to his friend. 'Isn't that an idea?'

Walid, undermined by that eagerness, relented and smiled.

'A splendid idea! I'm staying the night, anyhow—your uncle very kindly invited both Soraya and me.'

'With all the rest of us it makes a little party to welcome you back,' Khalil explained to Anton.

Under cover of Khalil turning to say something to Soraya Walid murmured to his friend, 'We'll have a chance to talk tomorrow.'

This time the significance of the statement was not lost on Anton, and he knew a faint under-the-surface surge of excitement, as when years ago Walid had spoken of getting to Dahiriya in the spring.

Then they came to the gates of the Dar el-Salam estate and the servant who stepped out of the lodge and opened to them was the one Anton had always known. The man saluted and Anton wound down the window and leaned out to shake hands with him.

'*Maharba!*' the man cried. 'A hundred welcomes!'

When the car drew up at the verandah of the house Anton saw that the entire family, with the exception of Nasri, was assembled. The first to greet him was his Uncle Farid, and for a moment Anton was startled by the family resemblance—it could have been his father. Putting on a little weight and growing much greyer had made Farid physically more like Butros. Majdeh, always inclined to fat, had become very fat indeed, but her smile was as warm as ever and her affection as abundant. Muna had also put on weight, but it merely added to her stateliness; she was still very handsome, Anton thought, and she, too, reminded him of his father. Nadia was as beautiful as ever and seemed not a day older; her three children clustered round her and a fourth was manifestly due shortly. The girl cousins, grown tall, and the eldest one fashionable, were still shy but no longer giggled. Anton kissed his aunts' and Nadia's hands and was himself kissed on both cheeks by his Uncle Farid, then Yusuf came forward, with his wife hovering in the background, and there were more *maharbas* and hand-shakings and tears-in-eyes, and a general happy confusion.

Yusuf and another servant brought cold soft drinks and the electric fan churned up the heavy warmth into an illusion of coolness, and everyone settled into bamboo chairs. White jasmine cascaded over a pillar and its scent was fanned across the verandah in soft waves.

Anton saw Soraya and Nadia sitting together and went over and stood by them.

'It's so beautiful here!' Soraya cried to him, looking about her, at the tall palms, the Bougainvillea arbours, the vista of orange groves. 'I've been through Jericho so often and never guessed there was this lovely place hidden away off the road!'

Anton smiled at her, happily.

'My father loved it. It was peace for him. His house of peace, *dar el-Salam*. He liked to tell how he fell in love with my mother here. And he died here.'

'I knew that,' the girl said, gently, 'but not the romantic part of the story. That makes it a happy place.'

'Why don't you show Soraya over the house?' Nadia suggested, not without guile.

'With pleasure, if she would like it!'

The girl rose immediately and Anton looked inquiringly at Khalil.

'With your permission?'

'Of course. Why not?'

'It's your house now. Is there anywhere we shouldn't go— anywhere private?'

Khalil laughed.

'My house is yours,' he said, in the Arab fashion.

Anton had a moment's panic that his aunts, or one of them, would insist on accompanying them on the tour, but Muna and Majdeh were chatting beyond ear-shot, and though Muna looked across to them when Soraya got up she did not inquire, as Anton dreaded she might, what was going on. He wanted to grab the girl's hand and rush off with her before there could be any intervention.

When they stepped through the French window into the house he had an impulse of a different kind to take her hand, then remembered that she was Arab, and that this was not England, and that in merely going off alone like that they were flaunting convention. He was very grateful to his Cousin Nadia, for he would never have dared to make such a suggestion, and he fully expected that at any moment one or more of the Dahoud girls would join them—or that Walid would. He could only hope—and he hoped it fervently—that Nadia would find means to protect her little plot.

He found the house almost unchanged from how he had remembered it. There were the same beautiful Persian rugs on the tessellated marble floor of the wide cool room, full of books, opening off the verandah. Logs had been laid in the fireplace for use when the evenings became cooler, just as his mother had always kept them, and there was a bowl of roses on top of what had been his father's writing desk. It was in this room his father had died, but he did not tell Soraya this because he was full of happiness and did not want to cast a shadow on it. At the top of the stairs there was the bust his father had had made of Marian by a Jerusalem artist in the early years of their marriage. She had never liked it and had left it for Khalil. Anton was glad, for although it had never meant anything to him it belonged in the familiar place at the top of the stairs.

He told Soraya, 'That is my mother when she was young. I was only about three at the time so don't remember her like that. I wouldn't know it was my mother, in fact. But my father liked it, and my Uncle Khalil likes it.'

Soraya touched the curve of the cheek.

'It's nice. It has a lovely feeling of someone young and happy about it.'

'Those were her best years,' Anton said. 'Before all the terrible things began to happen——'

'What is she doing now?'

Anton told her, and talking easily they went through the rooms and came to his own room, stripped of everything but the furniture, and then out on to the wide verandah looking through the cypress trees towards the Mount of Temptation, and on a hillside in the near distance the scar of the refugee camp, row upon row of tents[1] rising in tiers, thousands of them.

They walked to the other end of the verandah and looked across to the orange grove, and there was a scent of orange blossom on the warm air.

'It's so beautiful,' the girl said again, softly.

After a moment Anton said, 'This is where my father first saw my mother—really saw her and knew he wanted to marry her, and told her so. After we had to leave Lydda and came here and lived here all the time they often sat here. It was their favourite place until my father's heart got so bad and he couldn't go upstairs any more. I wish he could know I'm back here.'

'Perhaps he does.'

'Perhaps.'

1. Not until 1958 were the refugees moved into huts.

He hesitated, then asked:

'Do you think we could meet sometimes—now that I'm back? In Ramallah, at my uncle's house?'

'During the Easter vacation I expect I shall go there sometimes, visiting your cousins—but you won't be living there this time.'

'No, but I must surely occasionally have time off.'

She was disconcerted and looked away, and he added, quickly, 'If it were England we could just arrange to meet and go for walks together. It's so different here.'

She looked at him then and smiled.

'Yes. But people do manage to meet, and I'm sure that if we both want to we shall.'

'I do want to. But do you?'

'Yes. But now I think we should go back to the others.'

'I suppose so. I don't want to.'

They left the verandah and re-entered the house, averting their eyes from the beds as they passed, moving quickly and apart, not looking at each other, yet each intensely aware of the other.

2

LYING face downwards among the wild marigolds at the top of the Mount of Temptation Walid Hussein talked. Anton sat with his back against a crumbling wall and looked out across the broad valley which held the palm trees and olive groves and clustered white houses of Jericho, with the pale glimmer of the Dead Sea beyond, flanked by the tawny Mountains of Moab. He was filled with an immense satisfaction; this was the dream he had carried all through the English exile realized at last—to be alone with Walid and feel the communion of their friendship, with its shared obsession, flowing strong and deep between them.

Walid spoke in Arabic, being no longer concerned as in his school-days to practise his English.

'I couldn't write to you properly,' he said. 'I could only let you know I had your letters, and thought of you, and that nothing was changed. There was never much time for writing, and like most Arabs I'm not addicted to writing letters.' He smiled, rolling over on to an elbow. 'The English in you makes you a good letter-writer and I liked having your letters. Everything you wrote about your English life interested me, but the important thing for me was that you never lost sight of the road to Beersheba.

'As you know, since you left King Abdullah has been assassinated and King Talal abdicated, and we now have young King Hussein, and there has been the frightful massacre at Qibiya. But nothing has fundamentally changed. Palestine is still occupied—the west bank by Jordan, the Gaza strip by Egypt, and two-thirds of it by the Israelis.

'Every year the Palestine question comes up on the agenda of the UNO Assembly and the right of the refugees to repatriation is reaffirmed, and nothing is done. And nothing ever will be done until we Palestinians do something for ourselves. This we know. Our problem is to find the way—and the means.

'Our wellwishers assure us that repatriation is not practical, that we should be realistic and accept the fact that two-thirds of our country has become the Jewish state of "Israel" and likely to endure for a long time yet, and that we should lose our national identity by becoming absorbed into the life of the host-countries.' He paused, then added in English, 'Rehabilitation, not repatriation.' He pulled the head off a marigold and flicked it into the view and continued in Arabic, 'That is their idea of being realistic. That having lost our country we should then surrender our nationhood. As if it's not enough that the six hundred thousand or so of us in Jordan are officially Jordanians! Then they ask us to continue in our refugee status—in our own country. To forget that we are Palestinians, with homes and lands and money somewhere else, but to be absorbed. To become the forgotten people!'

His deep voice was harsh with bitterness. He sat up, cross-legged, his expressive hands dangling between his knees, his young handsome face dark with anger.

'You and I are among the lucky ones. But for our fathers having a little more money and education we would be down there rotting in a camp, living on UNRWA rations and the dream of one day going back.

'We are urged to take the historic view—that "Israel" is only a passing phase in history and will pass like the British Empire, Hitler's Germany, and, if it comes to that, life itself. The people who urge this on us are themselves in possession of all they own and are living in their own country, or somewhere of their own choice. Did you meet this kind of talk in England?'

'Yes,' Anton said. 'I even felt heartened by it!'

'But if you had been living in a leaky tent in a camp it might not have seemed so heartening, might it? It might even have seemed a depressing point of view, don't you think? I have a friend working at that community centre for the blind you're going to. His name is Talib Hamadi, and when I met him two years ago he was living in the big Dheisheh Camp, near Bethlehem. I was on a visit to the camp with my uncle. We went round with the Camp Leader and an UNRWA official and Hamadi was one of the people we talked to. My uncle liked him and thought him bright and asked him if he wouldn't like a job outside the camp and to live outside—he was eighteen then. At first he said no, because it would mean giving up his ration book, and the more ration books in a family the better, but his father said that he should accept, telling him he would be a fool not to. My uncle got him the job at Mr. Shapley's place. Last year he married a girl living in the camp, and she still lives there, though he has permission to bring her to live with him at the school, but she prefers to stay in the camp with her family. Whenever he has an hour or two off he goes off on his bicycle to visit her. He told me that though he is very comfortable at the school, and well-fed, and everyone is very pleasant to him, he still feels more at home in the camp, among his own people. It's the refugee mentality. The girl has it too. She knows she would be more comfortable and better fed living with Talib at the school, but apart from the giving up of the ration book she knows she wouldn't feel at home in the Christian atmosphere of the school, no matter how kind Mr. Shapley and his colleagues might be.

'I think we all have this refugee mentality, even those of us not living in camps. You lived a comfortable life in England, and your mother and grandparents were there, but you longed to be back here.'

'I thought of it all the time,' Anton said.

'It's the same with me. I am glad of the opportunity to study at the A.U.B., but I don't feel at home in Beirut—it's too Western, too Christian. I don't feel I'm in an Arab country when I'm there. I long to be back here—in the country that was Palestine. My own country.

'But the point about Talib Hamadi is that he comes from Beersheba and longs to get back, because he has a brother still living there. I got him interested in the idea of building up a resistance movement inside occupied territory. It's to his brother we shall go when we make the first move, and Talib will come with us.'

Anton's heart quickened. Until then the road to Beersheba had been no more than an obsessive dream, a fantasy, a symbol; suddenly it had reality; it was as real as the high hill on whose summit they lay; it was there, winding out from Hebron, and only a few miles over the border there was Beersheba. They were going along that road, as surely as in a few hours they would go back down the Mount of Temptation, retrieve their bicycles from the Monastery, and take the road from Jericho back to Ramallah.

'Does Talib know the terrain?' he asked, in an effort at casualness.

'He knows it very well indeed. His father had land in the valley below Dahiriya, and he has cousins in the village, which helps him in getting there.'

'Is it still difficult?'

'If you're a stranger you need a permit. We would get permission all right, through my uncle. Talib might risk going in on the bus, if one of his cousins comes in to travel back with him so that he can identify him to the police, if necessary. The police sometimes check the bus passengers to see if there is a stranger, and if there is someone must testify that he is a relative of someone in Dahiriya. It's better if he is accompanied by a relative. When my uncle comes in to Hebron it's not difficult for me to go back with him. It's not as difficult as it was in 1949. But you would need a permit—though as Butros Mansour's son that wouldn't be difficult.'

'What do you plan?'

'I plan to spend my entire vacation there in the summer, so that I get to know the terrain. I shall be out in the fields all day and every day with my uncle and Saïd and the old man and every day I shall go just a little farther, but always working, never just looking, and never going beyond the Demarcation Line, only to the very edge of it everywhere, so as to have an idea of what is beyond. And Talib will make a map for us.'

'How long will we stay in Beersheba?'

'I might stay for some weeks, but you and Talib will be able to stay only a few days, I imagine, unless you can get leave for longer.'

'You would have to come back alone.'

Walid smiled.

'That shouldn't be difficult—having done it once.'

'I would find it more of a strain doing it alone.'

'In some ways it's easier—you haven't to be worrying about what the other person might do. Do you feel nervous about it?'

'Yes. I didn't think I would be, but I find I am. But it doesn't mean I don't want to do it. All the time I was in England I thought about it.'

'It will mean a great deal to the Palestinians we'll meet there to have someone like you coming from outside. Some of the older ones will remember your father as a Palestinian nationalist.'

'Is it known how many Palestinians there are in occupied territory?'

'In Jewish-occupied territory about seventy-five thousand. They're treated as second-class citizens.'

'How can they bear it? Why did they stay?'

'Wouldn't your family have stayed, given the chance? My father wanted us to stay, but my mother was so terrified, and my grandmother, who was living with us. We left before the Jews came in, thinking we'd soon be back. Many did.'

Anton said, thoughtfully, 'I don't know whether my father would have stayed, given the chance. I think he might have left, as your father did, thinking we'd all soon be back. But we left when Lydda was already occupied, because we were told to get out, like everyone else, and after the fall of Lydda and Rameleh my father didn't believe any more we should be coming back. I don't think anyone believed after that.'

'Beersheba is only a start, you know. The nucleus of a resistance movement has to be formed in every town and village in Occupied Territory where there are still Arabs. We're starting with Beersheba because it happens to be Talib's and my home town and we've got to start somewhere. We need commando units, trained and equipped, stationed along the border——'

'Only governments can do that!'

'What government trained and equipped the Irish Citizen Army for its struggle against the British? And the I.R.A. after the Irish partition? And the *maquis* in France during the occupation in the last war? When a resistance movement is ready it finds the ways and means.'

He glanced at his watch.

'We'd better be going down,' he added. 'We told them at the monastery we'd be back at four.'

They scrambled to their feet and began following the steep rough track down to the monastery which bars the way to the summit. They reached it before four and their hammerings on the massive iron door producing no response from within they sat down to wait.

They sat in silence for a moment and then Walid said, abruptly, 'I noticed last night at the party you couldn't keep your eyes off Soraya Saba.'

Anton laughed, confusedly.

'She's very attractive!'

'I suppose so. But it's not a good idea to start a romance just now. Let's get this thing over with. I wrote you to London that all that sort of thing should wait till the end of your sabbatical year. Then you'll be back in England and free to do what you please.'

'Soraya won't be there.'

'Does it have to be her? There must be plenty of pretty girls in England.'

'I don't want an English girl. I didn't know that till I got back, but I know now.' He hesitated a moment, then, flushing a little, said recklessly, 'I want Soraya!'

There came from within the monastery the sound of footsteps on stone and then a clangour at the iron door.

'We're being let in,' Walid said and jumped up. He added, as they approached the door, 'Postpone your love-affair till we've done what we have to do. She'll still be there in the autumn.'

'The trouble is she won't,' Anton pointed out. 'She'll be back in Beirut!'

The dark-robed brother stood aside for them to enter and they stepped over the iron base of the door into a passage one side of which was the rocky wall of the mountain. Not until they had traversed the passage and gone out through the massive main doors of the monastery and down the worn steps and were descending the rough track to the base of the Mount did Walid make his final comment.

'Nothing must come between us and the road to Beersheba,' he said, firmly.

'Nothing will,' Anton promised.

3

ANTON wrote a number of letters home; he wrote to his mother, to his grandparents—jointly—to Gerald Johns; he even sent coloured picture-postcards to Lindley and to Edwards. In all he wrote he declared how wonderful it was to be back, but only to his mother did he mention Soraya, leading to it through Dar el-Salam. He told her how the same man on the gate had greeted them, and that Yusuf and his wife were there, and how it had all seemed 'so much the same as when we all arrived there together, except that it was nothing like so hot, and that the jasmine was in bloom'.

He continued: 'Uncle Khalil had brought Soraya Saba along to meet me at the airport. She is studying medicine now at the A.U.B. Last time I saw her she was only a schoolgirl. I hardly knew her this time, she has become so attractive. I like her a lot and I think she likes me. I hope we can manage to meet sometimes, but, as you know, it's not so easy to arrange that sort of thing here as in England, even among Christians.

'Soraya thought Dar el-Salam beautiful, so I took her over it. I took her on to the upstairs verandah and showed her the view across the garden through the cypresses to the Mount of Temptation, and I told her that it was there the romance between my parents had begun—where my father really saw my mother for the first time, as you told me. I had a curious feeling that the same thing was happening to us. I haven't told anyone else this, and I haven't seen Soraya since, for she has to be home for Christmas and only spent one night with us. She will have left Ramallah by the time we get back at the end of the month. I wish she didn't have to go back to Beirut.

'I went over to see Mr. Shapley the day I arrived. Uncle Khalil drove me over, and Walid came too, so I was able to introduce him to Amin, who wears a moustache now, like Walid, and teaches handcrafts at the school. We were very happy to meet again. It is so hard to realize he is blind. He took me round the place and showed me the cottage I will be sharing with him when I start there; it's a little adobe house with a thatched roof; inside it's all very bare, with white-washed walls and stone floors and only the minimum of furniture. Mr. Shapley's house is almost as bare, except that he has books. He is tall and thin and grey, and very gentle and kind; Amin says everyone loves him, and that he is a truly selfless person. He admires Gandhi very much and told Amin once that Gandhiji, as he calls him, although a Hindu was more truly Christian than many so-called Christians.

'The place is more of a community centre, really, than a school, as it is a collection of cottages, and there is a small farm and market-garden. There are workshops and there is a weaving centre. Mr. Shapley is not married, which Amin says is all part of his Gandhi-ism. There is an English lady, a Miss Rees, who is a kind of matron or housekeeper; she looks after the clothes of the boys who live there, and the laundry, which is done by some girls who come in from the Dheisheh Camp. She is quite old—about sixty I should think—and I thought her a bit brusque, but Amin says she's all right, really, once you get used to her, and that Mr. Shapley is such a dreamy person that it's a good thing to have someone practical like her around. She remembers Grandpappa from the Jaffa days and sends him her regards.

'As well as the blind boys who live at the centre others are brought in every day except Sundays. Miss Rees goes out for them in the school van. Amin says the centre is a very happy place, and though I felt a bit nervous about it at first I think now I will be happy there and manage all right. At present Mr. Shapley gives the English lessons, but I am to help him with them and he hopes in time I will take them over entirely. The centre looks across the valley to the Dheisheh Camp, which you can also see from the Church of the Nativity. Please tell Grandpappa that I gave the old tree in front of it his salams, as he asked.

'All the Dahouds, and Uncle Farid and Aunt Majdeh and Cousin Nadia all send you their love and wish you would fly out and spend some time with us in Jericho; I wish it too, but I know Jericho and Dar el-Salam finished for you when Daddy died. I haven't been to the cemetery yet. I wanted to wait until I could go with some flowers; also when I go I would like to be alone, or have only Amin with me, so will wait until I start work at the centre.'

As a report, Marian thought, it was entirely satisfactory, but the mention of the girl was disturbing. She knew the Saba family slightly and was sure that Soraya would pass even Elspeth's critical social standards as a nice girl, and it was right and proper that turned eighteen Anton should find himself attracted to a girl, but at the end of a year he would be back in England for two years at least, taking his course at the London School of Economics, and the girl was committed to the much longer course of studies at the American University of Beirut for her medical degree—so that the further outlook was one of separation, frustration and heart-ache.

Her father with whom she discussed the matter dismissed her misgivings as over-anxiety.

'Let the boy enjoy his romance for the year he's there—it'll keep his mind off any infiltration nonsense with Hussein, and when he gets back to London the new life at the university will absorb him and the thing will die a natural death. He'll end up marrying an English girl yet!'

'Is that what you want for him?'

'I want that he shall make a happy marriage, but if he marries an English girl it might keep him here, and that's what you want, isn't it?'

'Like you I want him to be happy, but if he could be happy in England I'd be glad—naturally. But I don't think he could be. He's too much his father's son. England was exile for him, as it would have been for Butros. Going back was going home, and with this girl he'll feel it more strongly still, send roots down deeper——'

'The boy had to be himself.'

'I know. I do realize.' She brooded a moment, then said, her smile rueful, 'Anyhow I'll write and give him my blessing.'

'And mine,' Melby said. 'Sufficient unto the day. It's as sound a philosophy as any.'

Anton did not write his mother in any detail about the Jericho Christmas, only that it was lovely having it at Dar el-Salam, 'which is just the same,' and that, 'with the exception of Uncle Khalil, of course,' they had all gone to church in Jericho on Christmas morning, 'and I thought of all the times we three had been there together, and when I closed my eyes I thought that when I opened them I would see you both, you seemed so close. I felt sad and happy at the same time.

'I wish Soraya could have spent Christmas with us. Although there are so many of us there the house seemed somehow empty when she and Walid had gone back to Ramallah the day before, and there is no chance of seeing either of them again now till Easter.

'I feel there is a kind of understanding between Soraya and me, but we had so little time together, and I don't see how we can ever have any opportunity to get to know each other properly, because the Easter vacation is as short as the Christmas one—only a week. There is the whole of the summer, but that is six months away. Perhaps when I start work in Bethlehem the time will pass quickly. I can only hope so.'

He hadn't felt able to say more than that because what was between him and Soraya was still too tenuous to be translated into tangible terms. With four girl cousins around, one of whom was her special friend, it had been difficult to get her alone in the little time available between showing her over the house and her departure for Ramallah next morning in the car that dropped him and Walid at the foot of the Mount of Temptation. They had strolled in the garden after the tour of the house, but the Dahoud girls and Walid had been with them and only occasionally was it possible to lag a little behind or get a little ahead for a few precious minutes. Once, greatly daring, he had taken her hand when no one was looking, and she did not immediately withdraw it; when she did so she smiled at him, and he felt that she accepted him. At the party in the evening they exchanged brief glances and fugitive smiles across the table; it was progress of a kind.

That night he slept badly, tormented by memories of Rosa putting her arms round him, kissing him on the lips, darting her tongue between; Rosa in the warm darkness of the cinema taking his hand and pressing it into the softness of her breast. There was no nostalgia in these memories of Rosa, only an emotional and physical disturbance. She had declared she would teach him to live; he thought now that if she had left him alone, or if he had never met her, which would have been better still, it would have been easier for him with Soraya.

Thinking about her—and he thought about her endlessly—he felt desperate and despairing. It was months to Easter, and how would they contrive to meet even then? The rest of the Christmas holiday had dragged. He had hoped Walid would be able to remain for a few days, but Walid wanted part of the brief vacation for his parents in Salt, and to fit in, also, a visit to Hebron. When he had gone Anton was impatient to get to Bethlehem, where there was Amin, and the unknown quantity that was Talib.

4

DESPITE the fact that he had been introduced and warmly recommended by his closest friend, Talib Hamadi did not trust this Anglo-Arab, Anton Mansour, and he did not want him on the Beersheba operation. True his father was supposed to have been a great Arab nationalist from before the Second World War, and the family were refugees from Lydda, but the son was half-English and was English-educated and had lived for years in England. He was, moroever, a Christian. Also he came of a wealthy family. He had too much against him.

Mr. Shapley was both English and a Christian, to be sure, but he had lived so long in the Middle East he had become Arabized; he might even end up as a Moslem; it had been known to happen. Even if he didn't he was a good man; he had lived almost all his adult life with the Arabs, working for the Arabs, and he lived very plainly, and humbly. Talib believed in Mr. Shapley. But he did not believe in Walid's half-English friend Anton, and when he had the chance to see Walid alone again he intended telling him so. In the meantime he saw no reason to be friendly with the newcomer, this rich man's son, this privileged refugee who, when his family had to leave one house, had another one to go to.

Talib had several chips on his shoulder: his family were poor, and had lost what little they had when they left Beersheba, and his father had succumbed to pneumonia during their second winter in a tent on the open hillside south of Bethlehem. They had buried him inside the tent, because to report the death would mean losing a ration book. They were not the only ones to do this; it was done all the time, but that his father, a good Moslem, should not have a decent burial for the sake of a handful of meagre rations was very bitter. It was bitter, too, that he who was intelligent and strong could have no regular employment until he was rescued from the camp and sent to work in a menial capacity at a Christian organization. He was not grateful for the rescue because it was central to the vaguely communistic philosophy he had acquired in the camp, from other young men as bitter and resentful and frustrated as himself, that the rich when they performed charitable acts were merely paying back a tiny part of their debt to society. He was not grateful to Walid Hussein's rich banker uncle, any more than Walid himself was, but he responded to Walid's friendly advances when he discovered that his branch of the family was poor and that he himself felt no gratitude was due to the rich.

Talib's marriage had not helped to make him less bitter; he resented the frustration involved in it, yet stubbornly resisted the idea that his wife's refusal to leave the camp was unreasonable; his attitude was that if she sacrificed her ration book she could make no contribution in its place, whereas he could. He took immediate fire from Walid's talk of infiltration and the starting of a resistance movement in Occupied Territory; it offered the outlet he needed and became the flame by which he lived.

He was a tall, broad-shouldered, handsome young man, of sombre expression and dour manner; with only a few people did he permit himself to relax, smile, and become ordinarily human. To Anton he remained offhand, and unfriendly. Anton was at first bewildered, and then resentful. He thought that perhaps it was the sort of jealousy he had encountered at school—that Talib was jealous of him as an intruder on his friendship with Walid. Then he began to realize that Talib had grudges against him, for coming of a wealthy family, for being one of the more privileged refugees, and for being half English. He gave up trying to foster the friendship and fell back on the gentle Amin.

Amin's was not a proud and angry spirit but a humble and resigned one; he had coped with his disability, made the best of his world, and was grateful for the help he had received from Anton's father. And Anton he loved. Vividly there remained with him the memory of his hand firmly clasped in Anton's as they stumbled through the wilderness together in that fearful summer heat, the pressure of Anton's shoulder against his own; and all his life he would remember Anton's refusal to reject him when his uncle's car came out to pick up the Mansour family, and how Anton had not wanted to get into the car unless he, Amin, the servant's son, was allowed in with him; and how at the Dahoud house he had demanded that they should be together, because, Anton had said, Amin is my friend. He counted himself most blessed to have so fine a friend, and it had seemed most wonderful that after the long absence Anton should now be restored to him, and sharing a cottage with him—even a room, for Anton moved his bed in with Amin so that they could talk in the night.

He did not tell Amin what Walid planned with him and Talib, but he did ask him whether he thought there was anything in the idea of organizing a filth column inside the Jewish state, a resistance movement such as the French had during the German occupation in the Second World War, a campaign such as the I.R.A. still waged against the British in an attempt to end the partition of their country. Amin didn't know anything about this, and Anton, who had learned of it through Gerald Johns, explained it to him, with enthusiasm.

The blind boy was interested, but not converted to the idea; why should the British government change its policy because of occasional outbreaks of violence on the part of a few people like that? The French resistance movement was something quite different; it had the whole of the French nation behind it, and a great leader, and arms, and British aid. What could the few thousand Arabs left in occupied Palestine do against the strong and efficient Jewish state? Surely no more than the few Irish organized in the outlawed Irish Republican Army could do against the British—a few isolated acts of violence and sabotage, how would that help? He could understand Palestinians infiltrating out of the longing to revisit their own towns and villages, see their old homes again, tread again the lands that were still lawfully theirs—it was crazy and dangerous, but it was understandable. But the idea of a resistance movement— no.

He concluded gently, and in the darkness Anton felt that he was smiling, 'Perhaps I am wrong. I am not clever and educated like you. But that is what I think. For us Palestinians there is no immediate solution. Time is on our side. We can only wait.'

'You are right,' Anton said.

When he said it he believed it; what Amin said made sense, and what Walid insisted so vehemently was all a wild, crazy dream. But he knew that even without the crazy dream of a resistance movement inside the Jewish State Walid would still attempt to get back to his home town; the road was there, drawing him, the road back, offering an act of defiance, an assertion of a right.

Lying awake in the still darkness, long after Amin was asleep, it came to Anton that perhaps in their hearts neither Walid nor Talib believed in any resistance activity, that that was merely the rationalization of something purely emotional. They would do this thing because they must, and he, Anton Mansour, would go with them although Beersheba was not his home town; but he would go because he was involved through his friendship with Walid and their boyhood pact, and because he, too, had need of the act of defiance and assertion. He had lived with the idea too long now to part with it for any rational reason; it had become an obsession.

But he was again no longer single-purposed, for now there was another obsession—the exciting tenuous thing that was between him and Soraya Saba, all a wonder and a wild desire, as in the Browning poem, but also all frustration and difficulty. He longed for her as intensely as he had longed for Rosa, but differently; because Rosa was physically accessible and Soraya was not, and outside of marriage never would be, and his attitude to her had to be adjusted accordingly. As feverishly as he had longed for Rosa's embraces he longed just to be alone with Soraya to talk with her. He had fantasies in which she came unexpectedly—contrived he knew not how—to Bethlehem to see him and they had a whole precious hour or more walking and talking in the grounds, or sitting in a secluded corner under a fig tree, looking out across the stony Fields of the Shepherds, her hand perhaps in his, and time flowing over them timelessly. He had fantasies in which he received ardent letters from her, beginning, 'My darling Anton', and in his mind he wrote to her constantly, addressing her always as his Beloved . . . between learning Braille, teaching English, assisting at weaving and basket-making classes, taking groups of boys for walks, supervising meal times.

Mr. Shapley asked him if he was happy and felt at home, and Anton with that warm, bright smile behind which he had hidden himself at school replied that he was, that he loved being there, and Mr. Shapley smiled dreamily and said, 'Jolly good!' his mind already on something else. Robert Melby's grandson was a good lad and shaping well and there was no need to think further about him.

Anton admired and respected the principal but never felt that he made much contact with him; it was as though through long years of association with the blind Shapley entered into their world and no longer saw externals. It was the brusque, mannish Miss Rees with whom Anton felt most at ease. From the start he had felt that behind that forthright manner she liked him, and it had compensated for Talib's offhandedness; he liked her because she obviously liked him, and because her affection for him, unlike his grandmother's, made no emotional demands upon him; she was a nice old girl, he thought, and easy to get along with. She in turn considered him a very nice well-mannered boy, and felt sorry for him because he appeared to her as lonely—which Arnold Shapley, for all his goodness, had a way of making his staff feel, as none knew better than she, who had worked with him for thirty years and still felt that she knew very little about him as a human being. She sometimes invited Anton to drive into Jerusalem with her to fetch supplies when it fitted in with his duties; he always gladly accepted—it made a break in the monotony of the daily routine, and he always enjoyed going into Jerusalem. He welcomed almost anything which distracted his mind from Soraya. Sometimes he came near to writing to her on paper something of what he wrote endlessly in his mind; once, even, he got as far as addressing an envelope to her, but the letter did not get written; it was too material an act for so tenuous a dream.

Spring flowed delicately over the Judaean hillsides with small white narcissus and pale patches of mauve cyclamen and the sudden reds and purple of anemones between the grey boulders, and the grey of the olive groves, climbing in terraces up from the valley, glowed again with the rosy clouds of the almond trees in bloom. Soon now it would be Easter and Soraya and Walid would both be back in Ramallah, Walid who insisted that now was not the time for a love affair, and Soraya whose very existence insisted that it was. He felt a restless need to talk to someone, but he did not feel able to discuss Soraya with Amin, and there was no one else close to him.

Then suddenly on an April morning in Jerusalem Soraya was there, looking through the window of the Land Rover in which he sat next to the driver's seat waiting for Miss Rees, who was in the post-office. She stood there smiling, the high warm wind blowing her dark hair, her eyes as smiling as her lips.

After mutual exclamations of surprise he scrambled down to stand beside her on the pavement, demanding confusedly what was she doing there before the Easter vacation had begun, when did she arrive from Beirut? She explained that the medical faculty's vacations varied from year to year and she had come from Beirut three days ago.

'Half the time gone already and we wouldn't have met even now except that by chance I came in this morning!' He was dismayed and wounded.

But then, most wonderfully, she was declaring that she had wanted to come out to Bethlehem to see him, but it was all so difficult, and she had been twice to the Dahouds' hoping to see him there, 'But,' sadly, 'you are never there!'

He said, despairingly, 'I have so little free time. What are we to do?'

'There's three months' vacation in the summer—it'll be easier then,' she comforted him.

'I wonder!'

'Of course it will. In the meantime we could write to each other——'

Then Miss Rees came up and he introduced Soraya and Miss Rees said oh yes, Dr. Saba's daughter, and there was a little polite conversation before Soraya excused herself, shaking hands with them both and holding Anton's hand just a little longer, to say, smiling, 'It's a promise then—we'll write!'

'It's a promise,' he said, firmly, and for a moment their eyes held each other's.

When he and Miss Rees were seated in the van again she said, without looking at him, as they drove off, 'Your girl-friend?'

He said, gloomily, 'I suppose so. But we never get a chance to meet. I haven't seen her since Christmas, in Jericho, and then it was with almost my entire family around the whole time! I don't know how anyone ever gets to know anyone else well enough to get engaged, let alone married, in this country!'

'Your parents met out here and managed it!'

'They were a lot older than Soraya and I. Also the man in the case was the close friend of the woman's father. There's no comparison.'

'Are you aiming to marry this girl?'

'I haven't really thought as far ahead as that. I just want an opportunity to see her alone sometimes so that we get to know each other! If we were in England I could go for walks with her, openly, take her to the cinema, visit at her home, bring her to mine——'

'Some of that takes place here, too. Young people do manage to meet. You're too impatient, young man! And you don't try hard enough. In this country the girls don't fall into men's laps like ripe plums into a basket; they have to be gathered carefully, at the proper time. Once gathered they stay put—which is more than can be said for your English miss, by all accounts! If you were Moslems you'd find the going harder still!'

Her tone was severe, but there was sympathy in her smile and glance.

He brooded silently, and she said no more until she had found a place to park in front of the Damascus Gate, then, as they prepared to clamber out made her final observation on the subject:

'The thing is to know what you want and then go all out after it. Make it happen. Nothing else must matter!'

'Supposing you want two things and they conflict?'

'You either do nothing and lose both, or you do what you most want to do! *Yalla!*'

Walid he met only once at that time, and that was by arrangement in Ramallah; he had telephoned Anton at the school the day he arrived and they met the following day. Anton had the afternoon off, by special permission, and was disappointed to find that Walid could only spare an hour, having been offered and accepted a lift into Hebron, where he planned to spend the night and go in by bus next day with his Uncle Munir to Dahiriya, where he would spend the rest of the week. He would have no time to see Talib this time, but it wasn't necessary; they would all three meet in the summer and plan the Beersheba operation very carefully. He was going this time, as he had been going several times a year for the last few years, as part of his campaign to establish himself with the local people and the National Guard. He considered that the risk from the Jordanians was much greater than from the Israelis. They were determined to stop infiltration because it led to reprisals.

'In principle they are right,' he concluded, 'but in principle we are right, also, for we have the right to return—the moral right, and the legal right as laid down by UNO.'

They met in a small café in the centre of the town and afterwards, in the little time that was left, walked about under the pine trees, still talking.

Inevitably Walid asked, 'How are you getting along with Talib?'

Anton told him, 'I'm not. He never speaks to me unless it's necessary—and it's very seldom necessary. I don't know whether it's jealousy, or whether he doesn't trust me——'

'He doesn't trust the English in you. I shouldn't have told him your mother is English.'

'I have an English grandfather who feels as strongly about Palestine as any Arab!'

'You wouldn't get Talib to believe that!'

'I wish we didn't have to have him in with us!'

'We need him. He's our guide!'

'I'm sure he wishes I wasn't in on it!'

234

'Perhaps. But he knows you have to be. There's no need to worry, though. When he sees you're serious he'll trust you all right. . . .'

They walked together to the depot where Walid was boarding the lorry which was giving him the lift to Hebron. The driver came in a few moments, and at parting Walid said, 'Tell Talib you've seen me and that I'm going to Hebron and Dahiriya.'

Then, as he climbed up into the truck, 'See you in June. *Ma' as-salāma.*'

'*Ma' as-salāma,*' Anton said, and wondered why, having seen his great friend and discussed the great plan, he should feel so heavy-hearted, or why, as he turned in the direction of the Dahoud house, he should have so strong a sense of a net closing in, inexorably.

5

Spring, which had flowed with such a tide of flowers among the boulders, on the hillsides and in the barren wastelands, retreated and left the red earth parched and cracking in the growing heat of the sun. Down in Jericho the heat shimmered like water over the dark green oasis of orange groves and banana plantations, over cypresses and palms; and in the coastal plain over the bitter harvest of weeds and rank grass of No Man's Land, and the lands of the exiled Palestinians, now cultivated by aliens from all over the world. But up in the Judaean hills, in Ramallah and Jerusalem and Bethlehem, there were cool airs and the heat was gentle.

All through that interminable spring Anton had told himself that summer would come because it must, that nothing could stop it. It would be mid-June, and Walid and Soraya would leave Beirut and be again in Ramallah. Soraya had written only once, but she had said all that had to be said, for she had concluded the letter with the command, 'Hold me in your heart, dear Anton, as I hold you in mine,' and, greatly daring, she had signed the letter 'Your Soraya'.

Now he could feel confident that all was well, that what had been tenuous was now confirmed as a reality. He was resolved now that Soraya should take him to meet her family and that permission should be sought from her family and his for them to be formally engaged. After receiving her letter despite his intense longing to see her again he felt more peaceful. There were many difficulties ahead, but when everything else was right, and it was, nothing was insuperable. Only the day must come when the written word was reaffirmed by the spoken one, and by the touch of hands, and perhaps, even, of lips.

Then as startlingly as she had been at the window of the Land Rover in Jerusalem in April she was walking towards him across the grounds at the school, accompanied by a slightly built, youngish man whom she so strongly resembled that he guessed immediately to be her father.

Anton was taking a class under a tree when he saw the visitors approaching, then, his heart plunging, he dismissed the class and went forward to meet Soraya and Dr. Saba. Soraya wore a white dress and high-heeled white shoes and looked, he thought, most beautiful.

'We want you to come back to lunch with us,' Soraya cried, when she had introduced her father. 'I want you to meet my mother and the rest of the family.'

Anton was not sure that he could; he had a class at three o'clock. Dr. Saba said he would speak to the Principal, either to give the pupils a holiday for the afternoon, or make the class a little later. He knew Mr. Shapley quite well. . . .

In the car Dr. Saba sat in front with the driver, and Soraya and Anton in the back. He reached out and took her hand and she turned her head and smiled at him.

He said in a low voice, 'Let us tell them we want to be engaged.'

She flushed and nodded, pressing his hand tightly.

Anton thought that never again, no matter how long he might live, would he know so intense a happiness.

After that there were only confused impressions of a fine house standing in a garden overlooking a broad valley, smiling faces, cries of welcome, an uttering of names he knew he would not remember, and a woman he at first took to be Soraya's elder sister but who proved to be her mother greeting him affectionately and begging him to regard their house as his home. There was a festive meal with what he thought of as mountains of food, and after-wards, at a propitious moment when it was possible to slip away without attracting attention, Soraya drew him out into the garden.

She told him, 'I have told my father we want to be engaged and he has no objection to it if your family hasn't, but doesn't want to announce it until just before I go back to Beirut; then he will give a party for us and we will invite all my relatives and the Dahoud

237

family and the Mansours, and perhaps, even, your mother would fly out?'

'It's a wonderful idea,' Anton said. 'I don't know if she would—she might——'

Then, because they found themselves under a Bougainvillea arbour out of sight of the house, stopped and turned to her and took her into his arms and pressed his mouth to hers. Her lips did not part under his kiss and when he released her she gave a little gasp and said immediately, breathlessly, that they must go back, before they were missed.

He insisted, 'I want to know that you love me—I want to be sure——'

'Of course I do. You know. I wrote to it you——'

He laughed, then, happily, 'All right. *Yalla!*'

Of all this Anton said nothing to Walid, who called on him a few days later on his way to Hebron. With Talib, surly because of Anton's presence, they held a conference in the shade of an ancient fig tree at the edge of the estate, from which they could see the Dheisheh Camp across the valley, above the road which went snaking past it to lose itself in the hills of the near distance.

Walid explained that he would not be returning to Ramallah before they carried out their plan. He wanted to be back in time to spend a few days with his uncle, and a few with his parents in Salt, before flying from Amman back to Beirut for the new semester. Operation Beersheba would be carried out the day after Talib and Anton arrived in Dahiriya; he would wait for them there. No one should write. Talib was due for a week's leave in September and they must settle the date then and there, fixing it to avoid the full moon. Walid produced a diary and they discussed dates.

Anton looked at the intent handsome faces and felt himself alienated, not by them but by something in himself. The thing he had dreamed about with such passion for the four years of his exile was now only three months away, and instead of his spirit leaping forward as it had that Easter of the Dahiriya visit it shrank away—because now all he wanted was to stay within reach of

Soraya. Nothing else mattered. He had returned from exile to find her, and the image of the Beersheba road faded, replaced by hers. Whilst the other two argued in favour of this date and that he recalled the softness of her closed lips and her little gasp afterwards, no longer the confident young medical student but a tremulous girl.

Walid's voice broke in on his reverie.

'Don't you agree, Anton?'

'Anything you say. I imagine I could get the same time off as Talib as we're quite separate departments.'

'We weren't talking about dates. That's settled. I was saying that from Hebron you and Talib should travel separately, Talib with his relatives from Dahiriya and you with Uncle Munir.'

Walid's voice was hard. As hard as Talib's eyes.

'I'm sorry,' Anton said. 'I was thinking of something else for a moment. Yes, of course I agree.'

'I hope you don't go thinking of something else on the day. We'll need to concentrate every inch of the way.'

Talib said, speaking in Arabic, 'Do not worry, my dear. On the day Anton Mansour will not be there.'

Anton flushed and demanded angrily, 'Why do you say that? Walid and I planned this thing years ago, back in 1949, before you had met each other! The chief reason I came back here was to carry out this plan with Walid. You had no right to say that!'

Talib said, his face still dark and accusing, 'If you are there on the day I will apologize, but not until.'

Walid said quickly, 'Of course Anton will be there. He's as much a refugee as we are.' He replaced his diary in a pocket. 'I must go.'

Anton said, 'I must go too. I've a class to take.' He hesitated a moment then added, 'See you in Dahiriya, then, in September?'

'*Insh'allah*,' Walid said.

Talib said nothing.

6

Marian wrote from London:

'My darling Anton,

'I am glad that things have shaped as you hoped they would for you and Soraya, and we are all very happy for you. There is no reason why you shouldn't be officially engaged, if that is what you both want and as the Saba family agree. I am only wondering about the two years' separation whilst you are at the L.S.E. If won't be easy for you, but as you will both be working hard perhaps it won't seem so terribly long. I am sure Daddy would have been glad of this link with a family he knew for many years. I wish he could know—but then there's all the time so much I wish he could know.

'The suggestion that I might fly out for the party early in October does not fall upon stony ground, for although I still could not bear to go back to Jericho I think now that I wouldn't mind going again to Ramallah, especially for such an occasion as this, and after so long I would like to see my Palestinian relatives again. There is a possibility I might be coming to Amman at the end of September, anyhow, for the paper; I didn't want to mention it until I was sure. I will cable you my arrival time in the hope that you will be able to come in to meet the plane. It will be lovely seeing you again and meeting Soraya-grown-up and as my future daughter-in-law.

'Grandmamma and Grandpappa join me in their congratulations.
'With all my love,

M.'

The letter made him very happy and he showed it to Soraya and her parents. All the Ramallah relatives were happy for him. And

Miss Rees, and Amin. Everyone except Walid, he thought, sadly, and him he dare not tell—not, at least, until after Beersheba.

Meeting Soraya was no longer a problem, for he had arranged with Mr. Shapley—with Miss Rees's support—to have every Sunday free and he cycled in to Ramallah and saw Soraya either at her home or at the Dahouds. They were not very much alone, but the girl did not expect to be, and Anton, by mental and emotional adjustment, came to accept it without a sense of frustration. Jordan was not England, and he did not wish it to be, and Soraya was no Rosa, and, by the process of adjustment, he did not wish her to be; she responded with gentle affection to the little love-making possible, and in the circumstances it was better that way. He was very happy, and it was an effort to bring his mind back to Walid. When he did so it was with a sense of guilt.

At first, increasingly entranced by lyric love, he could put it all away from him; in June, September seemed as remote as eternity, and by July Soraya had become so integral a part of his life that everything else had a curious unreality; he had, increasingly, the feeling of only coming alive when with her. But by August there was again the sense of the net closing in. September was by then only weeks away, and it, too, would come because it must.

He began to be worried, and finally in desperation discussed the subject, as nearly as he dared, with Soraya.

One day sitting in the garden at her parents' house, in an arbour overlooking the valley, he asked her what she thought about infiltration.

She replied that she was sympathetic to the people who did it but considered the Jordan government right in sternly opposing it.

'It's an emotional thing and it gives the Jews an excuse to do horrible things along the border. People get killed or imprisoned and it's destructive.'

'We have the right to return. When governments and UNO refuse to help us, or can't, why shouldn't we try to help ourselves?'

'The point is we don't help ourselves like that—we only give the Jews an excuse for killings.'

'What about the idea of infiltrating with the idea of starting a resistance movement inside Occupied Territory?'

'If the Palestinians in Israel were a majority, or even a big minority, there might be something in the idea, but with the Arabs only about seventy thousand, against two million Jews—it's crazy! As crazy as the Arab-Israeli war!'

He stared at her aghast.

'What are you saying? Do you mean the Arabs shouldn't have fought—should have accepted the mutilation of Palestine?'

'It was a war we couldn't win, and all it did was lose us still more of Palestine. But for it your home town would be in Jordan today—you'd still be living in your house. Your father might not have died when he did. Beersheba would be in Jordan, and Nazareth.'

He said, bitterly, 'If you were a refugee you couldn't talk like that!'

She laid a hand on his.

'Please believe my sincerity when I say that if I were a refugee I'd be even more bitter about that useless war.'

'We weren't to know it was useless.'

'We weren't organized, and we were outnumbered from the start. The war only aggravated the tragedy. I've discussed this a lot with Palestinian students in Beirut. Quite a few think like this.'

'It's what the British call being wise after the event! But rightly or wrongly we fought that war, and lost it, and unless we do something about it it's going to stay lost.'

'Not for ever. Time is on our side.'

'I've had that said to me a good many times, but I want results now, not a hundred years hence.' He added, bitterly, 'I suppose you'll say that's the refugee mentality!'

She said, gently, 'I think it is.'

It seemed pointless to discuss the matter further, and suddenly he longed for Walid's vehemence to bolster his faltering faith.

The conversation aggravated the conflict intensifying in him with every day that passed. He knew now that he hadn't Soraya on his side, any more than his mother and his grandfather, and Amin.

He tried Miss Rees on the question of infiltration, but she made it impossible to discuss it by declaring it 'a daft idea', at the outset.

'But supposing you had a brother or a sister or a dear friend in your home town—say in Lydda or Beersheba. Wouldn't you feel you had the right to try and get back?'

'Trying anything which it's obvious from the start can't succeed is daft,' Miss Rees insisted, and it was her last word on the subject. It seemed pointless to urge that infiltrators didn't all get shot by the Israelis or imprisoned by the Jordanians; that some took the road back and got there—and back.

He wondered what Mr. Shapley thought, he who had lived so long among the Arabs as to have become—so it was said—almost one of them. He had to wait for an opportunity, but it came one day soon after his attempt to discuss the matter with Miss Rees. Mr. Shapley wanted to visit a village family with a blind son who, he had heard, was becoming a problem in the home; he hoped to persuade the family to allow the boy to become a resident pupil at the school; he invited Anton to come with him. Anton readily accepted, and as they drove southward asked, abruptly, 'What do you think about infiltration?'

Mr. Shapley swerved just in time to avoid a large boulder in the road, then said in his deceptively vague drawl, 'Infiltration? Oh, very foolish. And wrong. Morally wrong.'

'Don't you think we refugees have the right to go back—if we can find a way?'

'Oh dear me yes! But not as individual infiltrators. That's unfair to the host country. Government is there to maintain order and is bound to respect the border. Can't complain of the other fellow aggressing if you agress yourself!'

'Is it aggressing to try and get back home?'

'It is if you do it in a way prejudicial, as they say, to law and order!'

'How is it to be done then?'

'I see it as I think Gandhiji might have seen it—as an opportunity for collective non-violent action. Remember the great Salt March? But of course you don't—you weren't born then. The British Raj had the monopoly of salt and required the people to pay salt tax. The refusal to pay it was part of the nationalist campaign of civil disobedience. Thousands of people marched with Gandhiji to the sea, where he made a handful of salt. A symbolic act. I have a vision of the great refugee camps in Jordan emptying, the people pouring out to march in a great ragged hungry army to the border, thousands of unarmed people, men, women and children, going home. Or trying to. They might get no farther than the border. Or they might go marching on over No Man's Land.'

'They'd be mown down by Israeli machine-guns, from the hill-tops. Perhaps from the air.'

'Would they shoot down thousands of unarmed people, steadily marching, an endless procession, do you think?'

'Yes,' Anton said, 'they would. It would be just one more massacre.'

'I wonder,' Shapley said, swerving again, this time to dodge a herd of goats. 'I just wonder. . . .'

So there was no one to whom he could turn for moral support, he reflected, gloomily. Only Talib, who avoided speaking to him and did not believe in him.

The question was whether he any longer believed in it himself; whether Talib was not likely to prove a true prophet. The thought filled him with shame and panic. There was a thing to do, and he would do it, a path he had known for years he must one day tread, and he would tread it; there would be no escaping it; it had become the path of his destiny.

7

TOWARDS the end of September, a few days before the appointed date, Anton told Soraya he was going to spend a few days with Walid and his relatives in Hebron. He might be away a week—not more. She was disappointed because soon now the long summer vacation would be over and she would be going back to Beirut until Christmas.

'You mustn't stay away so long,' she scolded. 'We have our party to arrange. I thought we should have it on your birthday, as a double celebration.'

He said, eagerly, 'It's my mother's idea, too. It's wonderful that she'll be with us!'

They were sitting in a secluded corner of the Saba garden and he put an arm round her shoulders and turned her face to his and kissed her lips, softly.

'I'm so happy,' he said. 'I wish I hadn't to go to Hebron! I want to spend every moment of the time left with you.'

'Then why do you go to Hebron? You don't have to!'

'I promised Walid.'

'Is he so important to you?'

'He's my great friend. My only friend. We were at school together, and we kept in touch all the time I was in England.'

'I know. But you have me now. He's no longer your only friend.'

He said, stubbornly, 'You are my love. That's different. It doesn't alter what I feel for Walid. I don't want to take time away from you to go to Hebron, but I promised him a long time ago, and I must! I believe in keeping promises—even if one regrets making them.'

She sighed.

'I suppose you're right. Don't stay longer than you need.'

'I'll be back in good time for the party, don't worry.'

'*Insh'allah.*'

'*Insh'allah,*' he repeated.

Anton and Talib left together, by bus.

'Have a good trip,' said Miss Rees, waving them off from the main building of the school.

'Come back soon,' said Amin, his hand on Anton's arm. He added, 'I'll miss our talks at night.'

Talib glanced impatiently at his watch.

'*Yalla!*'

Except to ask Anton what he was doing about a permit he did not speak to him all the way to Hebron.

The bus wound down through the valley, past apple orchards and patches of cultivation, past the refugee camp with its rows of tents rising in tiers on the hillside. Talib stared at it through the window with a set face. But for this Operation Beersheba he would have been spending his week's leave with his wife. Now not one day, not one precious night, of it would be spent with her. He had not told her he had leave or what he intended doing. It would be time enough to tell her when it was all over. Then he would give her news of Beersheba. . . .

Walid met the bus in Hebron. His manner was easy and relaxed; it was all right about the permits, they had only to go and collect them. His Uncle Munir was in the town and would travel back with Anton and himself. Talib said his own relatives from Dahiriya had arranged to meet him at the afternoon bus.

'When are we going?' Talib asked.

'Tonight,' Walid said. 'There's no point in waiting about. You and Anton have to get back.'

Anton asked, with an attempt at casualness, 'How long do you think it will take us to get there?'

'It's about twelve kilometres by road, but we have to keep off the road, and it'll be rough-going and in the dark.'

Talib said, brusquely, 'We might do it in three hours. We have to avoid villages. I have it all worked out.'

They walked in the direction of the town hall as they talked, three young men strolling in the morning sunshine, but with faces more serious than is usual for young men merely on the way to a coffee-house. Talib looked dour, as always; Walid's manner was relaxed, but he did not smile; Anton was depressed and unable to conjure up his protective masking smile. Walid and Talib glanced at him occasionally, Walid with anxiety, Talib with contempt.

Before they reached the town hall Munir had come up with them. He greeted Anton very warmly, and assured Talib, 'My house is yours.'

He accompanied them to the town hall, where he knew an official of some importance and they collected the permits without being required to wait, though the place was full of people, wandering in the corridors, sitting on benches outside closed doors, some squatting with their bundles on the ground, giving an impression of having waited for hours and being prepared to wait for hours more. The place smelled mustily, of stale air and humanity.

Anton and Munir rejoined Walid outside.

'We won't go to my uncle's shop,' Walid explained to Anton, 'because it's best no one should know we're going to Dahiriya. We can look in on them on the way back, though we won't be doing it together as I may stay in Beersheba till the end of the month.'

They went to a cheap open-fronted restaurant in a back street for a meal, and Anton who had been silent since they left the town hall discovered that he felt sick and couldn't eat.

'Scared?' Talib inquired, maliciously.

Anton looked at him, steadily.

'Yes,' he said. 'Aren't you?'

Talib attacked his food and did not answer.

Walid said, 'It's usual to get nerves before zero hour.'

But it wasn't only nerves, Anton knew, but that he no longer believed in what they were going to do, and had somehow to confront Walid with this betrayal of their pact—of the dream by which they had lived for four years. But if he did not betray Walid he would be betraying the promise he had made to his mother and his grandfather. And in a sense he would be betraying Soraya, who would have been horrified had she known what he contemplated. But it was not as simple as that, for with another part of himself he despised himself quite as much as he knew Talib despised him. Whether he would have continued faithful to the dream if he had not fallen in love—who could say? He had returned from exile unwaveringly resolved on this thing, but he had fallen in love on the day he arrived, and the dream had retreated into the background. Whilst Walid talked, lying face downwards among the wild marigolds at the top of the Mount of Temptation, crushing out their pungent scent, he felt already the slow seepage of the old enthusiasm and the onset of reluctance. He had felt guilty listening to his friend talking with such passion, and ashamed because continually his thoughts strayed away to the memory of Soraya standing beside him on the first-floor balcony of Dar el-Salam, as his mother had stood beside his father, and he had known, as his father had, the moment of revelation.

If he retreated now they would both think he did so because he was afraid; and if they glimpsed the truth they would despise him as much.

He answered Walid, despairingly, 'My nerves aren't from fear of taking the plunge into No Man's Land. People do it all the time and get away with it, and we have everything mapped out. The truth is I don't really believe in it any more.'

Talib laughed, harshly.

'What did I tell you?' he cried to Walid.

Walid stared at his friend.

'What don't you believe in? You've admitted that people do get away with it and that we're well organized. What don't you believe in?'

'The point of doing it!'

Walid's face became like a mask.

He said, with a glacial coldness, 'Have you forgotten that Talib and I have homes in Beersheba?'

'I have a home in Lydda, but I'd feel the same if we were trying to get to there! I just don't believe we could get a resistance movement going, or that it could be effective even if we could. I did believe it, all the time I was in England, but I didn't believe it when we talked on the top of the Mount of Temptation.'

'Because you were thinking of a girl called Soraya Saba!'

Walid all but spat the words at him.

Anton felt himself going pale.

'You don't believe in it now because it no longer suits you to believe,' Walid continued, violently. He pushed his plate away from him in disgust, the food only half eaten.

'There's a bus back this afternoon,' he said. 'You'd better get it. In fact you'd better get back to England, where you belong, and give up pretending to be as Arab as your father. You're as English as your mother! British to the backbone!'

Anton got up from the table. He was now very white.

'I'll go,' he said. 'There's no point in staying.'

'None whatever,' Walid agreed, bitterly.

Talib laughed.

'When they saw King Farouk off in 1952 they played *Rule Britannia*. Can't anyone whistle it now?'

Anton was spared the taunt, having already gone.

8

IN THE living-room over the glass and souvenir shop in Hebron Walid's uncle stood with a telegram addressed to Anton Mansour, care of himself, in his hand wondering what to do with it. He was not expecting Walid and his friend. Perhaps Walid had written a letter or sent a telegram which had not been received? Perhaps, Fuad suggested, they intended the visit as a surprise and would arrive on the evening bus. He would go to meet it, taking the telegram with him, so that Anton had it immediately. This seemed to everyone a sensible suggestion. The telegram was placed on the mantelpiece among the bric-à-brac and Fuad and his father went back to the shop.

When a telegram for Anton had arrived at the school soon after he and Walid had left Mr. Shapley similarly wondered what to do with it. He consulted Miss Rees—who reminded him that Anton had told them he was going to stay with Walid's relatives in Hebron; she did not know the name of the family, but they could easily find that out by ringing up the banker uncle in Ramallah. Mr. Shapley was of the opinion that in the circumstances they might first open the wire, in case it was anything they could and should deal with themselves. They did this and read: *Arriving Amman five-thirty tomorrow morning local time.* There followed the name of the airline and the flight number. The signature was 'Mother'. Obviously Anton would have to return from Hebron immediately. Miss Rees undertook to get the name and address of Walid's relatives and send the necessary telegram.

It was this telegram which rested among the bric-à-brac in the room over the shop whilst Anton Mansour first tried to resist and finally submitted to the destiny bound up with the road to Beersheba.

Munir Hussein and his wife were spreading their bedding on the floor of the room in which they slept when there came a knock at the door. Munir's first instinct was to reach for his rifle in a corner of the room, and Saïd came out from the adjoining room also with rifle in hand. It could be the National Guard warning them of a raid from across the border; it could be the raiders themselves. It could be the National Guard bringing back Walid and Talib and come to arrest the men of the house as well, for complicity.

'Who's there?' Munir called, sharply.

To his astonishment a low voice answered, 'Anton Mansour—Walid's friend.'

Rifles were replaced in corners and the door opened and a dishevelled youth recognizable as the boy Walid had brought there five years ago stumbled into the room.

'Walid and Talib—have they gone?' he demanded.

'Half an hour ago. You couldn't overtake them now. They said you weren't going with them.'

Anton came farther into the room and sank down on to a stool pushed against the wall to make room for the bedding.

'I'm tired,' he said. 'I walked in from Hebron. It's not so far, but I kept off the road in case of meeting a police patrol and it was hard going. I hoped to get here before they left. Walid and I quarrelled.'

'I know,' Munir said. 'They told us about it. We were sorry. It was always Walid's great dream you should go together.'

His wife, her head-scarf half drawn across her face, murmured something to him and then went out, with the old woman. In the dim light of the small oil lamp in the room Anton became aware of the old man standing behind Saïd.

'My wife and mother will bring food and drink,' Munir said, 'and then they will make up a bed for you here.'

Anton pressed his hands to his face for a moment.

'You are very kind,' he said. 'But I want to catch up with the other two before they've gone too far. Is that possible, do you think?'

'It depends how often they stop. The first part through No Man's Land is the most difficult. Talib knows it like the palm of his hand, and Walid has been looking at it for years whilst he hoed and weeded and tended the goats every time he was here. But the

Jews are up there on top of the hills. It depends how alert they are. Not knowing the terrain it would be madness for you to go alone.'

'I must,' Anton said.

Saïd asked quickly, 'Why did you change your mind?'

Anton sat with his face in his hands for a few moments, his elbows resting on his knees, before answering. Then he made an effort and looked up into the intent faces confronting him—three accusing Biblical figures they seemed to him in their long robes and head-dresses in that shadowy room.

'I was ashamed,' he said at last, a ragged edge to his voice. 'Walid accused me of being British, and Talib believed I was backing out because I was afraid.'

Munir said, 'Walid told us it was because you are in love with a girl in Ramallah and want to get back to her and that you lost interest——'

He moved aside to admit the women, his wife with a piled plate of flat peasant bread and some goats' milk cheese, the old woman with glasses of sweet milkless tea.

'But you must eat and drink,' he added.

Anton took a glass of tea and one of the thin pancakes of bread. The old woman urged him to take cheese, and Munir's wife went out and came back with a bowl of black olives. Anton pleaded that he was not hungry, that he would just drink the tea and be gone. To please the old woman he said he would take some bread and olives to eat when he was safely into Occupied Territory.

'It's impossible you should go alone, as my father says,' Saïd said. 'Even I who see the terrain every day would not go alone in the dark—and in daylight you cannot go.'

Anton swallowed the tea and stood up.

'I must go,' he repeated. 'But you can help me. Talib was going to draw a map. Have you got it?'

Father and son exchanged glances and Saïd went out.

'We have it,' Munir said. He made a gesture of hopelessness and added, 'But how can you remember?'

Anton told him, 'For four years I was in a military training corps at my English school. Reading maps was part of the training, and moving silently and invisibly over rough ground.'

'In the dark?'

'In the dark,' Anton lied.

Saïd came back with the map and he and Munir and Anton moved over to the lamp on the whitewashed window-sill. The old man muttered that it was all crazy and he was going to bed, and shuffled out.

Munir spread the map and began to explain.

'There's a *kibbutz* on the ridge across the valley. You can take your direction by its light. Keep over to the right when you leave my land and creep along behind the boulders—they are marked here. They go almost all the way down into the valley. Then you must come out into the open, with the spur of the hill where the Jews' lookout is on your left. If you can cross that open stretch and get close in under the hills you're out of sight. Once you're round that ridge you pick up the road again—here'— his brown forefinger followed it on the rough map. 'You must make a detour to avoid the village, but be careful, there are two roads which lead back to the border—Talib has marked them——'

The rough voice, speaking in Arabic, went on and the map imprinted itself photographically on Anton's brain. His spirits rose; he had always been good at maps, he told himself. Reconnaisance: the word came back to him from his cadet force days.

Munir finished speaking and Saïd asked, wonderingly, 'Can you remember?'

'I do remember,' Anton assured him.

Munir turned away from the lamp with a gesture of finality.

'Then Allah be with you,' he said. '*Ma' as salāma.*'

Anton sat for some time at the edge of the Demarcation Line accustoming his eyes to the darkness. The night was moonless but thick with stars, and the air clear, and it was not so very dark. The light in the *kibbutz* across the valley was like a beacon. There was no light on the ridge where the Jews kept watch. Away to the left, at the other side of the road, this side of the Demarcation Line, bedouin were encamped and there was the glow of a fire.

Munir Hussein's land went to the edge of No Man's Land; where his cultivation ceased the land dipped down into a rough bouldery wilderness. He could make out the nearest of the scattering of boulders. The problem, he reflected, would be to move silently over the loose stones. The need would be to go very slowly; to creep. It must be about an hour now since Walid and Talib had crossed the Demarcation Line and crept down there into the wilderness. They must be through it by now; perhaps resting under the bluff of the hill. When they became aware of someone creeping up to them they would be terrified; perhaps even they would leap out on him; but he would say Walid's name, whisper it, 'Walid! I've come. . . .'

He felt quite calm now, Talib's map imprinted on his mind. It could be done. Walid and Talib had already done it. The road glimmered palely away into the deep darkness of the hills; the road to Beersheba.

Quite calm and confident he felt, sitting there listening to the night, a dark brooding silence punctuated occasionally by small sounds, the distant yapping of a dog in the bedouin camp, starting up dogs in the village for a while, then silence again, broken by the faint reedy sound of a pipe in a shuttered house, the thin rise and fall of a phrase based repetitively on a few notes, remote and mournful; then silence again, underlined by the monotonous zizz of cicadas.

He looked up to the dark ridge commanding the road on one side and the valley on the other and wondered about the Israeli guards up there in their hutments. Did they pass the time playing cards between watches? Was there a path up there which they patrolled, night and day? Was there a patrol down there in the valley? That was the real danger, the unexpected patrol, not the hilltop lookout. He wondered how far Walid and Talib had got.

His heart did not quicken when he finally got up and moved softly down the incline, but his whole body was tense. Stones slid under his feet, but it was not a sound that carried; he bent low, using the boulders as a screen; between boulders he went down on his hands and knees; every few yards he stopped and listened. Once he stumbled into a thorn bush and the pain in his hands was so excruciating it brought tears to his eyes; in the next moment the pain was anaesthetized by his blood running cold at the sound of a barking near at hand and coming nearer; he stood rigid, and then to his relief the sound retreated and he realized that it was not as he had so terribly feared a dog but a jackal. When he crept on again he no longer felt the pain in his hands.

It was very slow going and the distance was greater than he had remembered it, looking across at it from Munir Hussein's land that sunny day five years ago. The stars seemed very thick and close, and the light of the *kibbutz* very distant. It never seemed to get any nearer, and there seemed to be always the same dark hump of hill on his left. Crawling across the open stretches between the boulders worried him; he was nervous lest a searchlight should suddenly swing out from the hilltop and pick him up, and he began to cover these distances in a crouching run. He wondered how the other two had negotiated them and longed to catch up with them; a vast loneliness began to engulf him. Once he fell flat on his face and it seemed to him a whole avalanche of stones came crashing round him; he lay still a long time, tense, listening; but there was no sound or stir; for a time after that he went crouching, nervous of straightening up.

He told himself, resolutely, that though it was not easy it was also not really so very difficult; just tedious—and a strain. He repeated the name of Talib's brother, and of the street in which he lived; he wondered if the brother was as dour as Talib; and whether the Israelis had modernized the little market town of Beersheba out of all recognition, as he had heard they had done to Nazareth. He wondered if he would have difficulty in finding the street; but then he might catch up with the others and they would finish the journey together. The road to Beersheba—well, this was it, this stumbling through the dark, and the lurking danger, and the loneliness. But the other two might be waiting, under the bluff of the hill, at the farther side of No Man's Land. Strange they should call it that, when they knew exactly to whom it belonged, to which Palestinians. When they knew that it was *Arab* land.

He looked up at the stars as a change from continually straining his eyes to peer through the darkness. The rough land continued to descend; perhaps, he thought, he was being too slow and cautious and now that he was used to the darkness should try to go a little quicker. He tried this and stumbled, and slowed down again. But now the dark hulk of the hills on the left had changed its shape at last and the beacon light of the *kibbutz* was perceptibly nearer. He was almost down. Then the ground was level and there were no more boulders of any height, and flat going across to the bluff—where perhaps Walid and Talib rested. He longed to walk upright across the open space, but dared not and went down on his belly, inching his way across.

Suddenly there was the horrible sound of the jackal again, coming closer. Then to his horror he realized that it was not a jackal but a dog, coming at him, with a fearful commotion of barking that seemed to reverberate through the hills. He picked up a stone and hurled it in the direction of the brute and repressed the impulse to shout; there was a yelp as the stone found its mark and then an intensified barking, and now, shadowily, he could see the dog, no longer coming at him but standing, barking full strength, ferociously. He hurled another stone, there was a yelp, and the dog retreated a few feet, then renewed its din.

The din was such that the first time the shout came Anton did not hear it; then it came again; there were words to it, but he did not distinguish them; panic seized him and he straightened up and pelted across the open space for the shelter of the hill. He had no thoughts; only the blind instinct to run for his life.

There was the sudden spatter of gun-fire, but its impact on his body excluded the sound for him; he staggered under it, swayed a moment, and fell. He was dead before he hit the ground.

A few hours later, whilst the air was still cold with dawn and the sun coming up quickly behind the bare hills, at just about the time when Walid Hussein and Talib Hamadi entered Beersheba, and the plane in which Marian Mansour was a passenger landed at Amman, the Israeli guard brought the body back to the Demarcation Line, where, as arranged, a Jordanian police van waited to receive it

People came running through the dust, word having gone round that they were bringing the body of an infiltrator back across the border. Munir Hussein and his son Saïd were among the tense silent crowd who waited, straining their eyes along the road to Beersheba.

Mannin, E.

The road to Beersheba